PEST

Ash Brunner

PEST by Ash Brunner.

Formatting: www.polgarusstudio.com

For more information about the Author and to receive updates on new releases visit: www.ashbrunner.co.uk

For Cristina

1

Masturbating, Fapping, Jacking off, Spanking the Monkey, Bashing the Candle, Basting the Ham, Beating the meat, Burping the Worm, Tugging, Flipping the Omelette, Choking the Bishop, Painting the Ceiling, Waxing the Dolphin, Polishing the Banister, Tossing Off, Civil War, Hand-job, Five Knuckle Shuffle, Mangling the Midget, Taming the Shrew, Bating -

I myself have always preferred good old *Wanking*. Nothing conjures up the same kind of sleazy innuendo as the 'W' word; it is dark, rude and suggestive and when vocalised at the right times, works as a huge turn-on. Whatever you may call it - it's a serious business for me, with the weekly calendar overflowing, safe in the knowledge that I have as many hours as is humanly possible of uninterrupted viewing at the computer.

The first thing to get right is what constitutes as 'The Set-Up'. The room is small with a bookshelf lining one wall, a desk beside the window with my laptop on and two chairs, one being a black, leather, low-back on chrome castors, which looks expensive, but isn't really, which is used for normal, wholesome activities – which are very few, thus rendering it redundant - and the other being a cheap, red, 'student' chair, covered in course material, without arm rests – less restriction that way - that is dirty, worn and marked with suspect stains that rests in one corner of the room, when not in front of the desk, which is rarely

1

the case as this is the one I use for wanking. Still, none of this deters me from holding on to the far-flung notion of the room as being an 'office'.

The computer is turned on, as is the internet connection. The blind is then pulled all the way down and the slats closed as there is a clear view of the houses at the back with a view straight into my room. This effect brings about a deep sense of isolation and were it not for the fact that I leave the door of the room slightly ajar, I would be completely cut off from the world. On this point about the door: it's important that I can hear any untoward sounds coming from the rest of the flat, this stemming from a deep-rooted fear of 'being caught' in the days when Sarah was still around.

I will generally have a look at the condition of the weather as this will have an effect on how I feel, regardless of whether it's rainy or sunny, although there is something about rain that justifies the reasons as to why I'm sitting here in the first place, coupled with the feeling of one defying the elements thus gaining a greater sense of power. In layman's terms: it's called blaming it on the weather.

With this being the only room in the flat that I allow myself to smoke, the ashtray is placed on the desk to the left of me, as are my cigarettes and lighter. On this point, it is imperative that I have a sufficient supply as a trip to the shop later will be completely out of the question; in fact, that applies to everything that I may need over the course of the session - specific foods, water etc. To my right, I have my cup with a supply of bottled mineral water on the floor beside the desk. I used to simply get up and fill my cup with tap water from the bathroom whenever I ran out until I read somewhere that drinking tap water can result in hair loss. It also eradicates the need to keep 'getting up' as opposed to just reaching down and pouring a cup without having to leave the chair. A small towel is then placed across the seat of the chair - any colour will do - but I generally prefer white. Likewise, the material mustn't be too coarse as this works as an abrasive on the skin over long periods of time. A 'cum-rag' is then placed on the right side of the table - I'm a 'left-hander' - which can either be normal paper towel or some kind of hanker-chief. No other electrical items must be on within the flat; this includes T.V and phone – simply to conserve energy and lower bills - although this doesn't include my mobile phone which sits on the desk, as again, there must be some semblance of contact with the outside world. All bills and any reminders of outstanding debts or 'troublesome' items must be put away and out of sight as these serve only to distract. The mind must be completely calm and unfettered. All these things can be dealt with at a later time.

Lastly, depending on the temperature, I will wear a t-shirt, preferably not too long in length and be completely naked from the waist down, with the exception of a pair of socks as bare feet on the hard wooden floor over a long period of time soon begins to grate, causing a dull ache that starts in the heels and moves up through the calves and into the buttocks, which again, only serves to distract. Only when all these boxes have been ticked, will I sit down, strap up and plug in.

The mandatory opening website is always my favourite, being the most explicit in terms of content within the categories provided and is used as the warm-up initially but will be viewed intermittently over the course of the session and is usually the one to finish me off. As with all the websites, they are split into a myriad of categories and niches that will cover just about anything you can possibly imagine, and I can, at any one time, have up to five windows open for easy access to whatever takes my fancy. I am not interested in chat-rooms or forums or anything that involves *actual* interaction with what's on screen – the power of imagination is usually a far greater tool than reality.

I check my watch.

Everything is in place.

I am roused to breaking point; this tantalising moment…

Dusk is beginning to settle as I work my way down the first page of films, not searching for anything in particular, just waiting to be moved by something. My choice can be triggered by anything from the look of a girl to the size of a cock or even the tone, colour and grain of the film itself. Something will always stand out a mile, and on this occasion I am grabbed by the rough and grainy image of a film from the 'vintage' era. I light my first, of what will be many cigarettes and stroke my rising erection. I move onto the next film and then the next and the next *and* the next, building myself up to the point of orgasm then stopping, allowing the iron to cool so as to prolong the experience. The entire act is centred on keeping one in a perpetual state of arousal until you have to eventually finish off to *something!* One could carry on like this for days! I find two hours have passed and I'm *still* only on the first website. I find an erection is progressively harder to obtain the more I go on, whereas at first, the slightest titillating shot was enough to excite me, now my hunger yearns for evermore explicit and extreme material to satisfy. I trawl through the abundance and pander to every desire that hits me: *HOTTIE TAKES THE JIZZ OF 12 MEN, HUGE BUSH MATURE, I WILL NOT STOP UNTIL I COME, GIRLFRIEND ASS-GRINDING, WEBCAM BABE DILDOS HER HOLES, GREY GRANNY GETS CUM ON HER GLASSES, MATURE SUCKS A 10INCHER, TEEN STUFFS HER ASSHOLE, TRANNY ASS, ANAL TOYING, THE PROLAPSE QUEEN, REDHEAD GETS HER FIRE-CROTCH EATEN, MILF BANGS SON-IN-LAW, AMATEUR PISSES HER KNICKERS, 3-SOME BATHROOM ANTICS, SMELL MOMMY'S ASS, BLACK ON BBW, RECTAL TEMPERATURE, LOVE-FUCK IN A HOTEL, COOKING THE SNAKE, SENIOR CITIZENS GO ALL NIGHT, FIST FOR THE MEMORIES, SUCK AND SWALLOW, LOVE*

POO, STRETCHED FOR LIFE, MOM WANTS A BABY WITH THE NEIGHBOUR…

The list goes on and on and only when I 'catch up' and begin recognising movies I've seen before, do I open up another website. I recall the girls at work and search for anything with a resemblance or something relating to the way they move or a facial expression I might have caught at some point. Then people I might have seen around town, in the bank, coming out of the pub, in the supermarket or at the petrol station and turn them into the stars performing on screen. Ex-girlfriends come to the forefront of my mind and the sex I've had with them and the ones that did the dirty things that the others wouldn't. I stop on a very cute skinny young woman having sex with a handsome guy with a big cock. Whilst they go at it, a mature woman suddenly walks in on them displaying disbelief at what she sees. We realise she is the mother of the daughter when she berates the couple with loud expletives, yet remains powerless to tear her eyes away from the action. Oblivious to her cries, the couple continue, punctuating their love-making with, 'sorry' and 'promises that it won't happen again'. The mother, relinquishing her post as caring, maternal guardian then strips down and joins them on the bed, promising to 'teach them both a lesson'. It's all pure fantasy, yet played out with such realism and genuine wantonness, that I bolt back and release my grip to prevent myself from peaking too early with thoughts of dead kittens and anything medical involving cold, surgical instruments.

A fly whizzes past my face, my prostrate slows to a cool and steady pulse. The fly works itself around the desk. I open up more websites until *everything* looks horny and I'm having serious trouble staying on one thing for very long. On top of that, my computer is beginning to get crazy as its memory capacity can't handle the amount of information being put forth at one time – it's an old model. I'm dragging my feet. The constant tension is giving me a headache. The entire evening is turning into a chore. My concentration is broken by the persistence of the fly. I stop; hand poised to deliver the fatal swipe and observe its zig-zagging flight pattern trying to comprehend the logic behind what seems a very deliberate set of manoeuvres. My guess is some kind of mating ritual. Whatever it is, before I know it I'm typing in 'why do flies fly zig-zag' on my browser. After some searching I discover it's something to do with their vision and because they perceive something to be threatening. The fly disappears, sensing perhaps that I am indeed a threat and not one to be trusted.

It's coming up to ten-thirty when I turn to my archive. This is a long and extensive list of all the films I've viewed and accumulated over the years, each one special in their own way - *something* I can turn to on tap in relation to a thought or person at any given time. Dubbed classics, I never tire of them. They are saved, labelled and listed in alphabetical order with a name referring to the main *theme* of the content – a succinct description of the pertinent facts - whilst retaining some kind of categorical element for easy finding. From here on in, it's down to my knowledge and familiarity of the material to decipher what it is I'm looking for. This is essential as the list becomes longer, as trying to find something specific in the heat of the moment without it, is too time-consuming.

Then there is '*WANTON MARY*' – the queen of My Favourites folder. She is a mature, amateur housewife who performs on her webcam and whose movies, often found in the 'Mature' section, excite me like nothing else on earth. She is not particularly pretty - but not ugly either – has a ripe curvaceous body, large breasts and huge loins set within a dense mass of black hair; her films are explicit, high quality and above all, acts of sheer uninhibited filth, coming from a woman who clearly enjoys what she's doing. I have 'finished off' to her more than any other and her updates, when found, are like gold-dust.

And it is to her that I turn to, hand hovering over the names listed simply as: MARY 1, MARY 2 MARY 3… Then changing my mind, decide to wait as they are films that cannot be overused, despite their brilliance, but must be seen and used carefully, lest they lose their lustre. I move on, concentration shot to pieces, back, arms, arse all ache and the underside of my cock has developed a friction rash. There is the constant buzzing of the fly in the room and the mad hum of the computer. To top it all, the cat is meowing incessantly for some unfathomable reason. And it's at this point, when for the life of me I can no longer see the wood for the trees, I pull up 'MARY 5' and finish off - not with a bang, but a whimper.

The bedroom is pitch-black. I adjust my eyes. The cat is lying beside me on the bed; a dead weight under which my arm has gone to sleep. I pull the numb limb out from underneath him and rub until the blood circulates once more. The clock reads 3:15am and I'm awake and thinking about the film I saw before I closed my eyes. Sliding out of bed, I walk into the spare room, turn on the computer and begin where I left off. There is interest - if not solidity - and for the next two hours, engage with myself, until I blow another load over a film involving mature lesbians. Then, realising I have a little under two more hours of sleep-time before I have to get up for work, I crawl back to bed.

At 7am the alarm fires off its first round before I hit 'snooze'. I turn over onto my semi and gently grind. Ten minutes later, the siren fires off a second round, forcing me reluctantly into action. I can hear the cat meowing on the other side of the bathroom door as I set about shaving and it's not long before he's scratching at the wood, working as a pest even before the day has begun.

My eyes are heavy and raw from lack of sleep and all I want to do is crawl back into bed. My appointment isn't until eleven but I've a busy day in store with Gemma on holiday, not to mention having to deal with the ebullient nature of Klep.

The water hits my face and I think about the two older lesbians with the huge strap-on - its graphic depiction of master over servant as being exceptional. The cat won't quit, his persistence scuppering any notion I have of turning on the computer and having another browse before I head out.

"Fucker…!" I hiss, yanking open the bathroom door. He bolts across the hallway and into the kitchen where he continues to make a racket.

With toast and coffee, I sit down to the news which is a huge distraction for me as I'm not in the least bit concerned about what's happening in the world but more about the dress wear of the female presenter. In the past there have been days when I have called in sick for work due to the 'urge' on account of what the weather-girl was wearing; this morning however, I'm wary of the fact that I have to be in to take the appointment. Another excuse would be inexcusable and I'm predicting bad traffic this morning, so decide to leave ten minutes early.

The traffic *is* bad. This does however give me the luxury of savouring the delights of the 'usuals' who go about their business every morning: the girl at the bus-stop with her quirkiness and glasses but impeccably shaped legs staring shyly at the ground before her, whilst the academic-looking forty-something stands behind her reading, the rigid look on her face enough to break any boner; the skinny Italian-looking girl from the coffee shop putting out her sign who looks like she'd snap at the slightest touch and the shapely owner of the local deli, simply referred to as 'bottom' for obvious reasons; the buxom bank clerk – always early - climbs out of her parked car baring huge breasts underneath a tight blue shirt and checks to see who's looking. She has one of those huge cracks that reaches all the way round… there's another and another and another, all are worthy, all are great.

The car behind me sounds its horn. I'm going to be late. To

make matters worse, the roads are clogged with arseholes, each it seems, trying to outdo the other with their idiocy. I speed up as a car tries to squeeze in from a side road, preventing it access. Horns fly everywhere and I notice the driver is a fat blonde woman with a red face and huge tits that wobble everywhere as she gesticulates wildly at me while I brazenly stare at the outline of the huge areolas that are visible beneath her thin jumper which infuriates her even more, sending her into a silent rant that is disturbing. The traffic begins to flow again and I pull away thinking about what she looks like naked and she gives me one last filthy look.

As I pull up to the Thorn Park Hotel and into the parking area designated for staff, the first drops of rain begin to fall. I am indeed ten minutes late and, to my surprise, Suzie is the only one in the office. She pours a fresh brew at the table whilst stuffing a chocolate Hob-Nob in her mouth. Unable to speak, she nods at me, masticating furiously as if emphasising the fact that she's got her mouth full and that some big news will follow after she's swallowed.

"Good morning Alex," she eventually says.

"You looked like you had something to say…" I tell her as I quickly check inside the door to Prasad's office.

"Nope, they've all called saying they're going to be late." she informs me. "Prasad said something about his wife's car, couldn't really make out what he meant and Lisa and Marcus are both stuck in traffic. Lisa's got an appointment at ten."

"You'll just have to do it." I tell her. "Make us a coffee will you."

"The hell I will…" she says, preparing another cup. "I've got enough on my plate thank-you very much."

I sit down at my desk, punch in my password, screen comes to life. I'm dying for a cigarette. As Suzie pours the water, I look approvingly at the way her skirt hugs her ample rear and the muscled tone of her calves in her tanned tights. She turns around and catches me wondering if they are tights or stockings – she looks like the stockings type.

"How many sugars is it?"

"Three please…" I say, turning back to face the console.

I hear her mutter something about sweet tooth as I open up my e-mails, but the system is slow and I'm impatient so I pull my cigarettes from my jacket pocket and grab my coffee, thank Suzie and head out to the smoking area. On the way down, I'm convinced she's wearing tights.

The first rush of nicotine hits me like a 'Puffing Billy' and goes straight to my cock. My head is bombarded with images of giant pistons working tirelessly in greasy continuation, great shafts of steel being ploughed into the ground and giant strap-ons being thrust into dark places. The intensity with which the images reveal themselves, make my head giddy as I look down at the only other occupant in the area, one of the younger Housekeeping girls from Romania or Poland perched on one of the cheap, garish, plastic seats specially brought in as a 'luxury' item for the smokers. Her back is turned to me and her head is buried in her phone, but from my vantage point, I can see her long legs crossed and the black fabric of her tights showing between the hem line of her trousers and her shoe. In keeping with my current fetish for feet I can only stare in wonder at what else is encased in her footwear. I puff again and sip on my coffee, slowly waking up amidst my own private fantasies before I'm interrupted by the voice of another housekeeper, either Polish or Romanian, who makes her way over from the laundry room to join her. This one is far older and uglier than her colleague and she completely blanks me before taking a seat. Ordinarily the scene would provide pleasure, but the ugly one is completely beyond repair and kills the moment, so I continue to smoke and drink my coffee and think about Suzie, but the conversation the two girls are having begins to irritate due to my lack of linguistic proficiency. I take it as my cue to leave when I see two chefs pulling out of the doorway and heading over with cigarettes dangling from their mouths.

I'm on the phone as Klep walks in, forty-five minutes late. Lisa is already in the office and in a shit mood bitching about how she's on the back foot with her preparations and the state of the traffic. I watch Klep from the corner of my eye as he sorts himself out before taking a seat and plugging himself in. I'm talking to a client who's looking to arrange a wedding and although I tell him he needs to go through the wedding coordinator, who happens to be on holiday, he still persists in questioning me. I run off some do's and don'ts and lie about how love is everywhere and what we can do for him and explain to him that Gemma is away and that she'll have all the answers but won't be back until next week and that all weddings are to go through Prasad who will be in shortly. As I put the phone down. Klep is facing me looking bemused.

"Should've passed him over – I would have dealt with it," he says.

"Prasad wants it that way," I tell him.

Lisa breezes past with her folder and tablet and heads for the door.

"Right, I'll see you lot later."

"Yeah knock'em dead kiddo," Suzie calls after her.

"Prasad is fretting – I'm more than capable of dealing with the wedding side of things whilst Gemma is away." Klep continues. "Make the problem your own. Take on the responsibility - remember?"

Typically, I ignore him and turn back to my computer as he pulls his little personal comforts from his bag. It's the same ritual every morning, two bottles of coloured liquid that he prepares at home and brings in as some kind of energy booster that looks like something he's drained from the toilet. He pours one of the bottles into a beaker and drinks before finishing off with a belch. Then, as if to galvanise us all into boosting our own energy levels, he's up and beside the flip-pad that stands on an easel beside Prasad's door with a marker in his hand for his little pick-me-up, motivational speech that we have to endure every morning. He looks out pleadingly towards Suzie. "Beyond perfection…" he begins.

The first sign of irritation hits me in the form of a twitching eye, followed by the desire to hear the cracking of his skull against my knee.

I'm sitting on the toilet trying to squeeze out the last of Klep's little pick-me-up and although he does it every day it never fails to infuriate me. I am resentful of him - *that's* my problem. I'm resentful of the fact that I've been with the hotel for two-and-a-half years whereas he joined eight months ago yet acts as if he owns the place. I am resentful of the fact that he is a sprightly, eager, twenty-two-year old and I am a jaded twenty-five. Lastly, I am resentful of the fact that I *know* he is gunning for the job that's come up in the Sales Department - as am I - with the possibility that he's actually being considered for the role as opposed to me. This isn't speculation as I'm savvy to the gossip that's going round the third floor and wary of the influence he has over some people. Klep is the pain in the arse that counters my comfort, my spleen - the nail that drives through the flesh. I wish he would climb up a mountain and jump off!

I push, trying to relieve myself of all ill-feeling before my appointment but I am bound by my own short-comings. My bowels are having none of it! I am accomplishing nothing with my denigration of Marcus, or 'Klep' as I like to call him – an abbreviation for a compulsive stealer, of another's energy in this case, *and* a derogatory term for a giant prick! Yes that's what he is – the moniker suits him well and I shall continue to refer to it in private. Nothing comes of nothing however; and as I push, I wonder if it's this that's the real reason behind my dislike of the little man?

Bored of waiting for my bowels to move and pushed for time,

I lift myself off the toilet and check myself in the mirror. This is not good as it leaves me feeling bloated due to a bad case of flatulence.

"Beyond perfect…" I mutter as I adjust my belt and observe the dark rings under my eyes.

So I'm sitting in the downstairs bar, shooting the breeze with my two clients whilst waiting for our drinks to arrive. It's all small talk and polite innuendo. They mention how good the hotel looks on first impression, the car journey and how long it took them to get down and where they're from and I try and sound enthusiastic and knowledgeable about the town they come from even though I know nothing about it and care even less. Then there is the business itself and how well they're doing and how we're doing, omitting the fact that we're well behind par and on and on until I'm wishing the drinks would arrive so we can get moving. It's the same standard package for all our corporate clients. They enthuse about the site's location in that it's central, as delegates will be coming from all over the country and this has often been a problem on previous occasions. They're impressed with the surrounding countryside and tell me I'm lucky to be living in such a wonderful part of the country. I explain to them that I live about a thirty-five minute drive away in a local town and agree about the scenery and how clean the country air is and that I'm originally from a city but that I have no regrets in leaving for greener pastures, which isn't entirely true.

Finally, I see the Waitress approaching with our drinks. I'm thankful that it's not Valeria but a very cute, young Spanish girl that I've seen around with an incredibly pert bottom that I've often thought about eating. She smiles warmly and greets us, then one by one, places the drinks down. The female client is still talking and I pretend to listen and seem interested in what she's saying but I'm waiting for the Waitress to finish serving so

I can get a look at that bottom. Luckily for me I'm facing in the direction of her return trip and when the moment does finally come, my client chooses to pull a map from her case urging me to have a look as she wants to establish some kind of detail involving directions. I am forced to take notice as the Waitress pulls away and cannot divert my eyes without making it obvious that I'm eyeing up the staff. My clammy hands clench up under the table as I listen to her bang on about some non-descript A-road, irked that an eye-full of that pert little bottom has eluded me. From here on in, it is down to business.

"How about we get going - let me show you around…" I say, pulling a fake grin.

It's coming up to two-o-clock in the afternoon and I'm in the canteen scraping together the last of the food for my lunch as the Kitchen Porters hover, waiting to dispose of the dirty dishes. The show-round went well but the clients are undecided, citing the Grand Ballroom as the brunt of their concerns in that it would have to be used during the day until late afternoon to which a quick turnaround would be required in order to be ready for the evening event. I bought them lunch on the hotel account and left them to it, agreeing to communicate early next week as there was another property they were considering and wouldn't know until then.

I'm tired and unable to eat the rest of my cold steak and kidney pie so throw it away, down the coke and prepare myself a coffee to take out with me as I smoke. I take the fire exit and walk across the small parking lot, reserved for the Directors, my eye catching someone coming out of the staff entrance; someone I seem to recognise, but don't. She sees me and waves as she walks to her car and I realise it's Caroline from Reception. I change direction and wander over, awed more than anything, as she's dressed as I've never seen her dressed before: tight jeans, slightly flared, with a flame-red blouse, dotted with flowers and unbuttoned to the crest of her cleavage, hair tied back, but untidy – methodically untidy - as if she's just straightened herself up after a bout of passion before going out, giving off the impression she's still getting some. Her shoes are retro, open and heeled in cork and there's an extra dab of make-up applied to her face, which is healthy and tanned and it suddenly clicks why I haven't seen her for the last couple of weeks as she's been on holiday. Despite the fact I get along quite well with Caroline and often stop for a chat if I'm passing Reception, never have I felt her exude any kind of sex appeal, mainly due to her fastidious nature and dedication to work to the point of being mechanical - until now. I also thought she was a lesbian – more a wish on my part than anything else - until she recently told me about a car-crash her 'boyfriend' had been in. Now, free of her insipid uniform, her humanness draws me in for closer inspection.

"Hey…Alex," she beams, pulling out a cigarette.

"I didn't recognise you." I tell her. "How was your holiday?"

"Ooo…nice…" she coos. "I'm dreading coming back tomorrow. I've just been to see Kathy and one of my night staff has just handed in their notice and one hasn't even bothered to come back which leaves me right in the shit," she says, getting straight to the point.

"That's not good…" I say, completely unconcerned about the state of her department and more interested about what kind of knickers she's wearing.

"I know…if people have a grudge with something, why don't they just fucking come out and say it, instead of not bothering to come in again? I mean, if they don't want to work here, why do it? Why apply for the damn job in the first place?"

I shake my head then sip my coffee. The last thing I want is a conversation about work and the complications and all the complaining from her, especially when she's looking so *human.* I'm about to bring up her holiday again with allusions to what she was wearing on the beach and what she did at night, but she gets in first.

"I've just spoken to Chef and they've had a crap result with their food and hygiene audit. He's still reeling and I've heard he's given everyone a bit of a going over. I mean it's not like it's his fault…"

On and on she goes until she becomes nothing more than a mouth, loose at the hinges and operating on auto until I am no longer looking at the siren with her 70's-glam-chic-lets-do-some-coke-and-fuck-look, but the moribund dispenser of working woes. I'm exhausted when we finally bid each other farewell but make a note of observing her ample backside as she enters her car and how the tight denim hugs her moons. It's an image I savour as I sit on the steps in the smoking area and I check my watch and will the three hours of work I have left to hurry on so as I can get home and think about it properly.

2

My entry rouses the cat from his slumber and he looks up groggily as I make a bypass straight towards the spare room where the first thing I do is turn on the computer. There is nothing more satisfying than hearing the sound of the front door close behind me, leaving behind the giant, infected, gaping gash of the world, and entering another where all manner of pleasures can be sought.

Hurriedly I remove my work clothes, wash my hands and face and slip on a t-shirt leaving my lower half in just my briefs. The cat has neglected his post beside the front door and is already in the kitchen awaiting his dinner as I make myself a quick cheese sandwich. I fill his bowl with food as he circles my feet and watch him eat while I stuff my mouth with the sandwich, attempting to fill the hole that's been grumbling away all day due to lack of food. Wanking on an empty stomach is *never* as satisfying as after having eaten, working as both a distraction and a negative effect on the size of your erection; and although the sandwich isn't exactly filling it will be enough to see me through the first half of the session. I can always stick something in the oven later on. I pull out a large bag of crisps and stuff them into my mouth quicker than I can swallow, gagging on the final handful causing the cat to stop eating and look up at me in consternation. After a reassuring glance from me, he continues to eat.

I pull a towel from the bathroom then head back into the spare room and drape it over the chair before moving it into position in front of the computer. Locked in, my heart racing, cock engorged with blood, I'm about to visit my first website when the mobile rings. Allowing five rings before I look at the screen, I recognise it as a work number, prompting me to eventually answer. It's Prasad, calling to tell me he won't be in tomorrow as his wife is ill and he's got to look after her and pick her car up from the garage and could I sort some things out for him that need doing. I tell him it's not a problem without delving too much into what ails his spouse and he thanks me and tells me to have a good weekend and that he'll see me on Monday.

"No problem…" I tell him, before settling back down.

'*Ducky-diapers*' is the first thing I see after the phone-line goes dead. "I've been a dirty girl…" the model informs me as I make a grab for my cock. Prasad's got me thinking about his wife's condition though, which is distracting me. This probably accounted for the stressful mood he was in today, where he had a few words with me about client expectation and what he expects from me and the team before going over the revenue figures for the month, telling me how the pressure will be on all of us if we don't keep things sweet, all adopted with a touch of apprehension as opposed to his usually chilled demeanour. This distraction prompts me to check that everything is orderly within the room as I sense something has been forgotten; some detail I've overlooked in my eagerness to get to the computer. When I realise everything is in order, I proceed… light up a cigarette, sink back into the chair, and click.

Searching for anything affiliated to Caroline's adopted look, I work myself over with fervour that brings about new alternatives. '*Vintage*' is an obvious niche, but nothing really stands out. I broaden my search: *hairy, 70's hairy, hairy flares, flower power, vintage webcam, retro anal, flower babes, coke and blow* – all without success. After an hour of browsing, my frustration is beginning to kick in due to the poor update in general. I pull up more, excitement waning, mind allowing unrelated thoughts, namely work and Klep in particular, to take over the process and fracture the moment. Another hour goes by and still I haven't hit full erection, balking at how the session began with such high expectation only for it to turn into another chore. I haven't eaten enough and I feel hungry and every website seems to be filled with the same rubbish doing the rounds that I've seen countless times.

Something catches my eye. A black fly perched on the window sill looking back at me. Without hesitation I reach over and swipe at it, causing it to take flight and disappear into the bowels of the room. I continue my search, digging up old movies, resorting to plastering imaginary heads on forms that vaguely resemble Caroline's, in the hope of replicating the image I had set my mind on - nothing works though. I forget about Caroline and move on to other niches and categories until I finally fall on a film involving women pissing their pants. This brings me to a sufficient level of excitement so as to get me into 'the zone'. Succeeding in upping the tension, the fly suddenly hones in from my left side and buzzes past my face. Not wanting to lose the moment, I continue with one eye on the movie and the other on the fly as it hits a dead-end against the wall, turns a hundred-and-eighty degrees and flies straight back towards my face. Its movements are laboured, as if it's just eaten and flying on a full belly and I'm certain I'll knock it to kingdom come when it's in range. Closer…closer… I think, releasing my cock. I swipe the air with a huge swoosh of the hand, missing it completely but creating some kind of vortex that sends it spinning past my ear with a loud buzz making me claw frantically at the side of my head.

"Fuck!"

I bolt up from the chair to follow its movements with cat-like precision until it finally disappears behind the bookcase. I can't be bothered with a pursuit to the death and re-engage with the computer, but the thrill is gone. With the time approaching nine-o-clock, I think about eating but realise I'm still too aroused for anything else. Pulling up My Favourites folder, I dig into past glories and look for something to finish me off. Within minutes, I'm perched on the edge of my seat and tugging furiously, using the film as a link to the explicit nature of pornography and the image of Caroline, until they flash alternately within my mind like the on-off switch of a light. I can feel my orgasm welling up from the base of my balls as I automatically reach for my 'cum-rag' realising I've forgotten to place one beside me. Not bothering to look around for something make-do, I point downwards and with a groan, release across the floor, convulsing at little snippets of remembrance: the flares, the garish, emerald-coloured eye-shadow, the flowered blouse, the hippie hair and the bottom, all work at finally bringing the session to an end. It takes me a few moments before I am able to get up and wipe the floor as post-cum lethargy sets in; there is, however, none of the usual enmity I feel, but instead a strange and greater sense of accomplishment and fulfilment. I attribute this to the fact that my yearning was all based in the reality of the image that Caroline presented to me earlier in the day, which works at justifying my actions. Indeed, this same image makes such an impression, that after cooking myself a pizza, I'm back in front of the computer for seconds, peaking intensely at one-thirty in the morning to a webcam of a plump woman with a huge bottom using a baseball bat. Only then and after much tossing and turning, do I finally manage to get some sleep.

I'm already back in the office - somnambulist state, functioning in slow motion - and all I want to do for ten minutes is quietly gather my thoughts. Klep is at his desk on the phone, talking I surmise, to either a relative or girlfriend due to the tone and nature of his conversation and much too engrossed to bother with me as I pass. Both Suzie and Lisa are also taking calls but at least acknowledge me as I sit down at my desk and log on. Prasad has e-mailed me the to-do list which I quickly browse over before heading over to the kettle to make myself a coffee. I am feeling dirty and unwashed and curse myself for waking up late and not showering. As I stand waiting for the kettle to boil I feel an intolerable itching coming from deep within my rectum causing me to squirm and clench my buttocks together discreetly in the hope of scratching it without actually having to reach behind me and root around with my fingers. It feels like a sweat rash, or a flare-up of the 'roids' that have been bothering me for the last week or so. No matter how much butt-clenching I do though, it isn't going away and I fear I am beginning to look conspicuously like a man in need of the toilet. Hurriedly, I make my coffee, spilling as I stir and Suzie puts the phone down.

"Alex, don't forget your appointment today regarding the model's convention." she tells me. "Marie called saying she'll be in at one-o-clock to go over the final details with you. That should cheer you up."

I don't say anything, instead haul myself off to the smoking area and scratch on the way down.

The smoking area however is the last place to retreat to if you're looking for sanity. The breakfast chefs are out in force in their whites and top hats and there are three or four girls from Housekeeping huddled together chaffing away like chimneys, all looking at mobile phones. It's a very depressing sight. I can't even get to my usual place as there are two Kitchen Porters occupying the space and when they see me, lift up slightly, indicating that they're willing to relinquish the space for me should I need it. I shake my head at them and turn away.

The coffee tastes good and the cigarette gets me feeling to something like normal again. I glance at the Housekeeping girls, but they're still busy looking at their phones. Whilst trying to work this image into something salacious, I'm subjected to the inane conversation coming from the chefs. This includes an account of the vast quantities of alcohol they had last night, bitching about the conditions of the kitchens, the quantity of work they have to put up with for very little pay, who is fucking who in the staff accommodation and football, all interspersed with the occasional fart. Blocking out the sound is nigh-on impossible as my mood is beginning to worsen and I light up another cigarette. I glance back over at the girls from Housekeeping - they are the most unattractive batch I've ever seen. My mind wanders to the other departments of the hotel. I think of Caroline again. Just the thought of her having reverted back to that old self fills me with dread and all at once the 70's get-up that suited her so well, seems a pleasant, but distant fiction.

Then Danute walks across the lot towards the staff entrance. Instantly my eyes hone in on her and I feel two little twitches inside my pants. Working in Accounts for the last six months or so, she's become a beacon of hope to me in an otherwise dreary environment. Coming from Lithuania and about my age, she is a glorious reason for me to excuse myself and hang around the Accounts department. On occasion, we've had a chat in the canteen at lunch or on the stairs if we pass eachother by and I'm certain she's interested in me as I always get the feeling she's waiting for something to happen whenever we engage but I'm simply too slow or stupid to commit. Whatever the case, I will *have* to make a move at some point soon. I have a very good reason. Her skin is unblemished and ghostly pale with a head of brown, reddish hair that is forever tied up in a bun. Even her eyelashes are unnaturally pale, accentuating the greenness of her eyes that hold you with a deep, intense stare that is often unnerving. She is of medium height, with a toned and muscular physique that fits the shirts and tight skirts she wears beautifully and it would be fair to say there was something even manly about her. But the thing that sends me over the edge, the detail that I have fantasised about more than anything concerning matters at work - the 'piece de resistance' - are the hairs on her legs that are just visible through the tanned tights that make up the entire outfit. Although it isn't the hairs on her legs that actually turn me on - they are a bit of a *turn-off* – it is the fact that these little wispy fibres are the dead give-away to the prize: the jewel that rests between her thighs in what I perceive must be the biggest *bush* to have ever graced a woman. This is the thought that has kept me up at night on so many occasions, having taken home the snippets of my voyeurism and concluded that there simply can be no other way. I have seen its massiveness from every angle, breathed in its scent and been left delirious with the way in which it maps itself out upon her body. I *must* see that pussy! I watch as she mounts the pavement with her quick step and modest manner and suck greedily on my cigarette until she disappears inside. I will pay her a visit today.

I get started on the list of to-do things that Prasad has left me but I don't feel like working. My first priority is the list of revenue figures as this means a trip to the Accounts department. There is also a prospective wedding to take place next year with the client eager to get the ball rolling which he has asked if I can look after in Gemma's absence. I am happy to do it, but wish Gemma would hurry up and get back from her holiday as I simply don't feel I have the right personality suited to dealing with the whole wedding fraternity and the sensitivity required to win the client over. Finally, function sheets left, right and centre need typing up. This reminds me that I have to get down to the A.V. department before my appointment for a chat with Mike just to make sure he's in the loop about what my client will want to go over with him. I make *this* my first priority.

"Are you sure this bill was paid?" Klep asks me out of the blue, eyeing the spread-sheet in front of him.

"Yes I'm sure. I billed it myself." I insist.

"It's alright. Relax. Chef was asking about it this morning, that's all…" he says offhandedly.

"Don't worry Marcus, it's done. I'll dig it out for you later."

"You seem uptight today…"

"I'm fine, Marcus."

"Well you seem it…" he says picking up the phone.

On my way down I stop off in the kitchen to check if Martin has come in yet just to see if we're still on for a drink tonight. I'm told he's due in at twelve. I continue on, past Reception where I see Caroline talking with a guest, delivering her routine recital in her monosyllabic tone that she's probably spouted five million times before without a word out of place. She quickly notices me as I pass but her mouth is working on auto and she doesn't really see me.

Mike is up in his office, a hive of wires and computers and tech boards and I can hear him in the room somewhere, but I'm damned if I can see him. I look out of the window that looks down into the Conference Theatre and catch the illuminated stage and a member of staff walking the lines of chairs dispensing water bottles.

"Mike?"

"In here," I hear him say.

My eyes follow the sound as he pokes his head out from under a table clutching some cables.

"Hi Alex…"

"Mike, I just wanted to see if you're okay with one-o-clock and the girl organising the models thing next week?"

"Yeah, that's not a problem. She wants to check the auditorium…yes?"

"Yeah she just wants to make sure she's got all her layout right and a couple of things on a presentation regarding sound and some of the film-work," I tell him.

"I'll be up here – just come and give me a shout."

"That's great – thanks Mike," I say, as he disappears back underneath the table. I stop to look around curiously at the mass of technology in the room.

"Mike, do you know what *everything* does in this room… what it's all for?

"Mostly…that's why I run the AV department…" he replies from under the table.

"Sure…thanks Mike," I say, before leaving.

In Accounts, I'm attempting to coerce Danute into moving from behind her desk so as to get a look at her legs, with a series of unimaginative ploys, but she isn't shifting. Behind me Ollie gives me a furtive look, probably wondering why I've been sniffing around a lot lately. Tittle-tattle spreads through the offices like a virus, infecting everybody; a toxic newsfeed that people positively welcome as a cure to the otherwise mundane tasks of their daily lives. I am different. I have other things to think about. I try not to get involved with the politics.

Just as quickly, Ollie forgets I'm in the room and returns to his work. I'm struck by Danute's pale lashes behind her round specs and the width of her mouth and fullness of the lips. A 'blowjob mouth', I think to myself. Her jacket is off, revealing a white blouse to which I can just make out the shadowy material of a frilly bra beneath as she stares at me with that deep and penetrating look that is hard to tell whether she's angry or just baffled, causing me to stall even more. I try again in offering up the papers, kind of pulling them towards me in a bid to get her to move, thus bringing her legs out from underneath the table. She doesn't comply, simply reaches out and forces me to hand them to her.

"What are they?" she asks, flicking through.

"They're the figures for the last three events – we just want to make sure they correspond with the numbers you've got," I tell her as I take in the colour of her hair and the way she's tied it back and how I recall I've always seen it tied up and not once cascading down her back, which I calculate would surely reach the crack of her bottom.

She looks up at me, flirtatiously, not really interested in the papers as I can tell, and distinctly observes my chest with that half-smile on her face as if she's seen something that I've failed to notice.

"Would that be okay?" I ask her.

"I guess so…" she sighs, placing the papers on her desk and returning to her computer screen. My presence is beginning to feel like an intrusion.

"Listen, I hate to be a pest but can you change a twenty for me?" I say, digging into my back pocket and pulling out my wallet. She's unsure at first, searching her desk in a confused state, her face suddenly becoming serious which really makes me feel like I've overstepped the mark. She pushes back a little, tutting, until her skirt comes into view, me sensing it's actually going to work, pushing back further, giving me a glimpse of the top of her tanned tights. At this point Ollie pipes up behind me like some Neanderthal man venturing out of his cave for the first time.

"I've got some change here…" he grunts.

I turn and glance at him, then back at Danute, just as I see her lower half disappear back from whence it came.

"Oh great…" I mumble as I step up and fulfil a completely pointless exercise at Ollie's desk, in the shadow of Danute's silence.

"Thanks for that…"

"No prob…" he grunts.

"Err…Danute…I'll get back to you on that…" I tell her.

"No prob…" she replies without even looking up.

After a meeting about the up-n-coming model's convention with Marie, a lovely, late forty-something ex-model who is pure class and who personifies everything good about the inevitability of growing old, I decide to make-do with a bag of crisps and a diet coke in the quiet and solitude of the empty canteen whilst mulling over when to call on Danute again. Martin finally shows up.

"Hey Alex…" he says, bounding past me and over to the vending machine.

"What time do you call this?" I ask, checking my watch.

"I've been here since twelve…"

"That's a lie – I checked at twelve and you were nowhere to be seen."

"Ok, half-twelve…" he replies, grabbing his coke before looming over me at the table.

"How's it going?"

"Christ…Chef is in a shit mood today," he says, as he throws the coke down his neck. I wish somebody would fuck this bloke, just so he cheers up…" he continues, his reflux causing him to burp loudly.

I balk as he presses his chest with his fist in an attempt to control the effervescence that rages within him.

"Busy?" I ask.

"Dinner for seventy in the Mongolian…" he says as he finishes the last of his drink.

We leave the canteen together with Martin stopping off at the kitchen door before asking me if we're good for tonight.

"Sure, eight-o-clock," I reply.

"Why don't you ask that Dante…or…Daphne…or whatever her name is to come along?" he says.

"She won't want to come," I quickly reply.

"Are you shy or what?" he asks.

"I think so…" I sigh, mishearing shy for sure.

Martin looks at me strangely before shaking his head.

"Fucked up…" he mutters before disappearing.

Fucked-up indeed! All I want to do is get home and enjoy the weekend. Everyone in the office it seems is feeling the same way - even Klep - and come five-thirty, the doors are locked and we're all drifting our separate ways.

Martin is telling me a joke about a guy who walks into a bar with his pet monkey but I'm not really listening, I'm looking across the pub at the blonde oozing out of her jeans. I catch snippets about the monkey sticking things up his arse and eating them, but I'm still looking at the blonde. I've never been a good listener of jokes, never know where to look as I'm listening, afraid it won't be funny then having to pretend it is with fake laughter. On this occasion at least, I have something to keep me occupied, something Martin could easily interpret in my face as being interested in the joke. And as I speculate over what type of underwear the blonde is wearing, Martin reaches the punch-line. I time my laughter perfectly as Martin reels back on his stool, almost spilling his pint. He seems satisfied enough with my reaction and we both drink.

"So where the fuck's Danute?" he asks, again.

"Get off it, will you…"

"Why didn't you ask her? She's probably at home, bored shitless right now…"he says, raising his eyebrows. "Check out the fucking hairs on her legs though – have you seen that?"

"The hairs on her legs…! Since when have you been looking so closely?" I ask him. "Come to think of it, you're nowhere near her office – when do you get time to see her?"

"Strangers passing in the night, that's all. Relax."

I drink my pint, desperate to get off the subject of Danute as I don't want some crude chef's remarks – friend or no friend – belittling the vision I have of her or affecting the way I want things to transpire between us.

"I'll do it…I'll get round to it. We'll go out for dinner or something," I tell him evasively.

"Sure…sure…" he nods. "Have you seen that new Italian girl in the Restaurant?"

"No."

"We'll you should. She's fit. I'd chuck her about…" he says, grinning.

I scan the pub as Martin continues with his assessment of the new Italian waitress from the Restaurant. A woman in her forties, with a huge head of hair and large breasts catches my eye as she holds forth with her friend. When it becomes apparent to me that I'm staring, I re-join Martin, in time to catch the end of his appraisal which finishes with something like: 'dirty bitch'.

"You're crude…and lewd…" I tell him.

"Don't come at me with your fucking airs and graces. I am who I am…" he says.

"I'm not so much talking about you…but the guys you work with…" I reply.

"We tell it like it is. We don't work in some office having to deal with twats like the one you work with all day." he replies. "We don't come at you with a smile and then stab you in the back when you turn around. If we tell you to fuck off – we *mean* fuck off."

I drink my pint.

"What's happening with that Sales job?" he asks.

"I don't know – I haven't heard anything."

"Fucking disgrace if they don't give it to you." he spits. "That's half the fucking problem in that place – they just don't promote internally. They'd rather scout around for ages and bring someone in, who within three months gets totally disenchanted with the place and leaves. In the meantime, the guys they *didn't* promote are just plain pissed off and leave as-well. That's why we're running a skeleton crew in every department and everyone's bitching and moaning. No incentives in that place."

Martin pauses to drink his pint and goes on.

"I won't suck up to them like Marcus – that's the problem," I tell him.

"That's how they like it, my friend." he replies. "It gives them an enormous sense of well-being…"

I nod my head absently as Martin urges me to finish up so he can get another round in.

"I'll get 'em," I tell him, getting up to go to the bar.

The pub begins to pick up and the level of noise forces the volume of conversation to increase. There are now a bevy of women scattered around the room for me to view whilst we talk and as Martin continues on the subject of work, we're both aware of a bit of a commotion at the table to our left with a young couple having a 'domestic'.

"You see, this is what I'm talking about. Who needs it?" I say.

"Comes with the territory, you know that."

"Really…? Do we need all that? I mean…my computer has everything I need concerning every aspect of my life, without the interference of others?" I say, tapping the side of my head. "All the information I need is stored right there in its memory banks."

"Not all. There's nothing human about a computer – and that's what we are my friend – human. What do you want to do – sit in your room all day wanking off, just so you don't have to deal with real life? There's no substitute for the real thing. You should know that."

"I'm not so sure…" I say, pulling my cigarettes out. "I'm telling you, there will come a day when we don't need people anymore. We will live fully automated lives." I say.

"Where are you going?" Martin asks.

"I need a fag." I tell him, rising from the table.

"Shit, now I understand your problem. I thought you swung the other way…"

"Hardy-fucking-ha…" I say, before heading out to the garden area at the rear of the pub.

The mature woman that caught my eye inside is now

outside, smoking with her friend. I make eye contact with her through the haze then she ignores me, uncomfortable at the weight of my stare. She really is a fine figure of a woman and I make a note of her assets, log them and store them away, before re-joining Martin.

"You're the only chef I know, doesn't smoke," I tell him. "Cigarettes, I mean."

"I quit. It's called willpower."

"Yeah, you'll be back on 'em in a couple weeks."

"Not this time – this time it's for good."

"Mmmm…"

"I'm getting back into my weights. Sorts me right out. Whenever I get the craving, I pump some iron - keeps my mind occupied *and* makes me look good." he says, to which I have to agree.

"I can't see any difference – you look exactly the same to me." I lie.

"Well it's not going to make a difference straight away is it – it takes a bit of time. It's what I *feel* that counts…right?"

He takes a sip of his pint.

"But anyway, as I was saying…" he goes on, his voice lowering. "I've pre-booked a date with a robot."

"What do you mean?"

"A whore robot… I've pre-booked a fuck with one. I found a place where they're working on the technology. Won't be long now before they'll have created a life-like robot, that looks and feels just like the real thing. That's what they say anyway. You want me to book you in?"

"I don't know…"

"Think about it…" he goes on. "This is the future - compliant in every way. No more arguments, no chit-chat, never tires, can be created to your own liking… plus, it will never get pregnant – it will never spawn screaming, baby robots."

"You never know…"

"Alright, perhaps years from now…"

"Now you're contradicting yourself…" I tell him. "First you say we're human and now you talk about fucking robots."

"I know…but you have to admit, it sounds good."

"What about Tasha?"

"I wouldn't be cheating on her, it's a robot… doesn't count. She could beat it black and blue – it wouldn't *feel* anything, therefore making it redundant."

"If it doesn't feel anything, surely that would affect the sex?"

"C'mon man, use your imagination…" he replies incredulously. "You in…?"

Another four pints and gone twelve and after more talk about fucking robots, in which he convinces me to try it, I'm standing outside the pub with Martin feeling more intoxicated than I had anticipated before the start of the evening. The last thing I want is a hangover tomorrow, rendering me incapable of performing any kind of task other than kicking back on the sofa with a headache. I walk with Martin to the cab-stand where he's told there should be something available in about twenty minutes and we talk some more until his cab finally comes. Upon his departure, he calls me a pussy for not asking Danute out and tells me that I'm too self-centred and egotistical to be a really good man, but because he's bigger than all that, still likes me. I tell him he looks like he's been whipped with an ugly stick his whole life and I hear him laughing with the cab driver as he pulls away.

I take a quiet, shortcut home, savouring the warm, night air, a part of mc glad that the evening is over and that I'm left to my own devices. I light up a smoke and listen to the distant voices of late-night revellers and the other part of me wonders if I'm ever going to have sex with a real person again.

3

As a rule, I don't sleep in on Saturdays and certainly not past nine o'clock, which today is not the case as its gone nine-forty-five. I clean my teeth then take in a vast amount of water to try and quell the negative effect I'm feeling before heading into the kitchen where the day starts with a big breakfast, made all the more pleasant without the rush of having to prepare for work. Ham and eggs, coffee, toast and jam with more coffee as I watch the cat, quiet and unresponsive this morning despite filling his bowl with his favourite food. He sniffs at me as I watch the T.V with the volume turned low keeping a check on the cookery programme that's playing – the only plus point being the female wine expert who makes a brief appearance. My exterior is calm, composed but inside, the anticipation is building.

I continue to eat slowly, teasingly and with the absence of a paper this morning, channel hop in the vain hope of catching more tit-bits to get the juices flowing. Only when I have finished eating, drunk my coffee and taken five minutes to digest, do I make a bee-line straight for the 'office', braced for another Saturday - the daddy of all wanking days.

It's 6pm and the computer is about to crash. The entire unit is about to explode and screams: OVERLOAD… OVERLOAD! And all at once, the deafening din in front of me, the whirring of the fan in its guts, spinning it seems at ten million revolutions per second, like some cataclysmic tornado carving up its insides with the cold, toxic resolution of its screen and the stifling air filling the room - makes me feel sick. It's a deep nausea filling me with bile that is ready to spew out of every pore. The room becomes hard and real once more, a place I recognise with all the familiar things inhabiting it, placed in all the places I remember them to be: the tanned slats of the window blind, perpetually drawn, the stack of pens in their ornate copper holding, the used batteries in the cracked jar, the ceramic Buddha statuette - enlightened and gently meditating – the 'vintage style' globe with the great expanse of the Pacific Ocean facing me, two toy cars passed down from childhood, the tea-light holder, waxed out and spooky and the small card propped up against 'Piglet' reading 'You're Gorgeous' – a token message from Sarah four Valentines ago. My eyes touch them all until they finally fall on the cum-soaked rag, pressed into the palm of my talon-like hand – a rag symbolising all the lust and passion of the preceding seven hours – all the meagre fruit of my mercurial labour!

The nausea recedes, replaced with the feeling of emptiness and nothingness and a sense of the *unreal*. The Buddha is no longer looking at me, but past me, into a place I know nothing about or could ever hope to understand. The Pacific Ocean is something I am vaguely aware of but unsure of its place in the world and the thin lines between the slats of the blind that once gave off daylight are now darkening. I listen to the still sounds of the room as the fan of the computer lulls and turn my eyes toward the desk-lamp, its head turned away at an awkward angle with the soft light emanating outward so as not to strain the eyes and fall into reflection. Then, climbing the bookshelf to my right, I catch various titles that I can't remember whether I've read or not. None of that matters. I realise it's all a deliberate ploy to avert my eyes from the one thing I don't want to see.

Inexorably, they are pulled back to the computer screen not more than two feet away from my face. The image is blown up - frozen in the moment - her catty eyes looking back at me so provocatively, so perfectly, they are impossible to ignore. His penetration is thick and deep and accentuated by the angle of the shot and one can only marvel at his size; a composition to stand up with any of the greats that have been before or ever will be again – and there will be more. It is a moment of perfection - the moment the world exploded across the universe at the speed of light in the form of a million stars. I hate the image, like I hate all perfection. I hate the falsity it represents; I hate the unblemished shape of her backside, the definition of the thighs; I hate the cock-sure look on his face and I hate the brazenness with which they both act. I hate the fact that they had sent me wild with desire and that they had succeeded in getting the best of me, having me relinquish all other duties in favour of gross self-gratification. I hate her with my throbbing head, with my numb arse, with my aching back, with the feeling of nothingness and utter uselessness, with my spent stars soaked up in that filthy rag. Yet despite all this, despite my loathing, I feel the stirrings of another erection.

Above me, the fly's omnipresence disturbs and diverts my gaze; its thick black body resting up in the top corner of the room. I'm not sure if it's the same fly that was there yesterday; the thorax seems to be of a much blacker constitution with white specks and the abdomen certainly seems fatter and more ovoid. It doesn't matter - it is filled with the same yellow pus and bile as the last. Lifting myself from the desk, I move in for a closer look, my flaccid cock and shrunken balls swinging against the inside of my thighs as my eyes hone in on the creature. It looks like it's cleaning itself, washing itself behind the ears with its front legs, much the same way as my cat does. It senses danger when I raise my hand and stops cleaning before I lash out! It's gone. The exertion leaves me even more exhausted; and with great lethargy, still clutching the wet rag, I re-take my seat and toss it into the waste-paper basket. The image on screen has finally lost its allure.

I open the window and welcome in the cool evening air, moving hungrily towards it, breathing in its vitality. A sense of reality returns to the room and to every other aspect of my life, the thought of which produces a giant gape of a yawn. Feeling angry and cheated, I move to the bathroom and perform my ablutions, thoughts turning to the previous evening with Martin and all the unspoken things I now wish I had said but didn't – a distortion that makes me feel even sicker. I'm tired. I check my reflection: wan, elongated and tired. I need a complete make-over - everything defective. I must sleep. It's all I'm good for.

Not so. At ten-forty-five, the force of my second orgasm racks my body, causing me to double over until my forehead rests on the table in supplication, a feeling something akin to having just completed a ten-hour shift on a building site. Shocked at the speed of the day's passing, I eventually wander into the front room and collapse onto the sofa in front of the T.V, waking up in the middle of the night, where I shift myself to the bedroom, crawl under the duvet and hibernate until just gone nine-thirty.

I'm convinced the cat has dementia. Looking up at the sky which is a grey blanket producing sheets of rain, a condition that dissuades me from venturing out for the papers, he harasses me for more food, so vociferously I have to stop and question whether I actually gave him the previous bowl I thought I did, due to it being empty. I've also noticed him walking around in a confused state, eyes vacant, unsure of his surroundings, trying it seems to latch onto something he recognises, a condition that perhaps suggests he's trying to emulate me. I assure him this isn't the way forward and decide to do some research on his symptoms – without feeding him.

Sunday is an altogether different kettle of fish. Whereas its predecessor comes with the promise of two days of leisure and all the time in the world, Sunday brings the spectre of work back to mind and the gnawing feeling that you're constantly fighting against the 'dying of the light', with melancholic effect. With this in mind, I forego the Sunday papers, wolf down my breakfast then head into the spare room and light up the first cigarette.

All forces are assembled and despite feeling tender and sleepy, I move from film to film exhibiting an exercise in tired stroke play as opposed to actually getting involved in the action. This changes, as time goes on, and by one-o-clock, I am suitably aroused thanks to a new update of webcams. My mood though, like the weather, is far from perfect and I find myself becoming irritated at the slightest thing: the women aren't doing what they're supposed to do, the camera angles are all wrong and won't go where I want them to and I find myself shouting at the screen urging whoever is behind the damn thing to take some time out and get lessons in camera work before uploading them! With my stomach in knots, shoulders tense, pressure on the heart and dismayed at my power of regeneration, I light another cigarette and continue until my mobile phone rings, a sound I welcome with quiet relief.

"Hey Martin…" I say, after giving it the five rings.

"Mate, it's time for a beer, wouldn't you say? I'm over here with Tasha and Becky. We're going to be in The Plough, so get yer ass out," he says.

"The Plough…?"

"That's where we're going. Meet us down there."

I consider the prospect of having to get dressed then go out to a noisy pub with a lot of people and make conversation when I don't feel like talking and laugh at things I don't feel like laughing at just when I was beginning to feel horny again.

"Hmmm…"

"C'mon over, yer lazy git!" he barks. "Becky's waiting for you. She wants to have a chat. She's got a problem with the zip on her jeans and thinks you might be able to help."

I can hear female laughter in the background and envisage Becky in some deliciously tight outfit struggling to unfasten her zip. I clasp my cock and add a little pressure.

"C'mon…stop expressing your sexuality alone and join us," Martin insists, sounding pissed already.

"I don't know…I've got some stuff I'm working on for tomorrow." I tell him lamely.

"Bollocks to that! You're making that up. I can tell by the tone of your voice. Becky really wants to see you mate," he persists.

I shoot a glance at the weather through the blind and then at the computer screen and the hairy muff staring back at me and realise the more I procrastinate, the harder it will be to turn him down.

"Well…what time?" I ask.

"Quarter-to-two." he says.

"No, I mean what time are you going to be there?" I say looking at the watch.

"Three-o-clock…"

"Okay, I'm not going to promise anything – I might be there, I'll see how I feel," I say, actually beginning to warm to the idea.

"Three o'clock…" he reiterates.

"I'm not promising Martin. I *might* see you there…"

"Alright…just put yer dick away and save it for Becky," he says.

"Sure…" I reply, to the sound of more laughter before the line goes dead.

By four-thirty I'm still sitting in front of the computer, struggling with the torment of not being able to get aroused, yet still persisting in remaining where I am. The phone doesn't ring again and I sense Martin's disappointment as palpable, despite his absence. It's not just Martin's - but my own. Coming to terms with the fact that one has a problem is never an easy thing and as much as I refute the damning evidence, concentration is impossible. I check my watch: Sunday hours, I need supplies; the Supermarket closes in precisely twenty minutes.

Outside, the sense of the unreal hits me like a brick as I scurry along with the dreaded feeling that I'm about to bump into Martin even though I'm nowhere near the pub. I check my watch and quicken my pace. Dog-walkers, Sunday lovers, grannies, pissheads, all regard me with their beady eyes, compounding the feeling of self-consciousness. My trousers feel too short, prompting me to hesitate every time I breach a curb, which in turn scuppers my momentum reducing the simple task of walking to a hobble. I look down and see my flies are undone. I zip up and move on.

I enter the arcade and round the corner to the Supermarket, which is on the first floor, and curse as to why it's always the 'up' escalator that's not working. It's cold inside, which brings some relief. I decide on the usual for quick and practical reasons, as opposed to anything nutritional: pizza, tinned goods, things that you can just stick in the oven, bread – although not the best time of day to buy this – cat food, cheese, some chocolate, crisps and tomato sauce. I'm already at the automated till in what seems like record time putting through my items until the machine informs me 'assistance required'. I wave to a woman loitering in one of the isles before I realise she's a customer. Then as I'm about to give up, a young girl comes to my aid and swipes her card, smiles artificially and tells me I can carry on. Bagged up, I realise I need more cigarettes which means heading over to the kiosk and waiting in line for an extraordinary amount of time as it seems every pensioner in town has decided to do the same thing. So much for cigarettes sending you to an early grave!

The walk home is always better than the outbound journey, having been instilled with the confidence that comes with having accomplished something. This doesn't rid me of the gnawing feeling though that something is very askew in my life and that if I carry on in the same vein for much longer, I shall go mad. As I approach the flat, I decide I need a holiday and will speak to Prasad about it first thing tomorrow, if I have the time.

As I wait for my food to cook, I can only reflect on what could have been: a momentous afternoon with real company in the form of Martin and Co, something I could have looked back on perhaps, years from now, with great fondness. My life could have been changed irrevocably. Did I miss out on a future wife, the mother of my children, the greatest fuck ever to bestow a man? How many weekends have been spent in much the same way? How many moments lost?

I observe the cat sitting elegantly upright and unusually silent, envying his simplicity before pulling my pizza out of the oven, suddenly feeling ravenous when I see the blistered cheese and pepperoni glistening under the kitchen light. After eating I watch some television but the act of watching alone only makes me more depressed, so I head for the shower.

I feel invigorated the moment the hot water hits the crown of my head as all tension falls away. Looking down, I see I'm urinating and standing in a puddle of bright yellow fluid. Hypnotized by its colour, it slowly becomes translucent as the jet of water hits the tub floor, diluting the discharge and sending it down the plughole in a slow and measured swirl.

In the bedroom, I dry off in front of the full-length mirror, observing my taut definition and come to the conclusion that I look good. Then looking down at the thatch of hair around my crotch, decide my pubes need trimming. Before doing so, I stick my cock and balls back between my legs and clamp my thighs tightly shut, giving off the impression that I have a pussy. Remaining like this, I begin to writhe until I'm gyrating, observing all the while the dense triangle of sprouting hair that looks very real, so much so I have to stop due to the swelling of my cock which springs back into position when I un-part my legs.

By eleven-thirty I'm tugging like a mad-man, as some kind of recompense for the lame afternoon session, to a French film I have seen many times with a woman in stockings and suspenders entertaining two well-hung men - all triggered by a man under the illusion that he knows what it feels like to have a hairy vagina. *"Ces't bon, ces't bon! Venez-baiser-moi! Venez-baiser-moi!! J'taime tellement ca putain de merde!! Oui! Oui…!!"* comes the barrage of filth spewing from the girl's mouth, enough to finally send me over the edge in a thundering climax that leaves me warm and tired and slumped in the chair, drifting on a golden sea of contentment – a night without end. Amidst this tranquillity, with Buddha staring back at me and the vast Pacific Ocean, spread across blue, comes the sudden intrusive thought of work and the research I had intended to do for a client meeting tomorrow morning, but have completely forgotten about.

"Shit!" I mutter, calculating, taking milliseconds to gauge whether I have enough information already to see me through.

Slinging on some clothes, I quickly bring up all I have on the company and the details of our preliminary meeting until it soon becomes obvious that the whole thing will take time and frankly, is the *last* thing I feel like doing at this time of night.

"Arsehole!"

I decide it's going to be a wing-job - down to the wire with the information I have, coupled with the experience and charm I know I'm capable of producing. It's a deal worth 40k and one I don't think the director would look upon too favourably if lost. Too fucking bad… I think, as the light goes out.

4

John, the hotel Director descends the stairs at a sprightly business-like pace that is way too quick for a man of his age and position. We meet on the landing where he raises his hand to me, as if stopping traffic and smiles in his perfunctory way.

"Morning…"

"Morning," I reply, smiling artificially.

He steps forward, chin jutting out.

"Are we all good with the guys from DatsComm this morning?" he asks.

"Yes…I've…"

"Good…good…"

He proceeds to prattle on about how they're a company and a little unsure of what they want, which means they're open to persuasion, but I'm not listening, instead adjusting my mind and body in preparation for entry back into the land of the living after a sleepless night where all manner of violent and criminal thoughts tormented me. I feel completely wanked out and not even the female news presenter at breakfast with her tight, pastel green dress and black tights aroused within me one iota of sexual desire. It's not a state I like to be in as a lot of my best work and impetus comes from the predatory feeling of seduction. It is *that* drive that urges me onto bigger and better things with a feeling of something to *look forward to*. Without it, life trundles along with a familiarity bordering on the obscene. Today will be obscene: Klep, boring show-rounds, catty girls incessantly talking about hunks, food unfit for slaves, more talk about nothing, a long and tired trek upon the treadmill, all nine hours with absolutely nothing to look forward to.

"Everything okay?" he finally asks, emphasising with his hand again.

"Sure…" I lie.

John is unconvinced.

"Are you okay this morning?" he asks again, scrutinizing my face.

"Yes I'm fine…"

"Good, let's do it then…" he says, still unconvinced, before descending in the same sprightly manner.

The office floor is already busy with people walking to and fro, all locked in their own Monday morning despair waving papers and passing me with a determined stride. The whole scene tires me enormously and a sense of the unreal washes over me as I approach the office. Everyone, it seems has made it in early.

Inside, Lisa and Suzie are already at their desks talking heatedly about a television programme they both saw last night concerning one of the male contestants and what a rat he was. Klep is with Prasad, talking in his office. Thankfully I've missed his usual morning presentation, but I do notice the words 'In the Loop' scrawled across the flip-pad, doubtless which has had little effect on the team's moral or impetus.

"Alex did you watch Love Nest last night?" Suzie asks.

"No…" I mumble, heading straight for the kettle.

This does nothing to deter her from trying to bring me in on the conversation, oscillating between myself and Lisa, formulating the notion that given the right circumstances, every man will eventually cheat on his girlfriend or spouse. Even her breasts do nothing to lift my weariness. I nod helplessly and spoon coffee granules into my cup, cursing the kettle for taking so fucking long to boil. Klep steps out of Prasad's office with a handful of papers and nods at me.

"Morning…" he says cheerfully. "Did John catch up with you? He wanted a word about DatsComm?"

"Yes, I've already spoken to him."

"He's taken a vested interest…" he says, sitting down.

"He takes a vested interest in *all* potential clients…" I reply as the kettle comes to the boil.

"How was your weekend?" Lisa asks, as I head back to my desk. "Do anything special? Climb Ben Nevis… go swimming with sharks… jump off Victoria Falls?"

I want to tell her I wanked all weekend to 'Wanton Mary' just to see the look on her face. I want to be completely honest with her and say I produced enough spunk to fill a bucket. I want to tell her I've got the spunkiest cock in the western world. How nice it would be to actually tell her the truth; to describe in detail every idiosyncratic step of the process, right up to its conclusion. What would she say then? I settle for some banal fabrication.

"I was with family on Saturday and on Sunday I read the papers."

"What all day?"

"With a rest here and there…"

"What a depressing way to spend the day," she frowns.

"What with family or with the papers…?" Klep butts in.

"Both - damn it!" Suzie says.

"Don't listen to it Alex. They do nothing better with their time; they're hen-peckers that watch reality T.V…" Klep informs me.

"*I* played Mahjong with my Steve," Lisa says.

"Martian…?" Suzie frowns. "You mean the film?"

"Mahjong! Like dominoes, with Chinese characters instead of dots," Klep says wheeling himself a little closer to me and leaning forward. "See what I mean…hen-peckers! Yeah, John was prattling on about DatsComm this morning…its worth a bit…you up for it?"

"I'm fine…thank-you, Kle…Marcus." I assure him, shaking my head.

Phones begin to ring simultaneously and reflections of the weekend are put on the back burner as everyone is taken up with work. I open up my e-mails, in two minds as to whether to go down for a cigarette, but decide not to. Messages from various departments fill the Inbox: Chef needs an update concerning the models convention on Thursday, new procedures implemented in the event of a fire – fire training to be attended by all; Accounts highlighting various outstanding charges relating to past events and what we intend to do about rectifying these for the future, the Director re-iterating this point emphasising that all parties involved will be held accountable, this reminds me to call in on Danute. Positions available within the company via our website - the position in the Sales team not yet advertised as it's not yet available - Health and Safety issues handed down from the HR department and what needs to be done, which include us up here in the offices; you never know, somebody might get their head stuck in the photocopying machine, somebody might eat the wrong Hob-Nob - Suzie needs to fill out a risk-assessment on this point; somebody might jump out of the window, *I* need to fill out a risk-assessment on this point, issues relating to backs and the height of chairs and the long-term damage of sitting in front of a computer screen all day long - I'm way past this one – how to lift a box and various other things that if you thought about for too long, would make you insane, so I don't. Various messages from future event organisers who want to meet up to go over final details, invoices, agency queries and invitations and finally, a company with a revolutionary new way of making your cock grow bigger – in weeks, guaranteed! This last one disturbs me as it's obviously got through the filter system as SPAM, although I do actually toy with the idea of looking into this before deleting it, and finally, a message from Prasad reminding me about the wedding appointment I have today.

I decide to head down for that cigarette, pulling every ounce of negativity down with me. As someone, so receptive to beauty – and I am – how did I become so ugly? A man can convince himself of anything and what he's doing as right, when out of control. And I am beginning to feel like a man out of control. Like those stories I hear concerning people who turn up in A&E with various objects lodged up their arses. How do you convince a doctor that your mobile phone got stuck up your arse by accident when you sat down? It brings new meaning to the words, 'talking shit'. What about a broken cucumber or garden gnome? What would you say then? A man will convince himself of anything in the name of self-preservation.

Before I know it, I'm stubbing out my cigarette and trying to look normal but having difficulty shaking the image of the garden gnome. And when I finally reach Reception and hear a guest explaining to Caroline that he's regurgitated all over the second floor – not been sick, regurgitated – and that it would make him feel better if we sent him the cleaning bill, I steady myself and take a deep breath, before approaching Judy and Brian from DatsComm, who rise to my outstretched hand displaying a look of menace that tells me I'm in for a rough ride…

After a long two hours, I'm back in the smoking area, recapping over what was a poor show-round, to say the least. And as much as I try, there's no getting around this fact, the excruciating details of which, return like little stabs in the belly: the coffee that tasted like chemicals – Valeria's attempt at sabotage for my lax performance in bed – answers to forgotten questions, a joke about post-coital smoking, T.V's without channels, views of the fourteenth tee as opposed to the fifteenth hole, the Maintenance guys staring at Judy's legs, the Restaurant with its décor of ostentatious-bordello-garish-kitsch-1920's-nouveau-modernist-opulence that gives me the creeps every time I walk in the place and Brian catching me out when I lied about it winning awards, topped by my general aloofness to the whole affair.

I suck in more smoke and turn nervously on the spot wondering how I could have played it differently just as I see Martin lumber his way into work, prompting me to stub out and move until we converge on the door to the staff entrance.

"Hey…" he says, clearly looking like shit.

I smile anxiously, waiting for him to lay into me about not turning up yesterday and not even having the decency to tell him I wasn't going to turn up. To my surprise, *he* apologises.

"Listen, sorry about yesterday…the girls decided they didn't want to go out after all so we stayed in and got fucking tanked," he tells me.

"Yeah, I was waiting for two hours and no-one turned up."

"You're joking?"

"I *am* joking," I tell him, just as Chef stops him on his way out.

"You maggot!" he calls after me, before muttering something about Becky still wanting a chat.

I'm back in the office after having taken some paracetamol, feeling battered and bruised and dealing with Klep.

"Well?" he enquires, after putting the phone down.

"Well what?"

"Were they bowled over or stamped out?"

"Couldn't tell," I reply quickly.

"You mean you left them undecided?"

"That's right – they were undecided…"

"In other words, you were unable to persuade them in…" he pauses to look at his watch. "…the last two hours, that we're the top hotel around and that they'd be mad not to use us," he says. "That's pretty lame."

"They were concerned about space," I tell him.

"Space – the final frontier or what?" he smiles. "Don't you want to know how mine went?"

"Not really…"

"Status – definite!" he pronounces, undeterred.

"Marcus, it was a sure thing. They had already booked with us – it was simply a case of going over old ground and making sure things were okay," I say, unable to ignore him.

"The *old ground* you're referring to can be slippery as hell if you're not careful – need I remind you of NOBA?" he smiles.

"NOBA was a one-off. How many other people have we ever lost that far in?"

"You're trying to belittle my achievements Alex." he says seriously.

"Give me some credit – I've got more important things to do." I tell him.

"God listen to them – just like a couple of women," Suzie interjects from the back of the room as Prasad wheels himself into the doorway of his office and beckons me over.

"Listen, I've just been on the phone with DatsComm – they're not going with us." he states matter-of-factly.

"Already…? Why?"

"It was between us and Chatham Manor - they chose them. She didn't go into too much detail. Size was an issue as was location. She also mentioned something about service not being up to scratch. What's your take on it?"

"I thought it went well…"

"Anyway it's done, no use crying about it, there's nothing we can do. Let's just get on," he says. You've got that wedding enquiry now haven't you?"

"Yes…"

"Okay, just thought I'd fill you in…" he says finally.

Unable to vindicate myself in any way, I head back to my desk and grab my jacket, just as Klep opens his mouth.

"IN THE LOOP…remember…?" he says pointing to the flip-pad.

"Don't say a fucking word…" I hiss, before leaving the room.

Weddings are an altogether different and more genial proposition to the cold, hard, formal world of business, despite the fact that thousands are being spent and that people consider their wedding day to be one of the most important of their lives to which enormous emphasis is placed on getting things right.

The couple I have seated in front of me are no different as I listen to their story of how they met, what they do, the infinite future and all it holds and what they want on the big day. Their almost enviable detachment from the fetters of the big bad world – a far cry from my own - is impossible to hold against them and has a calming effect on me. I take note of the bride to be, with her long, flaxen hair, virginal white skin and soft, fleshy features and feel almost pity for her in that it is I with whom she must entrust her most personal yearnings.

As I walk them round, they listen and look in awe, punctuating my facts with little ideas of their own; creating in their minds the perfect picture for which to look upon over a lifetime with the greatest reverence. Every decision made is a unified step on the part of the lady and her beau and the sparkle in her eye touches me when I tell her of all the possibilities the hotel is capable of providing. *He* is a little more shrewd and careful, with money being the key factor of all considerations. I humour him by telling him a woman never forgets – so make it count. We laugh in agreement and he mutters something about having second thoughts to which he receives a very dark look that puts him in his place once more. That's how she likes him, where she wants him; and the sparkle returns to her eyes when he walks obediently beside her, leaving me to recall in my mind the details of a movie that's been doing the rounds called 'Mistreated Bride' in which, on her wedding night her newly vowed husband is trussed up beside the bed, like a cuckold, as she, still in her bridal gown, is ravaged by three would-be suitors, whilst he can only look on. It's a film that's finished me off on more than one occasion and as I usher them back to Reception, a desperate yearning to see it again germinates within me.

We exchange final pleasantries and I make no bones about the fact that I am sitting in for Gemma and that it is with her that they will be dealing with, which I sense, to my surprise, the bride is a little regretful of. I reassure her that Gemma has vast experience in dealing with these matters, both of whom seem to buy into this and leave the meeting on a high and sense of great expectation. I sincerely wish them all the best and tell them I look forward to seeing them again as things begin to take shape.

As I bid them farewell, John the Director passes me with silent, unflinching brevity and I am again reminded of my previous meeting and whether he is aware of the outcome. I am also aware something needs to be done about the disease that is Klep.

5

'*Sluts know best*'! Sluts damn well know best! Or so she keeps telling me, her mouth as filthy as my mood. I'm not even *in* the mood, yet I've been stuck in front of the computer for the last three hours enduring a session that has seen me pummel Klep's head to a pulp, throw him into the garbage compactor, before pressing 'start', watch him have an 'accident' as he slips out of the third floor window, listen to Prasad fire him, listen to John the Director tell me he's sorry, it's all Klep's fault, walk in one morning and hear Klep's disappeared off the face of the earth and won't be coming back - all to the evil mantra of 'sluts know best'. She works her hands around her body as my eyes roll within my head furiously. My cerebellum is about to explode. "If sluts know best, why can't you fucking bring me off?" I retort. She produces more toys and spouts more obscenities and my fury grows with my flared nostrils and bulging eyes and distorted sense of the world as I egg her on and urge her to bring me off! The movie is good but I can't concentrate. What a fucking waste! Get me away from this filth. I spot a fly glued to the top far corner of the wall. Please no flies, not at this time of night - no fucking flies! 'Sluts know best…' she tells me again, and I believe, her mantra working over my tightening balls, heart pumping furiously. Nothing else in the world matters at this very moment – only the fact that 'sluts know best'. Yes - *you* know best! Teach me. Take me away from the horrors of the office; pluck me from my malignancy and lead me to the playground of the stars. 'Sluts know best' – yes they do! Move me, sail with me to Shangri-La, it won't be long now! SLUTS DAMN WELL, KNOW BEST!

At two minutes past nine I blow my load across my rag with such enmity, the gas-powered lever holding up my chair gives way and drops me a foot closer to the floor. The jolt down forces the tip of the stand, up into the base of the worn seat and hits my anus with the force of a cattle gun, sending me upright in spasms of pain. Hopping around the room thinking it's actually *penetrated* my arse I reach round and check for blood but thankfully the hand comes back clean. The movie is still playing and I continue to watch, however there is no great sense of the unreal, only deep anger and frustration at my impudence.

The 'slut' finally reaches her own climax and retires exhaustedly into her pillows. I fall back, reposed. Something has got to be done! Action must be taken. This will not go on unpunished. Closing the film, I pull up the archive and scan down the enormous length of content with the sole intention of erasing the list from my computer in one gigantic move towards freedom. I manage to hold this conviction for about five seconds as the various titles, commendations and codes I've written, scream out at me from the page, creating a mental picture of every great scene that has consumed, what seems like, the entire duration of my life. Deleting them would be impossible. It would be like cutting off an arm or a leg – or a penis! I am resigned to this thought, recalling the good and the great and decide that maybe deleting *some* of them might be acceptable. In fear, I begin to randomly click - titles I know I haven't looked at for ages and know I will probably never look at again, but remain, because I am a hoarder and afraid to let go. I delete…every click pushing me one step closer to salvation. After ten minutes I give up as the list is simply too exhaustive and think about other means of cutting myself free. I pull up information on filters and web blockers, chastity belts and manacles and decide against them all. Thoughts of seeing a psychiatrist enter the fray, regression analysis and trying to uncover some pertinent detail from childhood that I've blocked out or failed to remember, perhaps? Instead I remove myself from the terminal and hit 'shut-down'.

In the living room, I pace like a caged animal, conjuring up ways to occupy myself - all to no avail, everything a source of irritation. I need to get out of the flat, go somewhere, anywhere, call somebody, anybody. I walk across the room scratching my anus and the cat begins to follow me, sniffing the air, trying to reinforce his status to me as a mate and companion perhaps.

I finally give in to bed but it's too early and although I drift off into sleep, it is light and troubled and all I can think about is the 'Mistreated Bride' film that I failed to remember when I got in from work and whether I actually saved it, as it's a film I'm desperate to see again, made all the more potent by the elements of surprise and astonishment that come with re-discovery. Despite the urge being great, I refrain from getting up and turning on the computer, instead relieve myself with pure, positive thinking, all bathed in golden rays of sunshine caressed by the wind and the gentle sound of lapping water. Slowly I succumb to the vibe and with controlled breathing, drift into unconsciousness. All is well until dawn sheds her early light and the toll of my alarm sends my mind spiralling into a new set of maladies…

"PRESENTATION…!" Klep states, as he stands at the head of the room, admiring his green scrawl. "What do we look like? First impressions count…"

I stare out at the bright blue morning sky from the far window feeling like I haven't left the office at all. Then think about confronting Danute again.

"Let's look at Suzie." he goes on. "C'mon admit it - we all like to look at Suzie."

"I beg your pardon?" Suzie says, unimpressed, yet clearly relishing the attention.

I'm the first to turn and look.

"Hair healthy and beautifully clean…crisp white shirt…skirt pressed…sensible heels…and not over-doing the make-up. And look at that smile!"

"What smile?" She sneers.

I can actually feel the eggs benedict I had for breakfast making its way back up towards my oesophagus. I return to my e-mails, which I know will piss Klep off, but it's either that or an embarrassing display of projectile vomiting.

"My first impression of you is one of professionalism, confidence and a joy in what you do," he purrs. "If *I* think that, so do our clients."

I secretly chuckle at this, as *my* first impression, is that she gives a great blowjob, a train of thought I opt to pursue.

"What about Alex…?" I hear, from somewhere in the room. I look up and Klep is bearing down on me. "That head of dark brown hair, slightly overgrown and fashionably un-kept…a somewhat pallid complexion this morning, with dare I say, bags under the eyes…and is that a five-o-clock shadow masking the contours of your jaw line?" He says.

"Oooo…I think Alex had a late one last night…" Suzie comments.

Klep moves in for a closer look. I remain impassive.

"A very nice aqua-marine shirt, I must say, tucked into a belt whose stitching is slightly frayed…and I can't tell whether those slacks have been creased or not. Have those black brogues been polished this morning?"

The violation goes on with the irritation needle nearly off the scale, all fuelled by Suzie who punctuates his words with nervous laughter and little throw-away comments that make me feel like dropping the laminating machine on her head for the trouble, despite the fact she gives good blowjobs. Klep lifts his fore finger in the air - a light-bulb appearing above his head.

"What are my first impressions of Alex?"

"He's a bad boy…" Suzie purrs, in a way that sends a shiver straight to the root of my cock.

"No… does he care, I ask myself? Can I trust this man to provide me with everything I need? Would I trust this man with my money?"

"Marcus you're becoming annoying." Lisa informs him.

"We should never let our clients entertain thoughts like that. Everything must be perfectly in place before any discussion. Get that right and we've made a significant step towards success. Would you stay in a dirty hotel? Would you trust a dirty-looking man?" he says suggestively, staring at me.

"You're not implying I'm dirty, I hope?" I ask, to the sound of laughter behind me.

"I am simply saying there is always room for improvement…"

"Even for you Marcus…?" Lisa calls.

"Even me…" he says, stepping back. "If we all do our little bit, we can't fail. Synergy – the whole is greater than the sum of its parts…remember…" Klep finally says, taking his seat, leaving Suzie looking bewildered.

Slowly grinding into action, I'm at pains as to how I'm ever going to compete with the ass-licking, toe-sucking grovelling of Klep and his attempts at trying to impress all and sundry in his bid to make the Sales team. Quite content to brown-nose his way through life without fear of ridicule, it is this confidence and zeal that employers love and he knows it. How many occasions have I been witness to his powers of seduction over Prasad and Steph and watched them U-turn on decisions that were seemingly set in stone? Am I placing too much self-doubt and criticism upon myself just because Klep has had a pro-active moment? As the morning proceeds, the more ridiculous he seems to me.

In the canteen with Suzie and Lisa, I contemplate over whether Suzie makes the 'top five' or not?

"Marcus told me he had an argument with his girlfriend last night, which probably accounts for why he's being really annoying today," Suzie says matter-of-factly.

"I think he's gay." Lisa says.

"What makes you say that?" I ask.

"I don't know…he's just got that look about him."

"He's a softy…so what?" I say.

"I just said he had an argument with his *girlfriend*…" Suzie interjects.

"He just doesn't know it yet. He admitted once that he watches gay porn," Lisa goes on.

"He said *that*? Why would he admit to that?" I ask.

"We were talking about a newspaper story about the trend of setting up webcams at home which got us talking about porn. He was actually quite funny."

"I bet he's got a really small dick…" Suzie says, lost in the thought, leaving me lost in the thought of how big Suzie likes them.

"Still doesn't mean he's gay," I eventually say.

"Do all hetrosexual men look at gay porn then?" Suzie asks.

"I don't know…some curious men might," I say, recalling the few times I have resorted to it myself as a means to a fix.

"Curious of what: how to do it man-style?" Suzie scoffs. "Why would a man want to look at two *men* doing it if he fancies women, unless he was gay, or thinking about turning gay?"

As I chew on more chicken, I answer Suzie's question in my own mind, free from the cross-examination that would ensue regarding my own masculinity: it is simply the need for different or more stimulating material – at least that's what my own conclusions have found. There is no way Suzie will understand this unless I am prepared to explain the reasons why, which I'm not, especially in the hub of the canteen at lunchtime.

"Don't you look at lesbians?" I ask quietly.

"No, I don't! I don't watch porn - period! She replies, raising a few utterings from Maintenance.

"Are you telling me you've never looked at porn?" Lisa asks surprised, in a way that gets me thinking about what goes on behind *her* closed door?

"I have. Of course I have. I just don't want to talk about it."

I decide to quietly finish eating and not pursue the conversation any further and Suzie isn't saying any more either and when one of the girls from the Sales team sits down beside Lisa, I use it as my opportunity to extract myself from the scene.

"I'm off for a cigarette," I say.

Suzie watches me leave the table, still chewing and I indicate to her that at some point I still want to carry on with our talk, especially the bit about lesbians, but I'm not sure if she reads it that way.

The two hours after lunch pass with fluidity and lucidity: I am a well-oiled, effective machine and essential cog in the work machinery, performing tasks with no energy wasted on the frivolous or base. Then just as quickly, the rest of the afternoon drags.

To break the tedium, I decide to go over my 'top five' again just to see if the standings have changed. As usual, the same three rules apply: they must be an employee; I must know their first name and I must know which department they work in.

Now let's see…the top five girls in the hotel I'd most like to fuck… First things first…let's start with the obvious. Danute gets first shout. With a bush like that, it was never in doubt! That covers my pale and hairy department. That's *one*. What about Caroline? I've thought about her before, watching her claw her way up the table then somehow always missing out. My image of her was totally blown when I saw her in that seventies get-up though… I'll keep her on standby. Now work…meticulously around the departments … You're a dirty shadow, casting yourself in little corners of each room, quietly observing. There's the Spanish girl in the Bar with the pert little bottom, whose name I've discovered is Alba - surely she gets a look in? Let's move on. I can't. The significance of that bottom is too great. She's inducted into the hall of fame, no questions asked. That's *two*. Okay…young, petite and incredibly sexy covered. Keep searching the Bar… Valeria doesn't get a look in – been there, done that, worn the nightmarish t-shirt. What about that other one - she's worth spending some time over, surely? I don't know her name, besides which, she's below par. Up to the Restaurant…I'm confident up here… Hello Mora…you instantly spring to mind. It's your face more than anything. You're quite ordinary – not ugly - which is precisely what attracts me to you. You've got a slutty-pissed-off-moody-look suggesting you'd rather be anywhere but here – probably in bed having it off; the thickness of your eyebrows also indicate you're hairy. Surely you make it? Let's scoot onwards just to make sure I haven't missed anything glaringly obvious. No… Mora you're elevated to number *three*. Okay - my dirty-girl-next-door type. Now it starts to get a bit tricky. There's a plethora of girls out there, a whole host of different types, all kinds of permutations and only two spaces left. There is Suzie of course. What about her? You have both the figure and the attitude, yet there is something behind the veneer, behind the tits and arse and flame-red hair, deeply insecure, requiring much TLC and sensitivity, which is not what I need right now. I'm going to stick you on the back-burner. Lisa? No. What about Steph? Good figure, sexy eyes. No - *too* domineering…too cold…and my preconceptions of you looking good in leather are probably all wrong. There are girls more deserving of the space. Move on. There aren't enough mature women working in the hotel! There *is* that one that works in the kitchen – too fat and I don't know her name. What about Housekeeping? Way too ugly. Head back to Reception. What about that new skinny one? What about Caro… Wait! How could I be so blind? There's the blonde therapist over at the Spa! What a beauty: defined arse, young breasts and tight black leggings revealing the faint shape of a camel-toe. Picture the treatment room and all manner of events unfolding as she applies the herbal oils! She makes it to number *four!* That covers my fit, horny blonde… Wait a minute, what's her name? I have to know her name – rules are rules! Think man, think! Karen? Cary? Candy…Carmen …something stereotypical. Fuck it! I don't know. You know damn well you don't know. Balls to that! For arguments sake, we'll say it's Karen. Of course, yes, it's Karen! I remember now. Fucking Liar! You make number *four.* Okay…last but not least. I don't have to think long about this one. You've been hanging around in the back of my mind for a good few minutes now whilst I've been working on the more formidable equations preceding you. Back to the Restaurant we go. Thick-set with red hair and a spattering of freckles across your pale face – casual staff *are* permitted! Your name is Margot *and* I think you're Scandinavian. You make it in at number *five…*

I briefly enjoy the pleasures of each girl, taking each one for their own individual little features, succumbing to the idea that this is all I will ever need for the rest of my life. As I drift, I suddenly become aware that I'm drifting and that I've been staring at a computer screen for what seems a substantial amount of time. I gently shake my head as if shaking little wet dreams from the ends of my hair and the noise of the room re-establishes itself as the norm.

"Alex…" someone says, the word reverberating around my head like a lost echo. "Alex!"

I look up to see Klep leaning across his desk waving a paper at me.

"You might want to include that in the change-log for Thursday," he says. "It slipped my mind."

"Right…" I reply hastily, still undecided on whether I'm happy with my 'top five' or not.

With an hour to go before I finish, I meet Danute on the stairs - wearing trousers - who enquires about some late payments, which I take as a move to wean personal information out of me and *my* cue to enquire about more pressing matters.

"You know…we should go out sometime." I stammer. "I sometimes go for a drink with Martin – from the kitchen. What do you drink?"

Instantly her face brightens, with surprise.

"I like a glass of wine…and vodka of course." she replies.

"Done…. We'll make a date."

"I'd like that…" she says, turning very demure.

I decide to leave it at that on the premise that anything else said on my part might fuck things up.

"When…?" she asks, as I carry on up the stairs, pretending I'm in a rush.

"I'll let you know…"

As I step into the office, I conclude: if ever there was a 'sure thing', that was it.

I enter the flat, with my nose firmly out of place due to a late afternoon altercation with Klep over organic foods! After assuring me about the dangers of genetically modified food and the fact that it's responsible for many of the ailments that modern man suffers today, he then proceeded to call me ignorant due to my lack of knowledge about such things and that it was time I opened my eyes to what I was putting into my body. I told him to eat shit to which he responded by telling me that the bacteria in faeces are the same as those that live in our gut which play a healthy role in our bodies and providing the individual hasn't ingested any *bad* bacteria you shouldn't have a problem with eating it. Ergo, choose organic. I couldn't hear anything after that.

After making myself a cup of tea and eating some ginger cake, I get over it by applying the same diligence to my heads-down approach that I had at work earlier in the day and refrain from turning on the computer. Frankly I'm too tired to think about anything other than relaxing in front of the T.V. I've covered everything I need to for the models convention tomorrow and my body is crying out for a rest.

As I channel-hop, the cat jumps up and affectionately stretches himself over my lap, purring deeply, resonating through my entire body until it feels like a second tiny heart is beating in unison with my own. Slowly the mind and body acquiesce and the eyes begin to close. It will be a long day tomorrow, full of joys and surprises where my stamina will be pushed to the full. For that, I will most certainly reward myself when I return home – I will have earned it.

6

I was only eleven when my friend Bobby Goodright showed me the picture in that nude magazine he'd managed to obtain from somewhere of the blonde girl holding herself open with her legs apart. It was the first time I had ever examined anything like it over a long period of time, all other thoughts prior to it being nothing more than wild, puerile conjecture, whereas Bobby had indulged himself regularly – or so he told me - giving him licence to mock my green-behind-the-ears disposition, which he did with boastful and childish pride. I didn't care: I was confused and excited at the prospect of how females would look to me and the possibilities that came with it. It was my coming into awareness. To say it was the moment of conception or a hormonal imbalance associated with my age still mystifies, but the profound effect it had on me was unmistakable. It was to be the catalyst to a world of discovery that would hold sway over me throughout those formative years and fill me with a lust that still consumes me to this day. Everything subsequent to that moment was done with the sole intention of embracing that wonder – to eventually love and be loved. There was nothing else that mattered more. Yet somewhere along the way, that ideal became distorted, corrupted and bent out of shape. One could argue the transition into adulthood is a difficult one, forcing us to throw away the toys of youthful bliss and replace them with the burden of responsibility. Had I ever been ready for that? *Are we ever ready for it?* Was love possible in a world of micro-machines, computers, e-mails, money-making deals, cynicism and the constant flux of every conceivable source of information muddying the waters of the heart and the mind? Was I still clinging to those last pages of childhood, unable to let go, doing everything in my power to replicate the feeling I had on that summer's day behind the old flats and derelict Power Station with my friend Bobby Goodright? Where was I to find the love I had only read about, seen in the films, heard in the songs and seen in the picture of that girl all those years ago?

That same summer my grandmother died. I remember crying copious tears and my mother trying to explain to me that although Granny would never be coming back, she was safe and happy and in a place where she was able look down and watch over us and therefore important that we say a prayer for her from time to time; this didn't make me feel any better and I remember it taking a long time for me to reconcile with death and the idea of a heaven as being real, something I still can't get my head around. I also wondered whether her 'looking down' also applied during my bouts of touching myself, something I had curiously started to partake in. My brother always defined me as being too sensitive, looking too deeply, seeing too much instead of blindly accepting fate and getting on with things. "This one needs looking after…" he would tell mum at the kitchen table and then rebuke me for not standing up to him.

This changed during the latter part of my teenage years as the flower bloomed and turned its face to the sun, basking in the warm glow of new friends and emerging ideas. Yet as I dug in and 'accepted my fate', I couldn't help feeling that something was always missing, that somewhere the real me had been shunned and locked away, something beautiful yet too dangerous to let out for fear of it wreaking havoc and trampling over the carefully constructed and established order that had been mapped out for me.

Was this the bug that had crawled up my arse and set about the cogs in motion, propelling me towards a hiding place, intermittent blackouts, for fear of what lay ahead – a world of sterility, mechanics and conditioning? Was my porn use a manifestation of something lost, a yearning for moments as beguiling as when I first saw that picture all those years ago…?

My reverie is broken by more screams coming from the tiny figures playing - the 'tits and arses' as referred to by Martin yesterday - abandoning themselves in the sun, with more efforts of team-building. And as I observe from one of the secluded, upper windows of the hotel where the view stretches out far across the lawns of the estate, I watch not with greedy, lustful eyes, but an almost envious longing to have what they have, to experience the things they're feeling at this very moment. How carefree the tiny figures look - girls simply enjoying the great outdoors, connecting with nature and one another. It's a welcome break, but one tinged with melancholy at a time when I should be up and looking forward to the reward I will have earned by this evening. I haven't stopped all day…

Blondes, brunettes, reds, blues, pinks, gingers…faces white, black, brown, yellow, freckled…bodies thin…only thin…and bendy; rows upon rows of perfect white teeth, each and every one of them and legs that go on forever – each one lovelier than the next. That was the first thing that confronted me this morning, with Marie already pissed at the late arrival of coffee; Caroline at Reception, clearly noticeable she'd applied an extra coating of make-up to her face, which upon initial inspection made her look like a 70's porn star after which the sinister features of a clown began to take shape, making her look both ridiculous and evil as she tried to gain control of the melee surrounding her and testament as to why she always falls short of the 'top five'; me diving in headlong, trying to cram in as many different faces as possible for fear of missing out on something, shocked at how plastic the girl's complexions looked; more tits and arse. Then watching Caroline berate the Concierge for disappearing and leaving her alone, her no-nonsense, stressed-out state, turquoise eye shadow and its amateurish application, beginning to have a turn-on effect for me, to such an extent, that I jokingly told her we both needed a drink and that we should go out some time; then me watching the models file into the Conference Theatre, the same pathetic grin plastered to my face, concluding it would literally be impossible to come to a final decision with this lot in regards to my 'top five'. Smoking breaks amidst the smoking chimneys of Housekeepers, Porters, Chefs, staring through the blue haze, contemplating the factors that set models apart from the rest of us: wide-set eyes, perfect nose, large symmetrical mouth and legs…more length than us ordinary folk, deciding it's the confidence with which they carry themselves that really sets them apart, knowing the world perceives them as beautiful, thus bestowing upon them a sense of entitlement that is all too easily acquired; thoughts about their pussies and what they looked like: thin, hairless, bony, taught, tight, free of all excess flapping, pursed, pink and shell-like? Then it was up to the office until lunch, Gemma back from her hols, giving us the low-down of what she got up to and Suzie gushing all over the place telling her, 'it just wasn't the same without you'. Then back down at twelve-thirty, watching everyone steam into the Mongolian Restaurant for lunch, a slithering snake of bevvies spooning child-sized portions of food onto plates at the buffet station and examined curiously before being transported back to tables as if under the glaring eyes and flashing lights of the catwalk; everyone on a mobile phone as they ate, everyone taking selfies, green-eyed beauties asking me for fish without the sauce then thanking me artificially for my time; me staring at their almost non-existent arses as they traipsed back to their tables and Marie watching me, with a look of displeasure; the cacophony rising, a scream piercing the air, making me jump, raising a few laughs from the girls at the table nearest me; an argument breaking out between two girls over an Instagram picture, turning the air blue with squeals of, "bitch…fuckin' bitch…!" The fish coming out and me telling one of the Waiters to take it over, showing him the table, emphasising it was for the good-looking one which confused him even more, the redhead Scandinavian waitress appearing beside me, asking if we had more orange juice and me listening, realising I'd made a gross miscalculation, as it was quite clear she was in fact Scottish, giving me a new sense of wonder at the discovery of her provenance - she still makes the 'top five'; more cigarettes; models asking me where *they* could smoke; me escorting them downstairs, trying to chat them up - going nowhere. There was the moment I took stock and stopped for a moment, surprised at how bored I was of seeing the same thing over and over, one indistinguishable feature from the next, as if beauty had nullified herself on account of over-excess that left me yearning for the plain and the ordinary – not necessary ugly – but the 'amateur'. Nothing catches the eye like *imperfection.* Much like my porn and the reverence I hold over the amateur, the uncontrived, the unscripted, the ones deemed laughable in a world obsessed by what it considers to be perfection and the avidity of the masses. Porn is forgiving in that way - there's room for everybody. Everyone is welcome. Nothing displays more arrogance than something deemed to be perfect. Nothing works as more of a turn-off for me! Give me a scar, a touch of cellulite, a big nose, a flat chest, a belly…spots…give me the girl next door that hides her face and quick-steps her way through life with all the self-effacing charm she is so oblivious to. Someone *is* watching you, my dear…

There was the moment one of the girls lost her mobile phone, copious tears flowing down her face, me thinking someone had died, her friends telling her, 'it's going to be alright…we'll make it through…we'll work it out…' Then me, heading back up to the office, Klep and Lisa having an argument about ugliness after Klep had made some defamatory remarks about the Housekeeping girls, with Lisa threatening to take him to HR if he made any more comments; me calculating how much more 'fuel' I would need for a truly memorable experience tonight, then heading down to oversee the smooth-running of the girls leaving for their team-building activities with me watching them canter away in nothing more than shorts and t-shirts until disappearing over the grass verge. Then finally, more cigarettes with one of the Romanian Housekeeping girls opening up to me, recounting how dirty the bedrooms always are and how in this country people have no manners and how every morning the leftovers of the filthy habits of these people are left for her to clean up, then asking me something about myself to which I was startled to find I had nothing to say - nothing interesting anyway, which left me in a mild state of panic as I seemed to lose all power of speech and communication and a sense of who I was and all I wanted to do was get back to the sanctuary of home and away from all the interfering voices…

Come five-o-clock, the girls are filing in, all rosy cheeked and breathless. This time there is nothing insidious about my thoughts, only affection and that I've been instrumental in making their stay at Thorn Park Hotel as enjoyable as possible. A few acknowledge me as they walk past, like a kind of farewell march as this is the last time I will probably see them. I will hand over to the C&B Manager, leaving them in his more than capable hands as he takes over the night operations.

I offer a few kind words to Caroline, who looks like she's had a long day then move over to the check-in desk and await Marie just to ensure all has gone well and any predilections she might have for the evening will be catered for. When she does finally saunter in, she is happily relaxed and de-stressed and all the more alluring for it. There is very little else that can conceivably go wrong tonight - Gala nights tend to take care of themselves when there is booze in full flow and Marie senses this and thanks me for all my effort, telling me what a star I am and how she's about ready for a shower before putting on her party frock. I finally depart, savouring the image, until tomorrow, where the real picture of how events transpired will be painted out in the event debrief.

I'm a little sad about having left the party and remorseful that I hadn't connected more in some way with the people involved, if anything just to get to know Marie a little better.

"You looked shagged...in the *tired* sense that is..." Klep informs me at six-o-clock with his smug face and empty bottle beside him, confirming to me just how drab my life has become.

"Thank-you..." I say, packing my bag.

"You're welcome..." he says, beginning to swivel in his chair in that pre-occupied way that tells me something is on his mind.

"Sales job is up on the website. Have you seen?"

"No."

"Steph said they're in no rush...they just want to get the right person."

"That makes sense..." I say impassively, before hanging my bag over my shoulder. "See you tomorrow."

"Same time...same place..." I hear him say as I leave the room.

I arrive back at the flat with a horrible sense of foreboding, firstly due to the fact that the problem with my car needs addressing and secondly, the traffic was so bad I am convinced the majority of drivers on the road will soon be checking themselves into the nearest 'anger management' therapy facility before their murderous intentions become actual crimes.

And this foreboding is realised the moment I turn on the computer - after my mind having been impregnated with all manner of smut over the course of the day - by denying me access to my desktop with the words: PASSWORD INCORRECT. After numerous attempts at re-typing, it still won't allow me access, leaving me frantic and at a loss as to how a malicious website – which can be the only explanation - has managed to penetrate and infect what is a well-fortified device? The land-line suddenly rings and without looking to see who it is, I pick up.

"There you are!" the voice on the other end cries, instantly recognisable as my mother.

"Hi…mum…"

"Well we wondered where you were – we haven't heard from you in ages," she says.

"I'm sorry – I've been busy as hell," I bullshit.

"Well where have you been - I've been trying to call you, but the phone is always off?" she says, her voice rising.

"Oh really…?" I say, imitating surprise. "Did you try my mobile…?"

"Yes, but no-one answers!"

"Strange…there might be something wrong with it," I say, actually picking it up and turning it over in my hand.

The line goes silent for a moment and in the silence I sense her dismay.

"How have you been?" I ask.

"Oh we're fine – you know how it is…"

Whilst talking, I remove my boxers and place a towel on the chair beneath me.

"I've just sent you an e-mail with a picture of your dad and the huge fish he caught at the weekend." she says, her voice picking up. "He was so proud."

"Oh I haven't checked yet. Still fishing eh…?"

"Did you see the pictures of your brother I sent you about two weeks ago, in Canada?"

"Oh no, I must have missed that one too," I tell her irritably.

"Well what do you do – don't you open the mail I send you?"

I stare ahead and think about my 'top five' and realise I'm in a bit of a predicament with mum on the phone and having a conversation that could quite feasibly go on for an hour or more due to the absence of communication between us. I light up a cigarette and curse at the prospect of having to perform a 'system restore'.

"Are you still smoking?" she asks, after the first exhalation.

"I'm afraid so…" I tell her, prompting me to think about the amount I am smoking, which has risen considerably over the past year or so. "I didn't even know Scott had been away."

"He went with Helen. They got engaged."

"Oh that's good news – which one is Helen? Is she the one with blonde hair?" I ask, genuinely confused.

"No – dark hair!" she shouts, exasperated. "She's the Canadian one!"

"Right, right, of course…" I say, bringing her face to mind. "Wow…engaged…who'd have thought it?"

"When was the last time you saw your brother?" she asks. "Why don't you give him a call?"

"Well I saw you all at Christmas…"

"Yes, that was months ago…"

"I know…I've been working. It's been really busy…and then you come home and you're tired…I've been meaning to call." I tell her, initiating the first steps of a 'system restore'.

I can't hear anything as she prattles on about the neighbour's dog trying to get in through the cat-flap, whilst the computer performs very officious tasks, sending my heart-rate into over drive.

"Listen mum…I'm going to have to call you back. I've got a problem with the computer.

"Well for god's sake!" she cries.

"I know I know…I'm trying to multi-task and it's not working." I tell her, shaking my head. "I'll call you back."

The phone goes down as the computer finishes up and

restarts, prompting me to re-enter my password with bated breath. I've already forgotten about the conversation with mum. After a monumental wait, I'm finally in and the tension flows out of every muscle in my body as my thoughts gather pace once more. Without further ado, I set about preparing all forces before taking my seat and clicking onto the first website.

The screen remains white. The guts churn away. 'Resolving host'…still nothing! Then: 'webpage unavailable'. My heart sinks. I close the window and try again. Repeat: 'webpage unavailable'. The small, blue, globe icon in the bottom right-hand corner of the screen tells me I'm not connected in the form of a red cross. I check the 'bright-box' to see if I'm plugged in. I turn it off at the plug socket then back on and wait. As I wait, all I can think about are the models I've been looking at all day and I'm staggered at my capacity for memory and detail as the desire to turn it all into something tangible is suddenly overwhelming. Everything is systematically checked off one by one and still I can see no reason as to why I have no internet connection. I can feel the urge draining away as yet again I'm resigned to another technological patch-up job leaving me toying with the real idea of throwing the computer out of the window just to revel in the sound of smashing machinery.

"Fuck it!" I bellow, shattering the silence of the room.

Bolting up from the chair, I begin to pace the room frantically in the hope that the computer might relent when it sees just how desperate the situation is. After forty-five minutes, I realise the situation *is* serious. The last thing I want to have to do is call up my service provider, but I am resigned to the fact that this may be my only option. I try one last time before picking up the phone.

"Two hours! Are you telling me I have to wait for another two hours?" I wail, after having had a conversation that has had me spell out my name four times, incessantly repeat the ID number of my 'bright-box', been told it's an old one and needs replacing and that there are problems in my geographical location with regard to connection.

"It may be an hour sir – it may be longer," the voice says.

"And if I still have no connection, I have to replace my box? How long will that take?"

"We will send one out to you straight away sir…it should take four working days to arrive…"

"Four working days…!" I repeat, feeling the sudden rush of blood to my head, followed by the feeling of nausea. "That is quite impossible! Do you have any idea how much of an inconvenience that is? I work from home – my *life* depends on an internet connection. I need the internet to do my work. You're essentially asking me to take four days off work!" I tell him. "Would *you* be able to survive if I asked you to do that?"

I rise from the chair and search the room for something to pick up – anything to squeeze and absorb the anger that now courses through me.

"I understand sir…we will send one out to you straight away…" the voice continues.

Images of models and Marie and 'Wanton Mary' bombard the circuitry of my brain. In a millisecond, the contents of My Favourites folder tempt me with pictures that I have no access to, except in the overflowing memory banks of my mind. The prospect of four days, or longer, which I know will be the case, without a 'fix' fills me with a dread that seems insurmountable. I want to throttle the voice on the other end of the line.

"I don't think you *do* understand!" I go on. "It is imperative that I have that connection up and running by tonight."

"You may try again in an hour or two – the problem may be resolved by then. At the moment there is nothing we can do about it. I'm very sorry sir."

I stare at the computer screen in front of me, mute.

The voice pauses, waiting for a response, unsure of whether

I'm still on the line, before finally giving me the customary farewell. The line goes dead.

The shock of the news leaves me immobile as I come to terms with the implications of what this will have for me and my well-being. At a loss as to what to do with myself, I leave all connections on with a view to checking them at regular intervals to see if or when connectivity returns, before using the moment to prepare myself something more to eat. I side-step a pile of sick left by the cat in the hallway as I wander through to the living room, then gently prod him in the mid-riff for some kind of reaction, which does little in disturbing his slumber. I eat in a disturbed state, constantly up and down, doing nothing for my digestion, checking intermittently on the connection. Then, breaking my rule of where I smoke, due to exceptional circumstances, I light up in the living room, and sedate myself before checking again. The next two hours are spent combating fits of rage, pleas of forgiveness, bouts of pacing the room and one-sided conversations with the cat. And just when it seems there is nothing to do but accept my fate, connection is resumed.

At precisely nine-forty-two, 'The toilet antics of Hanna' tell me I am indeed back amongst friends old and new, performing on what I believe to be a rejuvenated and more efficient piece of equipment. Marvelling at how great an inconvenience, as was before, can be forgotten in the split of an eye and those responsible for said inconvenience referred to as simpletons and amateurs at their game – forgiven - I dive in headlong, recompensed with updates across the board that re-ignite my faith in the solemnity of justice, yet strangely omit the countless bods parading themselves around the hotel today, with the exception of Marie, who's shower comment, I can't shake. My solid erection reaffirms all this as the first orgasm hits me right between the eyes. Then, gorging myself with an appetite fit for a king, I'm back for seconds, firing off another wad at precisely ten-to-two in the morning.

A fly lands on the desk of enormous proportions, bigger than any preceding it and startling me out of my stupor. Lumbering towards me, it fixes me with its compound eyes, turning its head, this way and that. Powerless to move, I see it for the first time, not as some innocent invertebrate making its way through the unsuspecting houses of the world, but as my competitor and destroyer; it is no longer a fly, but a presence that binds and shackles me to the wonders of modern technology, making me a prisoner of my own compulsion. And as I search my mind again for some kind of recollection as to when and where our affair began and how it brought my life to this, I adjust my eyes to the gaping black pit I've fallen into and see no way out.

7

Perched on the edge of the bed gazing down at the space between my bare feet with the birds chirping brightly and the morning sun filtering in through the cracks of the blind, I decide I'm going to kill myself. Floating in this atmosphere of neglect and abandonment, the idea seems all the more tangible as I gaze across the room towards the door, knowing that beyond it, there is nothing. This is not some whimsical idea announced in a moment of confusion and fatigue, but the inevitable conclusion of one who no longer cares and is therefore one who shouldn't be. The only questions that remain are: *when* and *how*?

The pulled muscle in my back causes me to rise slowly from the bed then stoop to quickly alleviate the tension, as I curse at the four-and-half- hours of sleep I've had that wasn't really sleep but a nightmare with me suffocating between the legs of 'Wanton Mary'.

I move into the bathroom and pull down my pants and examine the raw underside of my scrotum where the weeping skin has coagulated overnight, leaving the pubic hair matted to the sac like a kind of gluey fur coat. My eyes sting from lack of sleep, as if filled with salt, scratching at the back of the eye-balls with every movement and I realise my bout of despondency has left me just over forty-five minutes to prepare for work. I must wash, feed myself and the cat and get dressed. Surely none of that matters now?

I wash then prepare my toast and coffee while the cat picks at the new plate of food I've set down for him. Somebody else will need to take care of him, one with a greater capacity for love. Perhaps I'll send him back to Sarah? As I eat and watch the news, the idea of taking my own life is still strong and I think about calling in sick for work, or simply not bothering to turn up at all. The crunching of toast adds to the tumult of worry filling my head as I contemplate the *how* and *when*. Am I *really* serious about taking the final step? Would I not have simply done the deed without thinking about it, if I were in earnest? Isn't that what happens? Doesn't the lowest ebb instigate the final course of action without any forethought? With every minute passing I grow weaker in my resolve to commit to the task fuelled by the enormous obstacle of the death itself: how does one kill oneself? An overdose of pills seems very favourable, but then which ones and how and where to obtain them. And what if they don't work only to find you wake up in hospital with a pumped stomach and your mother looking over you and crying, telling the nurse: "he was always playing silly games when he was a child…he gets it from his father." The slitting of the wrists requires a courage that I simply don't have. In fact anything involving a sharp instrument is out of the question: too fearsome an image and too bloody. Jumping from a height is an option, but again this requires great courage as there is too much time in the air to think about the impact that awaits you. What if you were to survive it, rendering you invalid for the rest of your life, or worse, being sectioned under the act of insanity? Driving into a wall at eighty miles an hour? Drowning? Hanging? The only quick and sure-fire way is with a gun. However the questions arise again, of how and where one gets their hands on a gun? And despite the fact that I've made this decision, are there still not things to be done? I have to debrief with Marie this morning. I have to get the car into the garage and fixed before it conks out on me completely. There is Danute and her enormous bush which I have yet to see, which surely makes dying out of the question. There's the new batch of webcams responsible for keeping me up last night that will most certainly require a second and third *and* fourth viewing if I am to fully appreciate their splendour. There is the small matter of my parents and the grief they would feel with my departure. The female newscaster is wearing a decidedly low-flung dress with black stockings. There's a job in the Sales department up for grabs, that I'm more than qualified for. At the age of twenty-five, surely I'm being premature about being unable to find ways of turning my life around? Isn't this all simply a cry for help? I have ten minutes before I have to leave for work. Have I really thought things through? Am I really at the end of my tether? The female newscaster crosses her legs as she introduces the next guest, showing off the wonderful shape of her calves as her stockings pull tightly on the white skin beneath. I'm blagging myself again, exaggerating the extent of my despair. Death can wait.

Prasad is in a foul mood and berates me for being late as I enter the office, after having convinced myself that my irascible nature all boils down to fatigue. I'm about to tell him to 'fuck off' but tell him about the problem with my car instead and how I'm going to have to get it seen to which mollifies him enough for a retreat back into his office, after he makes a point of how ill I look and whether I need to see a doctor? Lisa picks up on it aswell, as does Suzie which all makes me feel a whole lot worse.

In the Bar, John the Director, Marie and one of her cohorts are already seated around a table and engaged in conversation. I can see from the window leading down to Reception the flow of models forming a queue as they checkout with the young Concierge at the helm shifting Louis Vuitton, Chanel, Dolce and Gabbana and Burberry suitcases and bags to the side of the desk for collection with Caroline keeping a firm fix on him. I inhale deeply and smile a false smile before joining the table.

"Morning…sorry I'm late," I say, taking a seat.

"Morning Alex," Marie says, as John continues to chat with the other female colleague.

Marie double takes when she looks at me, but says nothing.

As the waitress comes over to take a drinks order John notices me for the first time and does the same with even greater concern and I realise how stupid I've been at having come in to work. Without thinking, I order first, asking the waitress for a strong coffee.

"I think I'll have one of those, aswell." Marie says. "Bit of a late one last night with a long drive ahead of me today."

"Cappuccino please," says Marie's colleague, whom I remember as Joanne.

"Ditto…" John concludes.

The waitress smiles and heads back to the bar as I open the folder on my lap and John produces a slew of bad jokes and more small talk about being welcome back at any time.

The girls laugh, but I can see Marie is struggling to keep up with a look suggesting she'd rather be back in a warm, cosy bed. As I try to smile at John's wit, I become acutely aware of the rash spanning the underside of my scrotum and the feverish itch that is beginning to take over, like the feeling of ants crawling around the entire seat of my crotch. Marie pulls up her details but she doesn't really look at them and comments on the food for both lunch and dinner. As I listen, I shift my bottom backwards in the chair trying surreptitiously to rub the base of my balls against the course fabric of the seat covering in an attempt to quell the itchiness. John flashes me a curious look. The waitress arrives with our drinks and sets them down. The itchiness engulfing my balls isn't going away and again as I reach for my coffee, I exaggerate the movement of my bottom against the seat, this time a little too forcefully, sending a searing flash of heat through my prostrate and up along the entire length of my spine, causing me to whimper, which I disguise by clearing my throat loudly.

"Dinner was excellent." Marie goes on. "My only minor niggle would be the wait from the starters to mains. But apart from that, everything was really good…"

The itch is becoming unbearable and all I want to do is run my nails across the red flesh until it bleeds. I begin to exercise my sphincter, opening it then closing it tightly in quick succession which seems to help. John nods. I remain silent.

For the next half an hour, I squirm and chew on fire, staggered as Marie, after highlighting the odd hiccup, eulogizes about the event with nothing but praise for all involved. This includes a personal thank you to me, from my initial dealings with her to the valiant effort of overseeing the day itself. Needless to say John remains impassive, as to him, I am simply doing the job I'm paid to do. It does however go some way in alleviating the feeling of depression I'm suffering. We go as far as to highlight plans for next year, which we promise will be bigger and better than ever with the same to be expected for the subsequent years to follow. This is what John wants to hear: establishing a good foundation with the client and building on it in a bid to keep them coming back. This is what keeps John stiff and his wife happy. This, above all else, is what he considers a success. After laughing at a succession of more unfunny jokes from John, we conclude the meeting with the usual pleasantries as Marie is tired and by all accounts, a little messy. I am tempted to kiss her on departure but decide a simple handshake more appropriate. Had John not been in the room, I would certainly have tried my luck. The Waitress comes over to retrieve the coffee cups as John gives his final director-hotel-spiel to the ladies after which both he and I leave the Bar. When we reach the lifts he turns and gives me three firm shakes of the hand.

"Well done," he says, as I catch a nose-full of his aftershave. "Good job, good job. That's what it's all about…"

I nod my head in agreement as the rub of material from walking sets my balls off again. John frowns.

"You okay? You look like shit," he says. "We haven't been over-working you, have we? You're not coming down with something?"

"I might be getting a cold or something…" I tell him, as he steps into the lift.

"Okay, well don't over-do it," he says, pressing the third floor button. "Oh and don't forget to get those drinks signed off," he adds, before the door closes.

I decide I'm going to take the rest of the day off work. I get the drinks signed off then stop for a smoke before heading upstairs; the questions of *how* and *when* still persist. The mood in the office is nauseatingly upbeat with Klep holding court, much to the amusement of Suzie, who stuffs chocolate Hob-Nobs into her mouth between her laughter. Thankfully, Prasad calls me in to his office before Klep can include me into his rhetoric. Feigning the most maligned expression I can, I watch as Prasad wheels himself back in his chair, eyes still fixed on his computer screen.

"Listen Alex, we're going to have to take a rain check on that holiday time you've asked for. It completely slipped my mind, but Suzie has already booked hers at the same time," he informs me.

It takes a moment for his words to register as I'm preoccupied with the excuse I intend to lay on him with regards to me leaving work. He looks up, expectantly.

"It's a busy time and I can't have you both off. Sorry mate, she got in first…"

He looks up at the calendar tacked to the wall. Running his pen along the dates, like some doctor about to prescribe another needless appointment whistling softly to himself, a tune I vaguely recognise from somewhere.

"I can do the fourteenth…up until the twenty-first…a week wasn't it?" he muses.

"That's fine," I tell him unable to recall the original dates I gave him.

He draws a line across the calendar, before writing my name below it then looks at me with concern.

"Debrief okay?"

"Fine…all good…very happy…" I tell him, impatiently.

"Sure?"

"John is happy…they're all happy," I reiterate, caressing my brow, before going in for the kill. "Listen Prasad…I'm really not feeling well. I know it's inconvenient…but I've really come down with something…"

"Well what is it? I mean you don't look so hot…"

"I don't know…I was sick last night and I'm feverish…" I say, fearful of him actually getting up and placing his palm on my forehead. I've just been sick in the toilet and my guts are playing up. I know there's a nasty bug going round at the moment…"

He pauses briefly, weighing up the implications.

"I've got nothing on today…" I add.

"What about Delios Group? Aren't they getting back to you today? I suppose Lisa could…" he thinks, leaning back in his chair, clearly not happy with the situation. "Well if you're ill, you're ill. There's not a lot we can do about it. Go home and get some rest. If it gets any worse, you'll have to see a doctor. Just call me later and let me know how you're doing," he says.

"Sure…" I nod pathetically, before leaving his office to gather up my things. Lisa looks confused.

"Home-time already…?" Klep smirks. "Part-timers…"

"What's up with you?" Lisa asks, as Prasad calls her into the office.

"Not feeling good…feeling really sick…" I mumble.

"Hope it's not too serious," Klep says, eyeing me suspiciously.

Not wanting to make a big song and dance with a lot of goodbyes, I wave to Suzie, who is talking on the phone, then leave.

My mood brightens considerably as I drive home, reaffirming the fact that it's an aversion to work that's ailing me and not a lack of sleep or depressive state. As I drive, I can't shake off the prospect of spending the day in front of the computer, leaving me at a loss as to how I can think such thoughts, when I was all but done and washed up at dawns early light. This doesn't detract from the fact that I am unhappy with life and that I can't continue in the same vein. How do I combat the unending urge for sexual stimulation *without* the aid of a computer? So entrenched has it become in my daily routine, I cannot see life without it. The idea of having to *cure* myself of something depresses me even more, whereas surely it would be easier to simply admit to the problem, accept it and even go some way to enjoying the fact instead of fighting it. As I near town, the lack of sleep is beginning to affect me and the idea of crashing out for the entire day and night seems even more appealing.

At home, the feeling of guilt at my absence from work, the soreness around my balls and the general feeling of lethargy, all battle with the delirium I feel as I view the new updates. If ever there were prizes given out for stamina in the field of wanking, I would undoubtedly be a recipient. However, being a seasoned veteran, I persevere even though a great deal of the session is spent 'twisting' the end of my knob absently - much like a pool player chalks the end of his cue - as my only means of stimulation. The act of actually being at the computer has become the primary objective, with the porn nothing more than incidental. My eyes are heavy. After half an hour, tiredness prevents me from furthering my quest for more despite the fact I haven't reached orgasm. Feeling confused and vulnerable, I crawl into bed and fall asleep immediately.

I wake disorientated, roused from my slumber by the deep yowls of the cat coming from outside the bedroom door, like a painful alarm, forcing me to address the real world once more. I have no idea what time it is, what day. I pull back the covers and drift towards the sound, unsure of what I expect to find.

Outside, the cat is sitting upright, elongated neck, emitting more sound, his tiny mouth forming what seem to be the vowels and consonants of some far out cat-speak. I search for signs of discomfort in his posture and across his face and wonder if it's the dementia kicking in and he's simply forgotten where he is. Then, without another sound, he turns and walks languidly away.

Drifting back into the bedroom, I check on the time, which reads: 6:15pm. After slinging on some clothes, I follow in the direction of the cat, dish up some food for him then watch him eat. Feeding time…I think to myself. That's all it was. I yawn tiredly and realise I'm not hungry but eat an apple anyway before heading back into the office to check on a website that's been niggling away at me for the last couple of days.

The website itself is of amateurish quality: bold blocks of text in garish colours interspersed between too many spaces of white with pictures of forlorn-looking people seated around a room that looks like a classroom teleported from the 1970's. The acronym at the top of the page reads: P.E.S.T – Porn Effect Support and Trust. Only weeks old, based just outside of Oxford, and addressed as the 'Old Pavilion', it claims to be for 'sensitive and open-minded people' who can gather together once a week and talk freely about 'porn-related issues' that have, one way or another, become a burden on their lives – 'simple support for a better life'. People are encouraged to reveal themselves to the 'class' and listen to the feedback and advice offered by others who speak from their own experiences. This is all held together by a mediator - the leader – a man to whom the website belongs, who claims to have helped hundreds of people over the course of time get their lives back on track with his warmth, knowledge and understanding and from having worked with people from all walks of life with addictive problems. "Thank god I found you – I owe you everything…" writes one devotee in the comments box.

Despite my urge to stigmatise all involved and frown upon the whole affair with a sceptical eye, I continue to browse and take in what the website has to offer as there are too many coincidences involved for me to ignore: the nature of the subject in question, the handy location, the need to talk about a problem with real people and so on. There are the forums that deal with the subject of porn addiction with other like-minded users airing their views online, but the problem is this doesn't get you away from the computer and you soon find yourself straying to the very thing you're trying to eradicate from your life. Also – not for want of looking - there is no such thing as a 'porn patch', something akin to the ones used for nicotine, which would be a handy solution. Meditation is not a line I wish to pursue, although I have heard it works for some.

I note down the venue, the date, the time and how much driving will be involved then read the footnote at the bottom of the page: 'Don't be afraid to share – other people are our only hope for salvation.' The website permits me to entertain positive thoughts, albeit briefly, before the idea depresses me once more. I close down the computer and head back to bed where the feeling of hibernation under the warm duvet is deeply satisfying and sleep-inducing and I think of nothing as I drift off and don't wake up again until eight-thirty the next morning thinking I'm late for work until I realise it's Saturday.

The market is in town and jostling with life. The sky is clear and blue and the air, morning fresh. I soak up the rays of the sun and fill my lungs with air, exhilarated and thankful for being outside and feel almost sprightly with the effect of having had a good sleep and wonder why all problems can't simply be resolved as easily as tiredness.

Inside, I trawl the aisles of the Supermarket, loitering beside the tinned tomatoes, the bananas, the spaghetti, the cold cuts of meat and pet food, watching mothers curse the behaviour of their glittering offspring. Even this does little to affect my buoyancy. At the checkout, the young girl flashes me a genuine smile before finalising the transaction. On departure, she gives me another look which I perceive to be a 'hit' making me wish I had been a little more engaging.

My mood is infectious as I stroll home, receiving more looks and nods of acknowledgement from people I recognise but have previously ignored making it seem all the more inconceivable that yesterday I should have entertained such thoughts as taking my own life when all around me is alive and well. Where do they come from, these mysterious influences, wrenching us first one way and then the other, keeping us locked in a perpetual state of anxiety? Perhaps meditation *is* the key, a way forward in controlling the patterns of the brain to a positive use. A young 'baby-maker', no more than eighteen, pushing a child in a buggy and swollen with another one on the way, passes me and looks at me flirtatiously. I can feel my pace quicken. As I pass the small green beside the church, a young lad, who looks homeless, or high, or both, sits on a bench smoking and observing me.

"Wanker!" he calls out as I walk past.

The insult sounds shocking amidst the sun and the sky and the clean air and startles me into turning to address his acne-ridden face as he glares at me menacingly. I quickly move on, convincing myself he was addressing someone else as he mutters something after me, only a whiff of which I catch, but equally as base. The word rings in my ears as I pace home, succeeding in having shattered my state of well-being.

Sadly, it's with relief that I eventually enter the flat once more. Of all the insults he could have used! Is the word plastered on my forehead? Is there something in my gait that suggests I'm a terminal tugger? Does my face give away the details of my pre-occupations at home?

In spite of the allusions made by the lad at the church green and my resolve to try and find a cure for my hopeless situation,

I head straight up to the office after breakfast and turn on the computer then set about preparing the room. With everything in place, I pull my boxers off just as the doorbell rings. Terrified it's the lad from the church green having followed me home and now making enquiries as to whether his aspersions were correct, I wrench my boxers back up then hurriedly attempt to convert the room back to its original condition. Tiptoeing through the hallway, I move to the kitchen window for a peek out onto the road to see who it is. There are no cars that I recognise and the front door remains out of view due to the impossible angle as the doorbell rings again. I reach out for a kitchen knife. Craning my head around even further, I vie for a better view just as Martin shocks me with his sudden appearance at the window.

"Open up!" he grins, thumbing to the door.

"Damn it…" I mutter, placing the knife back down.

Bugged at the intrusion, I give myself the once over, before reluctantly opening up where Martin's bulk fills the doorframe. He grins broadly.

"Thought I'd drop by and see how you're doing. Heard you were feeling poorly," he says, inviting himself in.

"I was…" I reply. "Who told you?"

"You know what that place is like – things don't stay quiet for very long," he says, as I close the door behind him.

We walk into the lounge where Martin sits himself down on the sofa and observes the cat as he slinks his way around my legs then darts from the room with all the stealth and guile of a furry ninja. I'm suddenly very conscious of my appearance and odour and realise I must look like shit which I consider fitting as I am supposed to be ill.

"Yeah…I was very worried when I saw Danute in the canteen and she said you'd gone home ill. So what is it then?" he asks grinning. "Touch of man-flu…?"

"Just a cold or something," I tell him lamely.

"You had Danute all worried. She said she was looking

forward to a bit of hanky-panky with you."

"Sure…" I say dismissively. "Do you want a drink?"

"I'll have a beer, if one's going."

"You driving…?" I ask, thinking it a little early for a beer.

I make my way to the kitchen.

"Yeah…one won't kill," he calls out as I pull a beer from the fridge.

"Not very cold… not been in there long." I say, handing Martin the beer then taking a seat in the leather wingback chair opposite him.

"You *do* look like shit mate," he informs me.

"Thanks."

"You not having one?" he asks before taking a swig.

"I'm ill…"

Martin's wry smile lets me know he's not really buying any of my grievances and I sense I'm in for a bout of cold interrogation. He takes another swig of beer.

"So were you in town? I can't believe you drove out just to see how I was doing." I say.

"Fuck no. I needed some paint. I've cleared out the garage and decided I'm going to give the walls a once over – it's beginning to look a bit shabby," he says.

Martin looks at me thoughtfully over the top of his beer bottle.

"To be honest I'm a little worried about you…"

"Worried about me?"

"Yeah…you seem a bit…down,"

"Down in what way?"

"I don't know…you don't seem happy. You don't laugh as much as you used to. Perhaps I'm just not as funny as I used to be," he says.

"I'm happy…I'm just busy with work,"

"Maybe happy isn't what I mean. You seem distant. You rarely come out anymore and when you do, you seem like you're somewhere else. You're staying indoors too much, I reckon. Not healthy. You know Danute likes you. How come you haven't made a move yet? Don't hang around too long mate…you're going to waste the opportunity," he continues. "I'm only telling you this because you're a mate…maybe I'm way off the mark…I don't know."

Martin's sentiment shocks me a little as this is not his usual style, prompting me to think up a host of elaborate excuses.

"You're not doing drugs are you?" he asks bluntly. "I mean…I've done enough of them, so I would know and…I don't think so."

"No I'm not doing drugs for Christ's sake."

"I mean if you were I'd hope you'd share some of that shit with me," he says.

We both laugh a little in an attempt to cover over the seriousness of his comments, but he soon looks pensive again.

"I mean look…I'm in no position to preach or anything, but are you really happy the way you are? I mean you're a good-looking bloke and I don't mean that in a funny way; you're intelligent, smarter than me anyway…I just think you could have a bit more," he says, drinking more of his beer.

I think about having one myself.

"Have you ever considered a wife…kids…getting yourself a home instead of renting this place?" he says. "I mean what are you doing? Are you looking at porn all fucking day? I mean, I'm all for a good session, sometimes I watch it with the missus, but not all fucking day."

"I'm not fucking looking at porn all day…"

"Well what is it then? I can't remember the last time you got your end away. Well except for that bird at work that you said went belly up. You want to start using your hips again. You're going to get fucking old before you know it and then where will you be? Dirty old todger you can't even get up."

"Martin, there's nothing wrong with me, okay. I'm just busy

with work and when I come home I'm knackered, that's all. I'm working on trying to get this job in Sales…" I tell him. "And I have asked Danute out by the way – just need a time and place."

"Bollocks…"

"True."

"Good! We're going out to The Horse Inn for dinner. I'll bring along Tasha and we'll have a night of it and I don't want to hear any shit about it. Next weekend…" he tells me.

I think about it for a moment before nodding.

"Ok…I'll tell her."

Martin takes another swig on his beer.

"Look… I'm going to get all philosophical now. I just don't want you left…unfulfilled," he says.

"Are you fucking joking me?"

"No I'm not joking. Wasting time is a crime," he says earnestly. "That's why we have ghosts…"

"Ghosts…?" I say, confused.

"I was watching a programme with Tasha last night. That's the reason we have ghosts; the people that can't let go. The ones taken away before their time; the ones who still feel they have more left to do; the ones who feel they didn't fulfil their time when they were alive. So they come back as ghosts, thinking they can still make amends, which of course they can't, it's too late for all that. So they suffer; eternal suffering for a life unfulfilled," he says. "Now I'm buggered if I'm going to have *you* come back to haunt *me* when I'm in the middle of doin' the wife or playing late-night 'Hitman' just because you couldn't be bothered to get off your fucking ass…"

I really can't tell whether Martin is being serious with me or not, or whether he's been smoking some of that shit I know he likes.

"Okay…I promise not to fucking haunt you." I tell him anyway.

"Next weekend…" he says finishing the last of his beer and

rising from the sofa. "I know the food is good because I know the chef there."

"I'll talk to her on Monday," I tell him.

"Good…" he replies. "Right, I've got stuff to do. I'm glad I stopped by. Short and sweet…"

I escort Martin to the door before he stops and sniffs the air like a curious animal.

"What's that funny smell in here? Alfalfa is it? You're not eating Al-fucking-falfa are you?" he asks.

"No."

"That stuff'll kill ya. Anyway I'm glad to see you're not dead and that whatever's got you writing sick notes will surely pass… right?" he says, making his way to the front door.

"I'm sure I'll be fine by Monday."

"Good. Thanks for the beer. Might feel better if you have one yourself," he says, about to shake my hand then quickly changing his mind. "On second thoughts…I don't want to catch what you got."

Martin finally steps outside, still muttering as he walks away and when I look up I notice the sun has moved across the sky with alarming speed. There is no time to waste.

8

The early afternoon sun floods the lounge with light via the large patio window that leads out into the small garden, infusing the room with a tranquillity that is utterly silent and still. Nothing moves unless it *has* to. It is after all, God's day of rest and the moment of a Sunday that for me is, and has always been, about as near to perfection as you can get. The Sunday supplements are spread across the sofa in what looks like a displacement of ink and colour but really, carefully organised in rank and file with the Sports section at the top of the pile; always the first to be viewed, always taking precedence. My belly is full and content from a late, hearty breakfast, procured with that little extra love and care that a Sunday breakfast demands. The television plays the Sunday sport with just enough sound so as to be able to hear the shifting tides of commentary and action prompting the occasional quick heads up. The cat basks in the heat like some crucified ragdoll tarred with a coat of shiny fur, his great panacea having finally arrived, leaving the burden of life scuttling to all four corners of the room until drowned in the cracks of the floorboards. The poetry of words and music and all-giving life cloaks the room selflessly and fills the air with a longing that leaves me hopelessly light.

Beside me I envisage a girl named, Emily or Sophie or Charlotte. She is an English rose: fair, gentle, a violinist in a string quartet, her pale, porcelain skin gently retiring in the curvature of the sofa as her bare feet rest lightly against the top of my buttocks. Lazily, we drift in and out of conversation, stories we've seen in the papers, a challenging move from the T.V screen or an off-hand remark alluding to the beauty of the moment; our moment in the glow of the near perfect sun-filled room where time has no place and where all memory is veiled in shadow leaving only the moment, only the *now*. Receptive to touch and smell and sight, our gentle banter brings us closer and we laugh like children and caress eachother with our eyes and touch with abandon the flesh of another, my hand grasping hers, until we have to break away and make gentle love in the home of our bed. Then after we've laughed some more, our bodies sated with the ardour of our sex, we return to the languid comfort of the sofa and to our rite, until our cupidity pulls us away once more. Who is she? I don't know; she's just a violinist - a girl violinist. The girl, the woman, the violinist remains; holding me with her love that seems everlasting; holding me with her beautiful sex, her music, her wide eyes, her soft flesh and her womanly life-force, breathing new life into…

The sounds of Mozart, Beethoven and Tchaikovsky are still caressing my ears when my eyes are forced to follow movement to the middle of the floor and to the cat squatting, trying with great effort it seems, to take a piss. His eyes are fixed on me staring at him, as if daring me to intervene as his back arcs into a grossly uncomfortable shape. Despite my observing all this, it takes me a moment to snap out of my reverie and realise what he's actually doing before I quickly jump from the sofa, grab him around his mid-riff and almost throw him outside into the garden where he adopts the same statuesque position before turning forlornly to look at the empty space where his discharge *should* have been. I let him remain outside thinking the air might do him some good as I return to the violinist and a world of peace and harmony with the Sunday papers, celestial light and the sharing of bodily warmth - but the thrill is gone, vanished into thin air, wafted out the door – nothing but a dream. Perhaps the cat's behaviour is something to do with yesterday. He just hasn't been the same since yesterday.

Things got hairy after Martin's departure yesterday - quite literally. After his interruption of little home truths, I was then introduced to a new girl called 'Zilla' in the 'Hairy' section of my usual website. Of Mediterranean origin, with a bush surpassing anything I'd seen before it, I remained engrossed for the rest of the day and early evening. Needless to say, as predicted and feared; after the frenzy came the feeling of despondency that again bordered on the suicidal. Filled with a new hatred, I spat and cursed with all the venom I could muster, pacing maniacally, until my navigation found me standing in front of the cat and unleashing a tirade of abuse. Astonishingly he sat through the whole thing with a kind of resigned and pitiful look on his face, that is, until I began shadow boxing the air, trying to knock seven bells out of the ghost of all reason. Eventually he loped from the room, seeking his own solace and respite, which I later observed was tucked away beneath my bed. There he remained, even as I finally came to rest above him at about midnight after taking heed of Martin's words and finishing the beer I had stacked in the fridge. Needless to say, he hasn't spoken to me since. That was yesterday – today is today. At some point I will have to apologise to him.

It's not just the Monday morning blues that trouble me as I walk across the parking lot towards the staff entrance longing for my Sunday back. The inside of my left forearm is killing me, which, being a 'left-hander', I put down to 'wankers elbow' or some other colloquial term used to describe damaged tendons or muscles, due to repetitive motion and overuse. My confidence in P.E.S.T is also on the wane.

I stop for a cigarette and notice one of the Kitchen Porters making his way over, a strange fellow from Hungary who natters away at you, irrespective of whether you're actually listening to him or not and doesn't stop until one of you finally leaves. I'm in no mood for talking, so as he approaches I pull out my phone and pretend to look very involved in texting somebody, which seems to work as he mutters a 'hello' before moping off to smoke in a corner some distance from me. When I finish my cigarette and look across at him, he strikes me as looking incredibly lonely and I feel bad for ignoring him. I wave, but I don't think he sees me.

"SELF-MOTIVATION – the desire to succeed…" Klep throws to a full class, as I walk in the room.

This is unexpected. I thought I was late.

"Mr Reed! Just in time…take a seat," he says, motioning to my desk as Suzie waves to me happily like a child from the back of the room, mouth full of chocolate Hob-Nob. "Glad to see you're back and feeling better."

"Welcome back Alex," Suzie mumbles.

"It all comes down to us to give our guests the best possible stay they can have," Klep goes on, underlining his message. "The only way this can happen is if we motivate ourselves. By doing this we are doing everything in our power to make things as good as they can be. What is motivation? It is the force that drives us to do things. For that to happen we must love the place we work in, take pride in what we do, care about what our customers expect," he says. "It all starts with us!"

I take my seat, already feeling ill again.

"Some key things to take into account: be aware of our thoughts, challenge negativity and replace with positivity, see problems as learning opportunities. Create a strong and vivid picture of what it will be like to achieve your goals. Set yourself goals!" he emphasises. "What do want to achieve today? Suzie…?"

"I'm going to close the deal with 5G Promotions today," she wails.

"Good. Lisa?"

"I'm going to call my sister…I *must* call my sister today. I haven't spoken to her in ages," she replies.

"That's very nice Lisa, but that's not exactly what I meant."

"That's achieving something isn't it?" Suzie pipes up, in Lisa's defence.

"It is, but I was thinking more on the lines of something work related." Klep stresses.

Lisa stutters her way through the thought process, failing dismally to come up with anything.

"Okay. Which part of your job do you love most…?" Klep pushes, from another angle.

"My two days off…" Lisa replies.

This gets Suzie reeling back with laughter, causing crumbs to fly out across her desk. Even I have to smile at this.

"Forget it." Klep says impatiently. "What about you, Alex? What do you want to achieve today?"

Again, the desire to reveal an honest answer is strong: No porn today… I think to myself.

"I have one more client to obtain to hit my quota for the period – I intend to bag it today," I tell him, trying to look as non-committal as I can.

"Good answer." Klep whispers.

"Teachers pet…" Suzie murmurs.

"Now we're getting somewhere. Gemma…?"

"I need to go to toilet. I think I'm coming down with the same thing Alex had," Gemma replies, rubbing her belly.

"Would you like me to describe what I had?" I say to her.

"No thankyou!" she purrs, taking leave of the room.

"You okay, honey…?" Suzie asks.

"Okay, okay, I think we get the gist," Klep interrupts. "The point is – keep motivated. Knowledge is the key for feeding your mind and keeping you motivated. Remember – self-motivation makes us feel fulfilled, improves our quality of life, therefore improving the quality of life for our customers."

The morning is unremarkable, spent on the phone, dealing with clients, hitting my quota, yearning for home. I don't even have time to go over my 'top five'. At lunchtime, I head down to the canteen alone. Looking at the dried out chilli under the hot lights I realise I shouldn't have bothered. Hunger dictates otherwise. As I spoon the mess onto my plate, someone nudges me from behind.

"Any good…?" Danute says, looking just as offended at the offering.

"Looks can be deceiving…" I say, handing her the spoon.

Her timing is perfect as the canteen is almost empty and I decide now is a good time to tell her about Saturday. I observe her matching khaki skirt and jacket with her hair up in a bun as usual and the flushed look about her that leaves a faint odour of sweat trailing behind her as we walk to the table; she looks like she perspires a lot, stuck in her office, all wrapped up in formalities, crunching numbers, I envisage her crying out in relief as she abandons her clothes at the end of each day before taking a shower.

"Are you feeling better?" she asks me, fixing me with her wolf-like eyes.

"Yes…"

"What was it…not the food I hope…?"

"It was a stomach bug or something – nothing too serious. I was sick most of the weekend though," I tell her.

"Well here goes nothing…" she says, before eating a mouthful of chilli.

I do the same. We both agree the food isn't too bad.

"You busy?" I ask.

"Not particularly. Ollie is on holiday as from today, so I'm covering him," she replies. "Which reminds me - there were some discrepancies last week, perhaps I could go over them with you a bit later?"

I suddenly realise I'm forking chilli into my mouth at a voracious rate, due to nerves.

"Sure, sure, no problem," I reply quickly. "Listen, are you busy on Saturday? Martin put forward the idea of eating out at The Horse Inn, apparently he knows the chef there who's supposed to be really good. I thought you might like to come? Hold true to my promise…"

"This Saturday?" she asks.

"Yeah…"

"Who's going?"

"Me, you, Martin and his wife," I tell her, just as Steph and two of her team walk in.

"I'd love to." she replies quickly.

"Good. We'll make arrangements." I tell her.

We both spend the next few minutes eating, pondering: her at the prospect of getting to wear something special on a Saturday night and me at the odds of taking it off. Steph joins us at the same table - not with us, but near us - and greets us both with a cursory 'Hello'. After some small talk about work related matters, I abandon Danute to the ever-growing numbers filling the canteen, telling her I've got a busy afternoon ahead and for her to stop by later on before heading outside for a cigarette where I try not to dwell on the prospect of seeing that *bush* for too long as it's an image that both excites and frightens in colossal measures.

At just gone three, Danute comes into the office to go over the figures she mentioned. As she leans into me, her arm stretching across the desk, I can smell her scent, heavy now with the added three hours of labour since lunch, sending me mad with desire and at a complete loss as to what she's talking about. Before she leaves, she places a piece of paper on the desk with her telephone number. Job done… I think to myself.

Come five-thirty, I'm the only one left in the office with Klep at his most exasperating.

"Have you seen the chap with Steph, on your travels?" he asks.

"No."

"Interview for the Sales position," he goes on.

"And…"

"Doesn't really look up to the job, if you ask me," he says.

"Why should that concern you?"

"I'm just saying it's a waste of time, if you ask me."

"Why is it a waste of time? You don't know anything about him. He might have the best sales record in the district. He might have sold rice to the Chinese for all you know. He might have brought in more revenue in the last six months than all of our Sales team in the last six years." I tell him.

Klep shakes his head vigorously.

"Then what would he be doing in a place like this?" he says.

"Well that's not saying a lot for us then is it? That doesn't exactly inspire or *motivate* me to go out and give it my best." I tell him.

"I'm not saying that…" he urges. "This place *is* what it is. It's not the top end of the scale, nor is it the bottom end. That's not to say we don't strive to become the best. Someone with a track record like that wouldn't find this place challenging."

"Maybe he wants to take life a bit easier. Maybe he's had his fill and just wants something to pass the time." I say.

Again Klep shakes his head.

"Doesn't work like that. Selling is addictive. The buzz is the *sell!* You sell one then you want to sell another, then another and so on. You don't just turn that off otherwise you wouldn't be in Sales," he says. "Besides, that would be obvious and it's not in the interest of the company to employ somebody like that."

"So what's your point?"

"I'm simply saying - I can tell instinctively he's not the man for the job."

"Okay Marcus…fine. I reply, sending my last e-mail of the day.

"I'll bet you if you like."

"No thankyou." I tell him, as he begins swivelling in his chair.

"I've noticed you seem very agitated lately. Have you noticed that?" he asks, still swivelling.

"I haven't, no. I don't know what you're talking about."

"You look tired. Are you sleeping? I have a great remedy for sleeplessness…" he says, stopping to observe me with even greater scrutiny.

"I'm sleeping just fine, Marcus. The reason I might seem agitated is because it's late and I want to go home and you're prattling on about Steph's interview, which to be honest I couldn't care less about."

"No I don't just mean today…I mean *lately*," he persists, rising from his desk to put on his jacket then gather his things. "There's only one man for the job…"

"Who's that then…?" I ask, regretfully.

"Me of course," he replies, before slinging his rucksack over his shoulder and heading for the door. "I shall see you tomorrow. Another day in paradise…"

Klep disappears, leaving me to pack up quietly in the deserted office. His overconfidence about the Sales job has left a sour taste in my mouth and again I ask myself what I want? Is life to be a succession of encounters with people like Klep? Is that all I have to look forward to in the world of Sales? What a depressing thought! Is he the product, the template by which we work and strive to become? Is it the Kleps of this world that get to worm their way into the moist folds of Steph's sheer knickers? Does the thought of *him* keep her up at night - perhaps they're in league already? Am I flogging a dead horse? I realise it's Klep's intention to wear me down and give up the chase, but that doesn't make his goading any easier to handle. The scent of Danute still lingers in the room – I probably just want it to. It is home time after all and I need something comforting to take back with me.

In spite of the fact that I can't get Suzie out of my mind for some reason and that I would do anything to see her naked, I resolve to spend the evening, computer-free. Still suffering physically from my weekend sessions and with a book - that I actually want to read - I should be able to negotiate a deal. Not the case! Whilst sifting through a bundle of papers in my attempt to get the office organised, I come across a picture of Sarah holidaying in Nice during our second year at University. It was our first real holiday together and it's a cracking picture of her in her bikini against the backdrop of the Mediterranean Sea: the whiteness of her flesh, the firm shape of her figure and the red hair evoke images of our love-making during our time together. Every detail, nuance, personal to me, entices me away from the mundane task I've set myself and towards the computer, where the promise of reconciliation is whispered in my ears like sweet-nothings. This intimate knowledge works as a temptation, impossible to resist, until I'm pulling up websites left, right and centre and all the resolve to desist, not even a memory - lost somewhere in the configuration of my mind.

As the session progresses, it is this same knowledge that begins to work against me. Rapture is replaced with distraction – confusion as to how I let her go and why I did nothing to try and get her back. My penis turns to mush and dread envelops me once more – dread of what the future holds and my inability to control it. Then Klep pops into my head and I think about giving *him* one and what his arse looks like and would he spout the same nonsensical rubbish with my cock buried in it? After a brief exchange with this, the idea repulses me and I'm back on familiar ground with a batch of webcams featuring sexy Russian babes, yet still continuing to vacillate from the feeling of unbridled joy to the impotence of a condemned man.

The flies are back - or rather *the fly*. A black mark in a blackening room, interrupting the flow with a nefarious will, determined to make life for me as difficult as possible, battering itself against the window with a sickening buzz, bouncing angrily off the frame like a mad, pernicious pinball. I cover my ears and the sound of my own heartbeat booms within me, the muscle pumping me with blood until it feels like my head is about to explode.

I dress, leave the flat and walk. The only way is to step away. I don't know where I'm walking to and it's dark, but the cool air is so good, it feels as if I'm breathing it in for the first time in my life. I take the quieter roads, working my way up and across the hill that overlooks the town, where I stop on a bench and look down at the lights then up, into the great black void, only the odd glittering speck visible and breathe, the mind becoming lucid once more. I am living, breathing tissue, flesh, bone and human. I *do* care, I have feelings; I'm not a pleasure-seeking machine; I am not simply taking up space and getting in the way - a pest! I *am* capable of love. The sound of approaching voices prompts me to leave my seat and move on. I work my way back down and into town and along the near-deserted high street where I decide to stop off in the pub for a nightcap.

The pub is quiet and Pete the barman nods and welcomes me when I walk up and order whiskey. I also recognise Chloe, pulling glasses out from the glass-washer and drying them. I take a seat beside the bar and they resume the conversation they were having before my intervention - which is about porn of all things. I sip my drink and accept the coincidence with sufferance as Chloe talks of her younger brother, who must be sixteen or seventeen, whom she says has developed a serious habit and who just keeps himself to himself these days, consequently worrying the shit out of their mother, who is privy to the filth stored on his tablet and who has threatened to throw him out if he doesn't change his ways. I want to tell her that it's probably just a teenage thing, that it'll pass, but I don't want to lie.

I finish my drink, thank them and leave. That settles it – tomorrow at P.E.S.T I will sit and listen with others to more of the same and maybe even tell them something of my own.

9

With a meeting place named 'The Old Pavilion' I struggle to dispel images of leg pads, grass-stained whites, groin boxes and the smell of linseed oil. Am I to expect stuffy old MCC members in their ties and blazers seated around, gin and tonics cooling in the palms of their hands discussing how things all went to pot after that infamous test match and how they all took to wanking in a fit of mutual despair? Am I to be reminded of my school days and the late afternoons spent playing cricket with my English teacher umpiring as I belted in and delivered my final ball of the over - an attempted Yorker, right at the toes of our most feared and respected opposition in the league? For two consecutive years I took the title of leading wicket taker, much to the chagrin of our talented finger spinner whose quest for his own personal triumph was often a good motivator in my own yearning for success. Indeed, it was instilled at an early age that the need for personal excellence was a vital contributing factor to the success of a team. Was there anything more pleasing, despite us losing the league, than watching him bite his lip as I collected my award from the headmaster in the final week of term before the summer holidays? Were those formative years an indicator of the lengths I would go to, to replicate the same feeling of personal pleasure in later life? Has pleasuring the self, become my sole occupation? I would have to answer: yes. At which point did I decide to neglect the team and how do I get it back? Is the 'Old Pavilion' there to welcome me in, make me one of the boys, allow my ego to run riot, if only for the sake of the team, or to expose me as some pariah?

As I drive in the musky light of evening towards Oxford, I argue that I'm not heading out for a game of cricket, but to try and curb my obsession with internet porn. As I near my destination it suddenly dawns on me that perhaps I should have telephoned before making an entrance, perhaps one of the unspoken rules? Perhaps there's no admittance to the group without first having made one?

I finally pull in to the car park of what looks like an old school of Victorian architecture, the ghosts of children's voices still echoing around the deserted playground, then turn off the engine and remain in the car. Two large wooden doors, paint cracked and flaking, serve as the entrance to what looks like a small, unmanned Reception area with a corridor, illuminated by long fluorescent ceiling lights with dirty shades that lead down into the interior. There is a placard beside the door, fixed to the wall that I presume displays the names of the various companies using the facility, but I cannot make out the signatures. The place looks devoid of life, even taking into account the fact that I'm early; and the longer I remain seated, the greater the feeling of seediness my presence seems to bring. I toy with the idea of getting out of the car and walking in but resist due to a sudden, irrational fear of bumping into somebody I know or recognise.

I finally unbuckle, pull the keys from the ignition and begin to open the door just as a car pulls in and parks a few spaces down, causing me to gently re-close the door. After a moment, a fattish man who looks to be in his thirties, steps out of the car, shoots me a look and walks in through the door, his chubby knocked knees carrying him forward until he disappears from sight. I finally decide to check on the plaque to see if I'm in the right place.

Various names of companies and organisations are slotted into the slats, all officially logoed except the very last one at the bottom that is crudely penned in displaying the name P.E.S.T. I check my watch: 7:30pm. If I turn around and walk away, get in the car and drive home, I will only regret it.

Above the Reception area is another, larger notice displaying the same names only this time beside a room of residence. Again P.E.S.T is the only one scrawled in pen, making everything about it seem cheap, transitory and half-baked as I observe the name 'The Old Pavilion' alongside it. Towards the end of the corridor I can hear the faint, murmuring sound of voices coming from one of the rooms. I follow the sound until I reach a door, then lean in and bring my ear up close trying to determine how many people are inside the room before something forces me to step back. As I do, the door swings open, revealing the chubby man I'd seen in the car park. His weight fills the doorway and he stares at me with a kind, gentle smile, as if he's been expecting me for some time. My first impression of the man is how oily his skin looks and how his pock-marked face, resembles something like the lunar surface. I catch a glimpse past him and into the room and instantly recognise the distinct, Jesus-like features of Jim Rodriguez, the man whose website has brought me here.

"Hi. Are you lost?" The chubby man asks me, in a soft, effeminate voice.

"I'm looking for…P.E.S.T" I tell him, voice wavering.

"You've found us," he says, stepping aside and inviting me into the room.

Jim stares up at me from his chair on the far side with a curious smile and in the room I count another three men seated on two large sofas placed at a right-angle. Jim steps up, welcoming me with his hand and I pause momentarily, wary of touching it, before shaking it, feeling his strong grip.

"Welcome…Jim Rodriguez…" he says.

"Alex…"

"Please take a seat."

He motions to part of the three-piece-suit that looks like it's been commandeered from some deceased pensioners home and will clearly take two people to move. The fat, oily-faced man is quick to lend a hand and helps me move the chair closer to one of the sofas, forming a kind of circle. My eyes quickly gauge the rest of the members in the room as they welcome me with a nod of the head, each one a little shy and wary of a new presence and instantly I regret leaving the house to venture out. I observe them all: the oily-faced man, a tallish, slim man, early thirties; a young lad that looks no more than twenty and a heavy-set man, slightly balding, somewhere in his late thirties or forties. Light-headedness prompts me to quickly take my seat for fear of collapsing. As my body sinks into the chair it causes the cushions to wheeze and puff out around my bottom, sending a dank, stale smell wafting up into my nostrils, conjuring up a series of lurid images of the people before me who've sat in the very same chair. I will give it another ten minutes before I find a reason to excuse myself; anything will suffice: a bad case of gastroenteritis, reflux problems, a weak bladder, aching colon - anything to find myself heading back out through those classroom doors.

"Guys…we have a new member of the group…Alex…" Jim says, offering a formal welcome.

The group herald me in with 'welcome' and 'hello' and 'hey there'.

"Alexander…welcome to the group. You're here, like the rest of us, for a reason…"

"Please, just Alex…" I interrupt.

"Of course…Alex," he reiterates, still smiling. "Please introduce yourself."

"Well I wasn't sure if I had to ring first…to book my place…or if it was okay for me to just turn up" I say, furiously thinking about an excuse for my being here, which I decide is heading somewhere along the lines of 'research'.

"It's quite alright you being here. You don't need to ring, you just need to know we're here," Jim says.

"Well…I'm actually researching a book…" I mutter, provoking a muffled groan from one of the 'patients'.

"We're all here researching a book," the heavy-set man chips in.

"Well now, wait-a-minute guys," Jim says."That's quite alright Alex. If you say you're researching something - fine. However, we're all here to share our feelings with eachother in the hope of overcoming something that has affected our lives in a deep and profound way. We've all placed our trust in each other by openly discussing our most personal feelings in a safe and respectful environment without fear of recrimination or judgement. May I ask what you're writing about?" he says.

"About the effect of pornography on people's lives," I tell him.

"Well that's why we're all here. Because pornography has affected the lives of everyone in this room, often with very damaging effect…" he continues.

For some reason I feel a sudden urge to cry; an irrational tightening of the throat, watering of the eyes. I remain silent, unsure of what to say as the eyes of the room bear down on me, especially those of Jim who studies me closely, searching for the truth, delving into my reticence for not being straight with him, doubtless which he knows already.

"How did you hear about us?" he asks.

"I saw your website – it just seemed the right place to start." I tell him. "I'm sorry, I don't mean to sound flippant…"

"That's quite alright," he replies. "However, I must add…if you wish to be a part of this group, you will be expected to contribute in some way, both by listening and sharing your thoughts about what you've heard and by disclosing some of your own experiences to the group."

"I understand," I say nodding.

His eyes finally loosen their grip and he turns to the room.

"Perhaps the group would like to introduce themselves to Alex..?"

The oily-faced man is the first to address me - a cherub face and excited smile and a child-like manner making it difficult to determine his exact age, which I put at about twenty-nine. I observe his shabby sweater and stained track-suit bottoms and the soft pudgy hands wiping themselves across the knees as he looks into my face. But above all, I observe the oiliness slathering his face and plastering his lank hair to his head. There's enough oil on his face to run ten Ferraris! How any woman could even contemplate sleeping with this man is quite beyond me, hence justifying his presence for what I presume has been a lifetime spent of chronic masturbation.

"I'm Gary," he says, extending a soggy hand towards me, which I reluctantly take. "I'm thirty-one years old, single and addicted to internet porn and…I'm seven days clean!" he says, matter-of-factly.

The transference of moisture to my hand causes me to wipe the side of my thigh as he leans back into the sofa, his confession leaving him with a flushed look. My attention passes to the next man, the thick, heavy-set man, who I can tell, just by looking at, is the most confrontational and vocal of the group.

"Rob," he says, remaining firmly seated in his place, giving me a quick nod of the head.

"Hello," I reply, finding it difficult to make eye contact with him.

"I've been watching porn going on ten years. I've a kid and a failed marriage behind me and I'm interested in very little else than whacking off which is why I've started coming here," he says.

Jim nods approvingly and I move on to the young lad who leans forward and lifts his hand to me almost apologetically.

"I'm Darren. I'm twenty-two-years-old and I've been watching porn since I was about twelve," he says. "This is my second time here and I find it helpful to talk about my problem."

Finally, the last man, seated on the opposite sofa, who to look at, you'd never have believed had seen a pornographic image in his entire life, lifts his eyes.

"I'm Matt...and I'm also addicted to internet porn. I'm twenty-eight years old and I work in the admin department for a courier company," he says, quietly.

I nod before Jim concludes the introductions.

"Jim Rodriguez, of English and Spanish decent - hence the name - and I was addicted to pornography for over six years. I've also had to overcome bouts of alcoholism, costing me my marriage, my work and the love and trust of my children. After educating myself and turning my life around, I decided about a year ago I wanted to help others who had been or were going through the same traumas I had experienced. I have worked privately and in groups with people of all ages and seen how talking about something and committing oneself to changing the way one lives, has brought joy and happiness back into their lives."

He pauses to look paternally over the group before continuing.

"This is a new group, only a couple of weeks old. We come together once a week in an attempt to try and understand the problems we face and how we can change them – we're a support group – here to help each other. Is this the place you're looking for?" he asks me.

"Yes." I reply solemnly.

"Good. May I ask you a personal question Alex?"

"Sure."

"Why are you *really* here?"

Burdened with the question and the stare of the class, I'm suddenly struck with the feeling of not knowing who or where I am. The walls come to life, adorned with motivational messages that I'd failed to notice beforehand: I DIDN'T USE PORN – PORN USED ME, IF NOTHING CHANGES – NOTHING CHANGES, GET RE-WIRED, AS LONG AS THERE'S TOMORROW – THERE'S HOPE and NEUROPLASTICITY – THE EXPANDING MIND, all reminiscent of Klep's roll-call every morning and sending my mind frantic as I try to unscramble the riddle of how my life has brought me here, to this room, full of people who openly admit to spending their time in a haze of sleaze and who consider me to be made of the same metal.

"Alex…?" Jim prods. "The first step in dealing with any problem is admitting you *have* a problem…"

I look down at my pale claw-like hands, gripping the fabric of a chair that is completely alien to me and for some reason think about the work of art called: 'The Physical Impossibility of Death In The Mind of Someone Living' by Damien Hirst as I wonder if in fact this *is* Jesus sitting before me, urging me to repent and offering me absolution if only I were to speak.

"Yes… I think I have a problem…" I finally hear myself say.

I sense a collective sigh of relief from the group as Jim nods in affirmation, before slowly rising from his chair and stepping up to the flip-pad he has set on an easel facing the room. Another fucking flip-pad! A feeling of revulsion hits me with the knowledge that my confession has indeed exposed the metal with which I am made; the same metal as the 'oily man', the 'thick-set man', the 'lad' and the 'quiet man'. Surely not!

'Admit you have a problem' Jim writes, before turning to the group.

"Let's re-cap. How do we know we have a problem? When do we realise we are addicted to something?" he asks.

"When we can't control it anymore…" Rob answers.

"Right – when we're unable to control the use of something and when it prevents us from operating in the daily running of our lives, are two signs of addiction," Jim says. "It's one of the toughest problems facing our culture today. However, people don't just become addicted for the fun of it. There are usually reasons why an addiction happens and it's these same reasons that make an addiction difficult to stop. Firstly, we become addicted to something because of the way it affects our emotions. Often we block out emotional pain thinking it won't come back, but as everyone in this room knows, it does. Gradually, we build up a tolerance where we need more and more of the behaviour or substance to achieve the same buzz, until it becomes *all* we want, resulting in a completely new character profile."

Rob nods furiously, staring into the void between his legs.

"The second important element is withdrawal: what happens when we take that substance or behaviour away? How does one re-adjust to living without those previous levels of stimulation and what effect does it have?"

He pauses, looks over the room.

"What are the factors that influence addiction?" he asks. "There are a few. Genetics: Is it in the blood? Are we influenced by the behaviour of generations before us? My father was an alcoholic. Did this have something to do with my own addiction to alcohol in later years? Yes I'm sure. It wasn't the only thing though. What else? Past trauma, suffering abuse as a child, events that have shocked or left their mark in a deep, profound way can all have a huge impact on the steps we take later on in life."

"Shame…" Rob chips in.

"Shame…" Jim repeats. "…A feeling of not measuring up, of feeling inadequate in some way. This is a very powerful emotion. I can certainly speak from my own experience as this being one of the root causes of my own addiction to alcohol: a lousy husband, not earning enough money, a bad father; all of these were instrumental in my feeling of being a failure and my attempts to numb that feeling with alcohol. When all of these things are stacked up against you, it can seem very difficult to overcome. So what brings us freedom from this dilemma?"

Gary raises his arm, closes his eyes and recites.

"Confess your trespasses to one another and pray for one another, that you may be healed. The fervent prayer of a righteous man avails much…"

I shift uneasily in my chair, as Jim re-takes his seat.

"Right…" he says. "At some point, we will have to confess to trustworthy people, *everything* about our addiction – only then can the healing begin."

"Amen." Gary concludes.

"We've all taken that first step, which is why we are all here," Jim says, his eyes meeting every member in the room until they fall on me. "All of us here have realised somewhere along the way, we have lost control. Why are we addicted to internet porn? We've established here that we've all come from a good home, that we had loving parents, a normal childhood, with the exception of Gary who suffered bullying and Alex, whom we know nothing about. Why is internet porn ruining our lives? Why have we succumbed to the nature of addiction?

Gary raises his hand triumphantly.

"Seven days – No Fap!" he exclaims, generating smiles from the rest of the group.

"Congratulations," Jim says, allowing him the moment. "Tell us about it then…"

"I bought myself a Scalextric set as a means of fighting the urge. You know, when I was a kid I was mad about Scalextric and I knew somebody local who was selling one – in perfect condition." he says. "So I drove round and picked it up last Thursday. When I got it home, it was just like Christmas again. It was a big track so I needed quite a bit of space and the only place was the living room, so I spent the entire evening assembling it there. It was perfect…" he says, thrilled at the recollection. "It was hard, especially yesterday because I was really feeling the urge. But you know, I forced myself to stay away from the computer and play on my Scalextric instead…and it worked." Gary adds.

My heart sinks after hearing this big, oily revelation from the kid sitting beside me, in the knowledge that it's simply a matter of time before the shine dulls and he discards the damn thing, like all kids eventually do, and returns to his sordid life of porn. If Scalextric is the best the group has to offer in terms of healing, then I'm truly fucked, I think to myself. I smile thinly and nod encouragement, nevertheless.

"Rob, what progress have you made?" Jim asks.

Rob shifts in his seat and stares thoughtfully at his hands.

"Well not so good." he says. "I had one day where I was doing alright. I woke up and resisted turning on the computer which was good in itself as this is the time I feel most turned on. I then spent the rest of the day fighting the urge, my mood gradually becoming more and more aggressive, until at one point I had to pull my cock out as I watched an episode of an old T.V programme that I used to watch with a female character that I really liked. Anyway, I managed to stop myself and make a cup of tea instead…"

"So no computer…?" Gary asks.

"Not yet…" Rob replies, before continuing.

"That afternoon I got a call from an old girlfriend, whom I hadn't spoken to for some time. We got talking about all sorts of stuff then her voice dropped and she got kind of sad and told me she just needed someone to talk to as she'd recently been told she had ovarian cancer. Anyway we spoke about it and she got upset and I kind of reassured her that everything would be alright, until we eventually put the phone down. I went upstairs and sat in front of the computer – without turning it on – and pulled my cock out. The sound of her voice and listening to the way she spoke suddenly brought back all the memories and all I could think about was fucking her in the arse there and then.

The image in my head was so strong, it gave me one of the best hard-ons I've had in a long time. I mean forget about the fact that this person has been diagnosed with a life-threatening illness; forget about the fact that she was in tears on the phone and turned to me in the hope of finding comfort and some kind of reassurance. Forget about the fact that this was a human being in the midst of suffering and scared of where life was going to take her. All I could think about was fucking her in the arse again. How fucking low is that? What kind of human being does it take to stoop that low?"

The group reflect on this for a moment, each member nodding, like a circle of pigeons.

"Any semblance of humanity disappeared the moment I turned that computer on, which is precisely what happened next," Rob continues. "My promises and will-power and all that shit just went right out the window. I was back on it until gone midnight."

"Why do you suppose that was all you could think about as opposed to what else you could have offered in the way of support?" Jim asks him.

"I don't know. I couldn't help myself, I couldn't stop. My hand was actually shaking as I turned the damned thing on. I knew it was wrong, but the image of her triggered my response and I couldn't stop, regardless of how shit I felt about it." Rob says.

"I had the same problem some time ago with something setting me off…" Darren chimes in. "I had some bird come round collecting for some charity – young bird she was – so I answered the door and she's standing right there in front of me and she's prattling on about some people in Africa and where the money goes and I'm not even listening, I'm thinking about what her arse and tits look like with this tight t-shirt and jeans she's wearing and she's got this really sexy smile - which is why I suppose she gets sent out - and in the end I tell her I'll think about it then close the door and quickly leg into the kitchen to look out the window to get a look at that arse and that was it. I couldn't think about anything else and I was straight onto the computer and fapping for the next three hours. I mean is that a one track mind or what? It ain't fucking natural."

Again the class nod in unison.

"Well let's look at this," Jim says leaning forward in his chair. "Is this a normal reaction to something we see in the street, to something that evokes memories of a past relationship? Are we as men naturally being turned on by things we see and hear? Of course we are - but is there something else happening? Both of you were confronted by people talking about serious issues that required a serious response. Why, when pressed, were you more concerned about sex? What was the brain telling you?"

"I've got an over active libido," Darren says.

"Because we're all a bunch of fucking perverts that think about nothing but sex…" Rob adds.

"Not necessarily," Jim says, rising from his chair and turning to a fresh sheet of paper before scrawling the word 'Dopamine' across it.

"Let's talk a little bit about this word. We've mentioned it before, but we haven't really spoken about it," he says. "Dopamine is a neurotransmitter – a chemical released by nerve cells that sends signals to other nerve cells, much like transmitters send signals to our mobile phones and televisions etc. Research has shown, that in all addictions, in spite of their differences, high levels of dopamine affect certain neurochemicals which bring about changes within the brain. These changes reveal themselves in different ways through our behaviour. Do we remember what the 'three C's' are?" he asks, opening up the question to the group.

"Craving, Control and Consequence," Rob answers.

"Right…" Jim says. "Let's look at craving."

"The need to spread the seed…" Darren chimes in.

"Yes, that's an important factor. One of our first priorities is to procreate. But it's more than that," Jim replies. "We are dealing with how sexual novelty can influence behaviour; how we can tire of one thing yet still find the energy to go on when presented with something new…and so on and so on…"

Jim pauses and leans back in his chair, before continuing.

"What has this got to do with internet porn you ask? Everything!" he says. "The desire for sex arises from the neurochemical dopamine. Dopamine is 'love', dopamine is 'lust', dopamine is 'gambling', dopamine is that fucked-up-crazy-arsed-far-out party you went to last night; they should have called it 'pleasuremine'. Dopamine plays a key role in all of these and the part of the brain associated with the 'reward system'. In a nutshell - this is where we experience our cravings, pleasure *and* importantly, where we become addicted."

Jim rises from his chair and adds the word 'Reward' to the paper.

"Rewards or Reinforcers increase the likelihood that a certain behaviour or response will occur again; sex is one of the primary rewards, like Darren said, compelling us to pass on our genes, ensure the survival of the species. Food is another. Chocolate, cigarettes, marijuana, racing around a track in a two-hundred-thousand pound sports car will all release high levels of dopamine, telling you: 'this is pleasurable'. And the bigger the dose, the more you want. Without dopamine, we would feel very little. What dopamine does, is send us signals to those predicted rewards, something that 'needs to be paid attention to'. The sight of a computer screen coming to life will release high levels of dopamine in response to this as your brain predicts the reward, like watching porn whilst jerking off. It is important to remember though that dopamine is about *searching* for pleasure, not the pleasure itself. This is the key factor in our relation to internet porn."

Jim reflects on this for a moment before adding the word 'Novelty' to the paper.

"Something that is new, fresh and interesting…" he says. "I'm sure this definition strikes a chord with everyone in this room. Internet porn ticks every box going!"

The group nod fervently. He goes on.

"Some of us here are old enough to remember the days before computers and how the internet has changed the way we live today. Gone are the days of trundling down to the corner shop to buy a porno mag…"

"It wasn't just one – it was usually three," Rob chimes in.

Jim nods.

"And how many times did you look at them – three, four? The novelty didn't stretch very far before you found yourself heading back to the shop for more. As with everything new, the thrill fades away as your dopamine levels fall."

"Videos aswell - remember them. Always a stack on hand; I've still got a lot of them." Rob adds.

The more I observe Rob, the more depressed I become as it is clear he is by far the most 'gone' of the group, a position I sense he relishes in some perverse way. I stare at his bulk and balding head and watch as his nostrils flare, creating two huge black orifices in the middle of his face whenever he speaks. He looks like he's got a huge cock with heavy balls; an image that has me vacillate between awe and a sense of pity for the women who've crossed his path or guys for that matter - he looks like he'd fuck anything given the chance. Jim continues.

"Modern technology has changed all that. Internet porn works because novelty is always just a click away; one continuous, streaming film of every niche, fetish and taboo you can think of at the click of a button, with updates on a daily basis. Whereas before you actually had to leave the house and venture out in search of porn, at least requiring you to *move*, now you can simply wake up, turn on the computer and spend the rest of the day in complete, static, isolation. If one film doesn't do it, you simply move onto the next, then the next and the next! Fancy a change…click…click…click. This is what has made internet porn so addictive – an endless *search* for hit after hit that keeps our dopamine levels on a high, constantly giving us promises of pleasure, keeping us searching for the next best thing."

A corroborative groan from the group sees me nodding at the simplistic interpretation of what has been said.

"Oh man, that feeling, waiting for your computer to boot up." Darren says, waving his hands in the air. "Light up a spliff, kick back and enjoy the ride. Start off nice and soft as a kind of warm-up just as the smoke kicks in, knowing you can move onto whatever takes your fancy whenever you like. Mate, is there a better feeling in the world than that?"

"Marijuana and porn – a lethal combination…" Jim says.

"I used to smoke and watch porn…" Gary begins, "Until it became counter-productive. I would literally become too stoned to get an erection. I once spent nine hours on one session alone… What's the longest session you've ever had?" he asks Rob curiously.

Rob thinks for a moment.

"Bout the same…" he replies.

"Darren?"

"You mean on one category or one sitting?"

"Either."

"Oh mate, I've done twelve hours in one sitting," he says. "My dick looked like a fucking red-hot poker at the end of it. I couldn't use it for two days afterwards."

I can see where this is going and I'm already in two minds whether to lie about the thirteen hours or not. I wait, intrigued as to what Matt - the quiet one - has to say before making a decision.

"Matt?"

"I couldn't say…" he says thoughtfully. "Time seems to just fall away and have no meaning and become something I seem to lose track of. But I would hazard a guess at about six hours," he says.

"Alex?"

A quick look at Gary's oily face, forces me to reply.

"It must be about five hours…" I lie, catching Jim observing me, knowing damn well he's seen through the falsity. Gary, on the other hand, nods satisfactorily, as if proud of the fact that he's been the first to prize some information out of me, the image of a pig wallowing in mud, deeply satisfying to him.

"The problem is you get to a point where that's all you want and no bird will ever be able to compete with that." Darren goes on. "So you continue to watch porn. It's like having a thousand birds in your bedroom all lined up for you; when you finish with one, you grab the next, then the next. It's like having your own virtual harem."

"Exactly…sexual novelty influencing behaviour…" Jim says, turning to another sheet of paper and writing the words: 'Sensitisation' and 'Desensitisation'. "It keeps us *searching*. Now we know that dopamine is a key part of the 'Reward System' where we experience pleasure and cravings." he goes on. "What happens when we overdo it…? Desensitisation is a reduction in the brain's sensitivity to dopamine. It's like a numbing effect. It's like a mini immune system blocking out the everyday pleasures, leaving us constantly hungry for things that get our dopamine levels back up, all for the sake of pleasure. In both substance and behaviour, it's probably the first thing we notice in relation to brain changes within the addict in that we need another 'hit' to achieve the same buzz, otherwise known as tolerance. One line won't do it anymore for someone addicted to cocaine. This will quickly have to be followed up by another then another in quick succession. The same can be said for violence – watch enough of it, we become numb to the horror, it no longer shocks us. How does this manifest itself in terms of internet porn? More time is spent in front of the computer. The sessions are longer. We 'edge' our way forward, bringing ourselves to the point of climax, before stopping and then continuing once more. Remember we don't want it to end - there's always something better around the corner! As we've just mentioned, there are some hefty times bouncing around the room. We view things that are harder and stranger and more perverse - things that once we'd never have dreamed of watching - to gain a greater kick or means to gaining an erection because the softer stuff just doesn't do it for us anymore.! Our tolerance levels become higher! We spend time putting off the shopping, paying the bills, socialising, working. Everything outside of those four walls becomes a chore and a burden and must simply be dealt with at a later stage."

Jim raises his finger to emphasise the point.

"The most destructive element of Desensitisation is that we no longer view women as real people; they simply become sex objects, fucking machines, not the loving, intelligent, beautiful creatures made of blood, flesh and bone with a sensitive soul…"

For some reason the Romanian Housekeeping girls at work pop up in my mind, provoking a sudden rush of sympathy that has me wondering what they eat for their dinner, how they feel when they watch a film, what they talk about with their families and what position they sleep in when they go to bed at night.

Jim goes on.

"What brings about Desensitisation is Sensitisation. In simple terms: we become sensitive to something. With repetitive porn use, we build up a huge memory bank of material that can trigger powerful cravings. It's like a little alarm bell goes off every time we see something or touch something: being alone in the house with time on your hands, turning on your computer, seeing a pair of crossed legs seated in an office, or something as innocuous as the way the clouds form in the sky – I've known it to happen. These can all trigger cravings for porn…"

"This is the most fucked-up part for me," Rob chimes in.

"Sometimes it gives me the shakes. I'm like an alcoholic – sweating, nervous. Everything I see turns to sex. It's like there's nothing else in the world, forcing me to go and turn on the computer. Then when I try and ignore it, it starts yelling at me: 'Oh yeah? Think about all the shit you're missing!'

"Those are symptoms of Sensitised addiction – neuro-pathways setting the cogs of your Reward System in motion, telling you to watch porn." Jim says.

"I reached a point where my whole personality changed." Rob continues. "I was constantly aggressive and moody if I wasn't getting a fix. Everything I did, from watching T.V with the wife, to going shopping, to being at work, left me feeling agitated and on edge, because I didn't want to be there, I wanted to be in front of the computer watching porn. My wife, or I should say my ex-wife, used to talk to me and I would have nothing to say. My head was filled with the shit I had been watching and I couldn't very well tell her about that. I couldn't concentrate on anything for long periods of time - I still have trouble - unless I was in front of the computer. I must have been shit to live with."

"Yes Rob, I know that feeling," Gary says. "I have mood swings all the time. I didn't even realise it until a friend pointed out that I had become depressing to be around and that I had changed so drastically he thought I was bi-polar. I'm getting better now, but it's like pornography *had* become so ingrained in the make-up of my life, that when I was without it, it felt as though I was missing a leg or something."

"In a nutshell – we are wiring up our brain's pathways to make us constantly want something, until we reach the stage where we've become conditioned to getting turned on by porn, instead of the real thing." Jim says.

A lapse in concentration has me watching the rest of the group as they fawn over Jim's every word, holding him it seems, as some kind of messianic figure providing the much-needed light. My cynicism has me wishing I had brought a pen and paper, had I known there would have been a torrent of endless information to get down. Jim rises from his chair and addresses the flip-pad once more.

"Here is your Reward System…" he begins, drawing a nucleus with two lines extending out from it in opposite directions. "Imagine your brain has two pathways – one pathway for porn, the other for a 'real' woman," he says running his finger along the two lines. "When we watch porn a lot, your brain is being wired for porn and not a real woman. Also remember the more shocking or new something is, the more dopamine is released, creating a stronger pathway…" he says, exaggerating the size of one line with his pen until it's ten times as thick as the other. "Now over time, where we continually watch porn, we will eventually develop a huge pathway for porn, where, as Darren mentioned earlier, a real woman simply won't be able to compete with, leaving you with a Reward System that no longer gets turned on by real women, but only porn," he says.

"How could she possibly compete?" Rob says. "Internet porn will always provide way more stimulation than a real woman; it's got everything you could wish for, like snapping your fingers. Anything goes! A real woman won't do half the things we see on the net. It makes 'real sex' boring by comparison. *This* is the fucking problem."

"I got to a point where I could no longer make love to my wife, despite her urges and my love for her. Why…?" Jim says.

"Because she didn't turn you on anymore," Darren says.

"She did…but I felt like I couldn't do anything about it because my brain had become so wired for porn. It left me impotent in front of the one thing that mattered to me most."

As I listen with a growing feeling of pity and repulsion – for myself - I am intrigued with the man opposite me - the quiet Matt, who like me has yet to say anything. His face is studious yet pained, burnt-out, unbefitting a man of his age. Yet behind the eyes, one senses a switchboard of mad, flashing lights, blindly sending and receiving; a maelstrom of information, nothing discernable to hold on to. And in this, I find something of a kindred spirit. Like me, he *seems* normal, young; handsome and at pains to be in such company, yet for the same reason has been forced to attend.

"Mate, there are times when I can't even get a woody without porn." Darren begins. "One time, I got off with some bird, went back to her place and couldn't even get stiff then! I kept trying to think of this one bird I'd been watching on the net which eventually seemed to work, but the sex was shit and I felt like shit afterwards and I know she told her fucking mates. That was when I thought, fuck this - I need help and joined a forum with other people going through the same shit."

"And did it work?"

"No. You discuss stuff, but it's not like being here where I can look into people's faces. There's no emotion to it - doesn't make me want to change fuck all." Darren replies.

"I haven't been with a woman for four years – with porn I never thought I needed one," Gary states, the sheen on his face, glaring like a radiant sun in the dinginess of the room.

I observe, as Matt nods his head with intent, wondering if he is finally about to say something. Jim turns to him encouragingly and after careful deliberation, he finally speaks.

"Well I'm also curious about this phenomenon of how we overcome our wanton desire of the uninhibited and beguiling monster of internet porn over the flesh and vital force of a real woman. I myself have had no contact with the 'real thing' for a few years and reached a point just recently where I was so desperate for actual physical contact with 'something', just to make sure I was still capable of performing penetrative sex, that I resorted to what can only be described as desperate measures."

I watch as Matt struggles to lift his eyes to the group, the mind in great conflict.

"Which was what Matt?" Jim asks.

"Well I thought about the things available to me in the house: a cup or a toilet roll or something similar, but there was nothing. There wasn't even any fruit in the house, a melon for example," he says.

Gary nods eagerly at this, directing his enthusiasm towards me, as if fucking a melon is something we've all participated in at some point and that we're all in complete understanding of where Matt is coming from. He goes on.

"I ended up fucking a Spatchcock chicken," he says.

There is a pause for breath within the group as the information disclosed sinks in, laying foundation for a myriad of images to suddenly spring to life.

"Shit…a live one?" Rob finally asks.

"No, no…" Matt answers. "From the Supermarket… I bought a few more items and drove back home. I remember the excitement of pulling it out of the cellophane and then having to clean the herbs and seasoning off its back – the smell of food is never conducive to good sex – before taking it into the bedroom and sticking my cock in."

"Shit…" Darren mutters.

"I suppose I should ask if it worked or not?" Rob asks.

"It did work, yes. I was able to gain a full erection and it was pleasurable. There was only one drawback and that was the jagged breast bone. I had to be extremely careful so as not to shred the topside of my penis."

"Of course…" Rob mutters.

"Anyway…it was good for two sessions, after which I had to dispose of it." Matt concludes, before hanging his head once more.

The character study I've cultivated of Matt is suddenly blown into orbit as I realise he is as much a freak as the rest of the gang, making me feel very alone and highlighting the hopelessness and futility at my coming here.

"This is our mind telling us that we must do what comes naturally – to seek out a mate, someone to love, to hold and take care of. Not wire ourselves up for sitting in a room watching the fake world of porn." Jim says.

"By that, I hope you don't mean a Spatchcock chicken," Matt says, modestly.

"No Matt, I don't mean a Spatchcock chicken."

Jim looks at me for a response, as if I have a piece to add to the puzzle, some juicy confession that stacks up against Matt's and endears me to the group. I remain silent.

"Of course this all leads to conflict within the brain, weakening our willpower when confronted with strong cravings that ultimately cause the self-loathing I know everyone in this room has experienced." Jim goes on.

"Don't knock a man when he's down…" Rob mutters to himself.

"Precisely… In this weakened state, it is usually the addicted pathways that inevitably win." All of these points are key players in the role of addiction…"

For the first time in the session I check my watch and put aside my prejudices, working over the mechanisms of what I do every day and how I might change them. I suppose I was expecting some kind of instant cure - a prescription of pills to be taken twice daily after food then left to wait for the results to kick in. However, the notion of simply rewiring my brain to exclude the likes of 'Wanton Mary' et al seems a mountainous task requiring a huge amount of willpower to overcome which in the present company seems ridiculous. My head is beginning to ache as Jim goes on, talking more about the science behind some of our cravings then recounts days of how his relationship with his wife deteriorated over the course of time due to his extra-curricular porn activities and how the fact that he lost her worked as the catalyst in getting himself clean. Did this not mirror my own experience with Sarah and the fact that porn had been partly responsible for the break-up or was that simply the capriciousness of youth? Rob becomes confrontational when pressed to disclose to the group what he's done in the way of abstaining over the course of the week. Gary tries to calm him. Darren talks more about a girl he was with and her sexual preferences and Matt hangs his head for the remainder of the session. Without barely having said anything myself and not having been pushed to, time finally catches up with us.

Jim leans back in his chair to reflect then checks his watch. Gary smiles at me with his oily face, clearly overjoyed with the company he's in, clearly believing he's found his route back and there to encourage others to follow.

"Remember guys, this is all about trying to regain control…that's why we're all here." Jim says. "There is no easy fix and the healing process can be long, so a couple of things before we finish up."

"Yoga…!" Gary exclaims, beaming.

"Ah Yoga…" Jim nods. "Gary's Nova ingressus…!"

"I can really feel it working." Gary enthuses. "Twice a week without fail and I have to tell you, it's not just about stretching, it helps the mind to focus. Please guys, if anyone wants to join me, let me know."

Despite another notch being etched into the stick of revulsion with this confession, I listen with interest as this is a line of exercise I have thought about pursuing, having previously looked into the details at my local sports facility. Aside from this, the thought had occurred to me that it might be a good place to meet women. Yet, as Gary goes on, describing in lurid detail some of the moves he's asked to adopt, my heart sinks picturing this big oily-face kid in full whimsical flight, forcing me to reconsider.

"If Yoga works for Gary – so be it," Jim says. "The first step is to give your brain a rest from the shit you watch every day.

And not just for a few days – a few months or more. Embrace 'real life' again and try to remember what it was like without an endless stream of porn. Our goal is to start gaining pleasure from interacting with real people again and to open our eyes to the joys of life and love."

"Amen…" Gary whispers.

"Seems pretty fucking dull to me…" Rob says.

"Compared to watching porn, sure…" Jim says. "But the more you refuse to allow porn to clog up the pathways of your brain, the more you will gradually see change. How do we begin achieving this?"

"Delete *all* porn from your hard drive." Gary emphasises.

"It doesn't work." I suddenly blurt out.

Silence descends as the entire room fixes its eyes on me. Gary moves in closer and in a hushed tone tells me: "It does Alex – all you have to do is press delete. Open your folder, all the back-ups, bookmarks, history, don't think – just act. The whole fucking lot…!"

The ensuing silence requires a response – one I'm unable to fulfil, before Rob fills me in.

"I know…difficult isn't it?" he says. "Think of the years it's taken you to get that folder together; all the babes and pussy you've methodically stashed away, ready to be taken out whenever the mood hits you. Today it's Brenda, no Tracey, no Wendy, Carla, Jackie, Maureen, fucking Maggie! Shall I go on? You've got a seriously intimate relationship going with every one of them. Are you going to just cut them loose, chuck'em out into cyber space, never to be seen again?"

Gary shakes his head and goes on.

"Not one and keep the other. We'll get rid of those ones and keep that batch as they're *really* good and frankly irreplaceable… Delete the lot Alex – it's the only way."

"I'll try."

"Don't try – do!" he emphasises.

"Okay, I'll do it," I tell him, actually believing.

"Feel the consequences before they happen," Jim says. "We all know how blind we become *before* we watch porn - lost in the excitement, stuck in the moment. Think about how you're going to feel *after* viewing it - exhaustion, depression, guilt, wasted time. You know damn well you're going to feel shit. Next time you feel the urge - focus, think, close your eyes and walk away. It won't always work, but get into the habit of doing this. Keep thinking about the negative aspects you're bringing upon yourself every day and the effect it's having on your life."

"Yeah, stop living the lie – to yourself and others. Just tell yourself it's all a lie." Darren says.

The group nod in unison.

"Remember, the more you walk away, the easier it becomes to walk away." Jim says. "We've covered a few things this evening. Try and remember them and maybe do some research of your own. Use your imagination to help yourself… be creative. Do anything - but preferably things that don't involve the computer. In today's world, that isn't easy. Use your imagination, interact with people. Don't exist in a private hell. Not as much fun as watching porn? It's not meant to be. The point is you are doing something else. Remember we are all here to get ourselves off internet porn. It's going to take time. Set yourself targets. Start with an afternoon, then a day, then two days and so on.

"Seven days – no Fap!" Gary reminds us.

"Above all, keep attending these sessions. We all know the invaluable effect of talking to someone, in the flesh, about the problems we face and what we can do to help eachother. Reboot! Jim says, pointing to the poster on the wall.

"Amen…" Gary adds.

This heralds the end of the session and the group finally begins to disband, gathering up their belongings and dusting down.

"See you all next week…" Jim says, unfastening the sheets of paper from his flip-pad.

"Cheers…sound…" Darren mutters, as he brushes past me towards the exit.

Matt also offers me his goodbye with a pensive nod of the head. Unsure of quite what to do, I loiter near the exit as I watch Rob and Jim converse quietly leaving Gary to approach me on his own.

"Here," he says, pulling some leaflets from his 'retro' holdall and handing them to me. "Read through these. I found them really helpful."

I glance down at the hand-outs: Neuroplasticity, The Nature of Addiction, Cognitive Development and The Mind and Meditation.

"You can include them in your book," he adds, smiling, drawing in and giving me a faint whiff of the heady smell about him. "Don't give up. This is a new beginning for you. I hope to see you next week," he ends, before delivering his final goodbye to Jim.

Rob is quick to follow and simply grunts at me as he passes, leaving me alone with Jim.

"Was it more or less what you expected?" he asks. "Did it meet the requirements for your book?"

He places one hand on my shoulder and walks with me a little.

"Alex…I don't mind you telling us you're writing a book and doing some kind of research. I don't care if you're from Mars. What matters is that you are *here*. Just don't lie to yourself."

"I'm sorry…"

"Don't apologise. If there was an easy way of getting around this, we wouldn't need places like this. I hope you take away some of what you've heard today and use it as a tool to begin the healing process. You're here because you want to be healed – remember that," he says. "Keep fighting and see you next week."

He offers me his hand which I accept and we shake on it.

As with my trips to the supermarket; the return journey home is always more upbeat, proud in the knowledge of having just accomplished something. Yet as I drive, the idea of shedding the persona that I've come to know over the years is a frightening prospect. Again I question the strength and conviction needed to eradicate something that seems too big and beyond my control.

My head is heavy with information, flitting from one anecdote to the next, recapping on all the things that were covered in class, calculating where to begin. Were it not as simple as simply walking away from the computer, I would have done it ages ago. Where to begin? In spite of all my frowning upon the group as geeks, freaks and hardened masturbators, there is no denying my own need for the same help they seek, a fact ironically undermining my decision of whether to attend another session.

10

There is a flip-side to everything, I ponder, indisposed, gazing at the computer screen. There is noise and there is silence; there is dark and light… there is the noisy sound of routine at work all around me but I'm busy totting up the plus points of what watching porn has done for me in defiance of everything seen and heard last night. What about the cultural benefits? What fucking cultural benefits? Have I not seen beauty in all its guises, in the skin-tone and the diversity of ethnicity, from the continents of Africa and Asia to Europeans and beyond? Have I not learnt a little something about the indigenous people of these lands - *not* in spite of what they do on screen? Have I not developed a greater appreciation of the female form, carried in the weight of the multitude of shapes and sizes that they come in, watching then seep their way into the world of the real? What joy! What a thing of beauty the body is! What about the *male* form…my own form? From a biological point of view, have I not learnt something about how the human body works and reacts and opposes and welcomes in all its various capacities or am I just a voyeur to some mad, freakish circus? It is staggering what the mind will allow and what the human body is capable of doing, of sucking in, absorbing and releasing! What about languages? Have I not developed an ear for the resonant sound of speech, accents in all their strange, beguiling, mysterious and discordant intonations? What about: 'Fick mich in den Arsch und nicht aufhoren, bis Sie kommen,' for starters. Or: 'Sucer ma bite avant que je baise!' Surely this holds me in good stead amidst this multicultural world we all live in? Has not my ignorance been lifted from its complacency and my eyes opened to these countless tributaries flowing over the face of our earth, inspiring new life? What about sexual performance? Although only moderately endowed, have I not digested the various positions and speeds with which to satisfy and prolong the act of love-making, thus utilising my modesty to greatest effect? Am I not capable of performing like a rampant bull, much like my esteemed virtual colleagues? Am I not more adept at pressing the right buttons covering the female form, tickling the right spots in my quest for mutual satisfaction; have I not become more receptive to what women want! Where else would I have learnt such things - in a science lab? Is porn not just getting a bad rap?

I'm forced to divert my gaze as Suzie breezes past, her breasts looking bigger than ever. Why fight it? It's too big to overcome, so why fight it? Life *could* be worse. What are the alternatives? Boring endeavours, watching T.V, getting shit-faced with work colleagues then crying about it the next day; having to *work* the next day; trading in your hours to become a man like Klep! I am simply watching the rock stars of our generation performing every day to the beating of my heart and make no mistake about it, they're here to stay. This is the future. Do I really need P.E.S.T?

Prasad calls me and Klep into his office.

"You're in trouble…" Suzie teases.

Klep who's been relatively quiet all morning with his own dealings shoots me a look before we both converge on the doorway.

"Shut the door…shut the door," Prasad urges as he swivels round in his chair to face us.

"Right guys…I've just spoken with John the Director and

Steph…" he begins. "Steph's booked in a client who are possibly looking to hold an event here over four days, within the next couple of months. They're a company called Alpha6, high end, with a worldwide client base and looking to make a home for their twice-yearly get-together."

"What do they do?" I ask.

"I've no idea – they sound like something out of Star Wars. Now John's got his knickers in a twist over this as it's potentially worth around two hundred K, per event. Steph's done a lot of work cuddling up to them and it's just a case of getting them over the line. Now Steph's got a shitload on her plate at the moment *and* she's going to be away on holiday when these guys are in for their show-round, so John's come up with the bright idea of assigning you two to the task."

Klep shoots me another look, his mouth curling into a smile. Prasad goes on.

"It's a show-round like any other show-round and it's up to you guys to sell the hotel, to convince them that this place is *so* perfect for them, that they don't even *think* about going anywhere else. Only John doesn't see it that way; he sees it as some kind of 'burning bush' moment."

"Piece of cake…" Klep blurts out.

"Then why doesn't John look after it himself? Why does he want us to do it?" I ask.

"Because it's what you do for a living. Besides, John is no good at all that crap: hello and goodbye are about as far as his talents stretch concerning show-rounds." Prasad insists.

"John is smarter than I thought!" Klep says, feigning a yawn.

"Is *he* going to be serious on this or do I have to go crazy in the process?" I ask, referring to Klep.

"Look, just work together okay? At the end of the day, it's just another show-round. Talk to Steph and find out a little about the company. Go and do your homework. Work out how you're going to play it and who says what and when. Work together as a professional team…yes?" Prasad tells us.

We pause for silence. Prasad offers us the papers detailing the company and its criteria to which Klep is quick to make a grab.

"Steph will catch up with you and give you a briefing…" he adds. "Just make us look amazing. This is a chance for you both to shine and send a message to John from this department that says – 'ON THE CASE'! Clear?"

"As a whistle…" Klep says, before looking at me then leaving the room.

"Close the door…" Prasad sighs, taking the moment to confide in me personally.

As I close the office door I can see Klep is already at his desk, scrutinizing the paper.

"Alex, you've been here a while…you know the score. Just look after Marcus on this. We all know he gets a bit excited and shows off a bit, but you know better. Work together and make us look good. More importantly, make yourself look good. John specifically asked for you two, which means he has faith in you and trusts you'll do a good job. It's no secret you and Marcus want the Sales job and a good result on this will go a long way in deciding who Steph takes on."

"I've got no problem with that Prasad. I just don't want him thinking he can run all over this and go off in his own little world without consulting me."

"That's why I want you to take the initiative. Look, Marcus is good at his job - as are you - put aside your egos and everything else and work as a team. That's why we're here. That's what we do, right?"

"So what, are we under scrutiny here? Whoever performs best gets the Sales job?"

"You're always under scrutiny, you know that," Prasad smiles. "You make your own guess as to what they're looking at. At the end of the day, it doesn't matter. You need to be treating this appointment just like you would any other."

I pause reflectively. Prasad wheels himself back to his desk.

"Go on…Steph will be in a bit later…" he concludes.

Klep is on the phone when I walk past his desk, but he reaches out and hands me the brief, urging me to read. I take it and smile at Suzie, who with second sight, is shaking her head as a matter of condolence, foreseeing a bloody battle of wills that will have nothing to do with catering for our client.

"We'll go through it after lunch," Klep informs me as he puts the phone down.

"I'm too busy." I tell him. "We've got plenty of time to deal with this…"

"Okay, it's up to you, mate…" he says.

Suzie joins me for lunch which works as a nice distraction, although it does get me thinking about P.E.S.T again. Unable to open the windows due to some needed repair work and the issue of health and safety, the canteen is stiflingly hot with the smell of roast beef and potatoes heavy on the nose. Groups from every department grumble and mutter their discontent about the conditions whilst stuffing their faces with what is actually a bit of a treat.

"So tell me what he said - about Alpha6? Presumably that's why Prasad dragged you and Marcus into his office." Suzie says.

"What's there to say – he wants us both to take care of it," I tell her. "How do *you* know about it?"

"I spoke to Steph earlier this morning. Lisa now has to see in your IPP appointment in your absence."

"Fair enough…"

"Good luck with Marcus. I have prior experience of doing a show-round with him and I couldn't get a word in edgeways," she warns me.

"Yeah I can believe that." I say, struggling to divert my eyes from Suzie's breasts which I conclude *are* bigger and wonder if she's managed to hide the fact that she's pregnant.

"I've got to tell you though Alex, I know Steph likes him. She keeps prattling on about how he should be in Sales, how he's got enough bullshit floating around in him to see off the big boys. Maybe it's that crap he drinks every day." she tells me. "Speak of the devil…"

Steph walks in with one of her colleagues and sniffs at the hotplates. After serving themselves, they join us at the table.

"Just the man…" Steph says, placing her plate down and taking a chair opposite me. "This looks nice. How's the beef…?"

"It's actually good," Suzie tells her.

Steph takes her fork and prods at the food curiously like it was something spread out on a table in a science lab before gingerly placing a piece of meat in her mouth. She fixes her cold eyes on me as she masticates then nods after swallowing.

"Prasad told me about Alpha6 this morning…" I say.

"I told John you and Marcus would be fit for the job," she begins, her eyes unwavering.

Steph proceeds to fill me in on the details: a show-round of mega proportions featuring a high-end client with a huge network around the world, two delegates to attend…thinks me and Marcus will look good as a team…wants us to spout off about past events that have gone swimmingly well…it's a big day for the hotel… She takes another mouthful of food, chews then swallows.

"Play off each other. Have a bit of fun. Work like a comic duo. Who are those two comedians…?" she says thinking, unable to come up with any names and none the wiser with our help. "Do you know what I mean?"

I think for a second, failing to see the correlation between a pair of comedians and two salesmen on a show-round, but nod anyway. Then just as quickly, Steph is talking with her colleague about something totally unrelated to the previous conversation, blanking me out as a given that I've understood everything and there's nothing more to say, a move typical of her slick guise.

Then, as if realising she's still keeping me on hold, asks me again.

"Do you know what I mean…?"

Steph's unremitting look leaves me exposed and I'm hit with the odd sensation of hot flushes where all I can think about is the fact that I've just recently attended a support group for internet porn addicts and whether this information is written on my face? I stuff some food into my mouth to prevent myself from speaking. Would this information sway my chances of nabbing the Sales job? How favourably would she look upon my parallel existence and the sexualising of everyone I see? Thank god we're not eating chicken! Suddenly I feel as if the whole canteen is staring at me, somebody having had knowledge of my discreet little tryst then spreading it like wildfire across the entire hotel. I swallow the gristle. Then without saying much more, I finish the rest of my food as the conversation turns very 'female', based around 'hunks' they've all been watching on T.V, instigated by Suzie, resulting in no-one really noticing when I eventually excuse myself and depart. The rest of the day is uneventful and nothing more is said about Alpha6.

The cat is weaving between my legs in the kitchen, curious as to what I'm stuffing into my mouth. I bring the cheese sandwich down teasingly and begin waving it in front of his face in a circular motion causing his head to do the same. I can't help but laugh when teased to the limit, he finally lashes out with his paw – with greater speed than anticipated – and knocks the food from my hand, before diving down to retrieve it – again with great speed – only to be met with disappointment. I look around and take stock, realising I am simply killing time because I don't know what else to do after making a promise to myself on the way home not to turn on the computer in respect of everything that was said at P.E.S.T. However, my life is compartmentalized, consisting of working during the day, five days a week and wanking during the night with the exception of weekends which can feasibly take up both day and night. Take one of these things out of the equation and I'm stumped with a whole lot of time on my hands.

The food begins to feed my cock as I envisage the new updates slipping away into the infinite void of cyber space, leaving myself short of what could be life-changing images. I move to the sofa and sit down, the hours ahead suddenly seeming like weeks. The idea of calling Martin up for a drink is out of the question as I just don't feel like it. Television is nothing more than one, giant advertising campaign and bores me to tears. A games console would go some way in alleviating the pain, but I don't have one, perhaps I will look into rectifying this despite Sarah always telling me it was even more of a time-waster than wanking. There is the small matter of researching Alpha6 that I promised Klep I would complete. It can wait. There are my long abandoned books gathering dust on my bookcase crying out to be read - inspiring pieces of work to be absorbed and turned to in times of need, something I once took great pleasure in doing and which right now seems the most appealing, despite it being a solitary one. The cat walks in and over to his corner where he flops down and assumes his curled up sleeping position, fiddles about for a bit then just as quickly becomes inanimate, a piece of furniture, one with the sparse décor of the room.

In the bedroom the idea of acting upon Gary's advice and deleting every shred of porn from my computer disturbs me as I familiarise myself with my collection of books, the words 'JUST DO IT' echoing around the inside of my head…easier said than done. Drug addicts, alcoholics are all weaned off the hard stuff gradually, because they know that severing the arm or leg in one blow will be too much of a shock to the system. The same must apply to internet porn? "There is a motive to every action…" I repeat to myself as I become more dubious about the prospect of reading as it allows the mind to wander too easily if not completely absorbed, coupled with the fact that one is usually recumbent, thus giving the reader way too much latitude for 'wandering hands'.

I decide I need to gather some information and make a new list of books to buy if I'm to settle for this option irrespective of the old novel I take to bed with me and begin reading. After about twenty minutes, as much as I try, I can already feel my eyes wanting to close, head nodding listlessly, limbs falling flaccid. Concentration is impossible. I force myself upright, leaning back against the headboard and place the book on my lap, buggered if I'm going to allow sleep as my only other alternative. Another fifteen minutes or so and I give up, moving into the office and turning on the computer to research Alpha6, running over pertinent facts, gathering information and generating a rough idea of what the function sheets will look like, all on the presupposition that we pass the show-round with flying colours and all done without deviating towards My Favourites folder – a duration that lasts about an hour.

This all changes after I receive a text message from Martin confirming that the chef he knows will be working on Saturday night for our evening dinner, which in turn gets me thinking about Danute, which in turn gets me deliberating over My Favourites folder. What if I were to *cut down* my viewing time as opposed to cutting it off altogether? The prospect of seeing Danute naked clouds my reasoning and weakens my will to carry through on Gary's advice. I simply can't bring myself to delete the entire lot, knowing I will never be able to retrieve them. Surely a quick look won't do me any harm? I've already made headway by attending P.E.S.T…one step at a time. I look over my notes concerning Alpha6 which don't interest me in the slightest. Besides, Klep will have written reams. I can feel my hands beginning to shake as the huge and endless extravaganza of porn buried deep within the CPU pulls at me like an angel-voiced siren, luring me to my death. I pull up My Favourites folder and run down the list of titles, reacquainting myself with literary classics like: '*HOUSEWIFE FISTED IN KITCHEN!!*' and '*GRANNY COMES OVER REPAIR MAN!!*' not daring to open them for fear of lightning striking me down. There is an option at the top of the page that reads: 'delete contents of folder', that fills me with a mix of fear and wonder. "Just fucking do it…" Gary's voice whispers, the entire contents of the folder flashing before me like some 'greatest hits' montage that finally sways the pendulum of my indecision to an emphatic NO! I watch as the clock ticks by, redundantly staring at my desktop, unable to open *anything* until I finally decide to spurn the urge and give my book another go. Before I retire to the bedroom I note down the exact time of my last visit to a porn website, which is about twenty-eight hours, including yesterday. Smugly satisfied, I manage to get in a good couple of hours of reading before my heavy eyes finally give in to sleep.

I wake up with a stonking hard-on after having had a dream about hiking somewhere in the Peak District with an incredibly sexy mature woman, the face of which I remember from seeing in town somewhere. How vividly I recall the secluded spot, amidst the beauty of mother-nature, locked in the bosom of the earth, her white nakedness laid out before me, the smell of grass and honeysuckle, dense and abundant. And I recall in my mind how appealing she looked in her shorts and walking boots traipsing across country with me in tow, only one destination in mind.

I stick my hand down the front of my pants and gently caress, staying this way for twenty minutes or more before reluctantly rising for work, heeding the advice of my associates at P.E.S.T by taking a cold shower which actually works in supressing the urge, yet fills me with a vitality that remains with me during my commute in, despite the rain that pours from the skies.

When the first rush of nicotine hits me, it's as if I've had a dose of electric shock therapy, instilling within me an extra-sensory perception that magnifies the minutest of things, leaving me even more confused and irritable than my usual self. Upstairs, I can hear the constant drone of Suzie and Lisa nattering away like some round-the-clock call centre that never wavers or ceases in its intent to provide. The sound is unrelenting and deeply irritating and I can barely hear the client on the other end of the phone, prompting me to turn abruptly and tell them to shut up, which seems to offend Suzie. This is added to the higher than usual pitch of Prasad's voice as he converses with Klep with his office door open. The room stinks like a sweat-pit and I'm in two minds whether to call up Housekeeping and ask them to do a quick job in cleaning the place up, and get it back to something like decent working conditions. I can also detect the heady smell of female at her time of the month and speculate over who it is as my computer works at a frustratingly slow pace. I grit my teeth and clench my fist and ignore Ollie from accounts when he places some papers on my desk and asks me to get them back to him ASAP. When Klep returns to his desk, we both agree to go over the notes we've made concerning Alpha6 which looks unlikely today, given our schedules.

"We'll play it by ear…" he tells me offhandedly. "Go with the flow and arrange a time."

"Fine by me…" I tell him.

"In my country we all smoke; my grandmother, my grandfather, mother, father, brother, sister, cousin - everybody smoke. It's a very unhealthy place. We like to drink aswell. We have a saying: when the drink is inside – the sense is outside…" the friendly Romanian girl I've spoken to before, tells me as I smoke my post-lunch cigarette.

"Why don't you give up?" I ask her, still trying to work out the meaning of that saying.

"I can't," she stresses. "When you start work at six-thirty and you don't stop pushing trolley around, then make bed, then clean toilet and push more trolley around, you need a cigarette at lunch-time, believe me."

"Yes I suppose you do…"

"We all die sometime…yes?" she smiles, taking a drag on her cigarette and playing with her mobile phone.

I squint at her, basking in the heat of the sun and watch the manner with which she smokes her cigarette and feel the effect that both are having on my cock whilst weighing up the possibility of her making the 'top five', which I finally reject due to her lack of sex-appeal.

"You have girlfriend?" she enquires, still checking her phone. "She English…?"

"Errr…no girlfriend…" I tell her.

"You live by yourself?"

"I have a cat," I tell her.

"Oh I love cats! I have two back home. My mother, she look after them. She send me picture last week, sleeping together. Look!" she says, bringing up the image on her mobile phone. "I miss them so much…"

"Well I hope you see them soon," I tell her, as she stubs out her cigarette and begins walking away.

"I hope you find girlfriend…" she replies.

I continue to smoke, agitated with the way this last remark was said. Women know instinctively when something is askew: a built in sensor that tells them whether a man is a suitable mate or not. They can determine very quickly if one simply shows up for a dip or if one is in it for the long haul; if he's big or small, if he carries the weight of life well with enough room for another? They are the bearers of children - they don't let any old prick in for free. As I smoke, I recall the times I've wondered what it would be like to be a woman, with all the trimmings. How I've yearned for a vagina – just for a week – so as to experience the feeling of satisfying the biggest dildo in the shop! Perhaps it's this simplistic nature of mine that comes across to the friendly Romanian girl – a vision that deters her from taking things any further. What about Danute? What does she see?

Suzie completely blanks me as I pass her in the corridor on the way back up. I didn't dare look at her breasts which are *even bigger* than they were yesterday, for fear of a reprimand. Perhaps I'm hallucinating. My suspicions tell me it's her who is menstruating. The office is swelteringly hot even with the windows open and my crotch feels like it's roasting in its own private sauna. Come five-thirty I catch Suzie on her own.

"You okay Suz…you seem a bit on edge." I ask her as she gathers her things. "Rough day…?"

"Prasad's pissing me off. He's been on my case all day." she replies, checking her mobile phone.

"Sorry I was snappy with you earlier. I was having a bit of a shitter…" I tell her.

"Don't worry. You're forgiven when it comes to this fucking place." she moans. "I'm going home to have a glass of wine…or three," she says, before saying goodnight.

I gather my things and soon follow her out. After stopping to buy some food, I enter the flat in desperate need of a shower. The weather remains unabated with predictions of another scorcher tomorrow. Just moving is an effort and after slinging my clothes in the washing basket, I step into the shower and gasp under the cool volley of water. After drying myself off, I decide to forgo all clothes and remain naked for the rest of the evening.

After fifty hours, the dam finally broke. And when I came, it was like a water cannon dousing the flames of a violent mob that had been vexing me for the last ten-thousand years. For four hours preceding it, all peripheral vision was defunct; the levee ran down in shattered ruin, flowing with the water into the dark, infinite abyss and there was nothing I could do to stop it; there was no sin or shame, no malpractice or misbehaviour attached, just a quiet word in the ear; a voice so lovely, it was impossible to resist.

Whether it was the cool interior of the flat against my naked flesh, or the indifference of Suzie towards me during the course of the day, boredom or the gaping, neurological highway in my brain telling me 'enough is enough, it's time to play' - I don't know. It didn't matter, I made a decision and I stuck by it. All that mattered were the images on screen and the way I felt whilst viewing them.

Now, at just gone past the witching hour, I decide I won't be attending another meeting at P.E.S.T, under the pretence that I can bring myself down without having to listen to a bunch of freaks lamenting about how the breastbone of a spatchcock chicken will shred your cock to pieces or how you just can't gain enough friction from the inside of a honeydew melon. This is simply a phase I'm going through – it will pass. I won't be stigmatised by the persistence of a few rogue thoughts.

11

Fiona Dunne is the last person you want to see when trying to keep your mind on the straight and narrow and away from the distraction of pornographic thoughts. However, this is who I find seated and waiting for me by Reception for an early appointment that I've completely forgotten about – a 'cardinal sin', as Klep so eloquently informed me. Upon seeing her, looking the absolute spitting image of a young Britt Ekland, I'm reconciled with a hundred images of our last encounter together and realise, I'm nothing more than putty, ready to be moulded and shaped into any excuse I see fit, preventing me from seeing my true self.

I *sense* the stunning shape of her figure at all times, under the cream blouse, no jacket, tight black skirt and the flat shoes that give off the illusion of her standing in bare feet, revealing her true height and play a little game with myself in seeing how long I'm able to deny myself the proper look it deserves. I sense the slight bow-leggedness, suggesting her legs are perpetually open, riding either horses or men - I can't decide which.

"Let's get a coffee…" I stammer.

"Great…"

It's early and the Bar still smells of the sickly-sweet scent left by whatever freshener the cleaners use, strongly permeating the room that is headache-inducing and when I ask Fiona if it's not too strong for her, she replies: "No".

I order our coffees at the Bar, showing no interest whatsoever in the fat but pleasant Barmaid before heading straight back to the table where I catch Fiona staring out dreamily at one of the far-off estate workers going over the lawn with his mower. It's a stunning image and one I want to savour for longer, which for my sins, she obliges me with. Seated opposite her, she pulls a folder from her bag and places it on the table as I set down my notes for Vista Publishing.

"So…how are things with you?" I ask.

"Really good…busy…busy…" she says.

"You look well," I tell her, stating the obvious.

"Thankyou… I'm moving house at the moment, so things are a bit hectic, you know how it is. It's amazing how much stuff one accumulates over time. I'm trying to get into the habit of giving things away…to charity. It's not good to hoard." she says.

Her insouciant, untroubled demeanour exudes warmth and effortlessly tames any ill-feeling I have with the world. Yet her otherworldliness is immediate, as if she's just landed from another planet; wandered in from a place where everything is beautiful and made naturally to perfection and where creatures like Fiona whisper and giggle, confiding in secrets the rest of us have no way of understanding. The fact that she's in publishing also sets her aside from the usual grey, corporate, hard-nosed business end of the spectrum that fills our calendar.

"You live in London?" I ask.

"Yes…I've moved into a flat in Fulham which has cost me a small fortune."

"Alone?" I ask, a little too quickly.

"Yes…" she says, hitting on that.

Her answer makes me think of three things: firstly, how is a woman like this possibly living alone, secondly, that she must be doing alright if she can afford a place in Fulham and thirdly, does she masturbate at night?

"No boyfriend?" I ask, sounding nothing short of pathetic.

"No…" she says, crossing her perfectly formed legs. "Not at the moment…"

The coffees arrive quickly and I can feel my hands trembling as I open up the first page of the file I've put together for Fiona's event next month. We discuss the formalities, me having given up on my little game and grabbing fleeting looks at various points of Fiona's anatomy at every opportunity. The taste of hot coffee only adds to my feeling of wellbeing as I take a moment, whilst Fiona looks down at her file, to assess the beauty of her legs and her shoe which is on the verge of slipping off the heel of her dangling foot. I adjust my seating position when she looks back up as my pelvis feels like it's in a constant state of propulsion, held in a sort of perpetual limbo, thrust out farther than it actually is. I take another sip of coffee as I think about what kind of lingerie she's wearing. It's a tough one as *anything* would look good on her. A few tresses of silver hair languidly fall across her face, partially obscuring her eyes which she has to run her fingers through to move as she pictures the scene: Hamburgers, Hotdogs, BBQ chicken, German sausage, a variety of salads, cold bottled beer, warm summer evening… I really want to ask her about the book I'm reading and how she thinks it fares in the world of literature and if perhaps there were some suggestions she could recommend as I'm in a state of rehabilitation.

"Any good reading recommendations…?" I ask, amending my notes.

"Sorry…?"

"Any good books out there I should be reading?" I repeat. "What's selling at the moment?"

"Oh yes…"

Fiona reels off a few names - none that I've heard of - and I nod enthusiastically, one eye on that dangling shoe. She tells me of a book that's become a bestseller about the story of a woman whose plastic surgery went wrong and who is now disfigured for life. For some reason, this gets my back up and I forget momentarily that I'm with a client.

"Another one striving for perfection…" I mutter. "I've no sympathy. They should leave themselves the way they are. I don't like the whole fake thing…do you?"

Fiona looks up, a touch of surprise on her face.

"I can understand…" she stutters, before I butt in.

"There's nothing fake about you is there…I mean, nothing been tampered with…?" I ask, trying to sound good-humoured.

This time she blushes.

"No…" she says awkwardly, running her fingers through her hair.

I look back down at my notes.

"The main Bar is always available should somebody want something else and will be there for any late night revellers…" I go on.

"I'm sure there'll be a few well-established, hard-core drinkers…"

My heart skips a beat when she says 'hard-core' as I observe the way her mouth forms an 'o', accentuating the razor sharpness of her cheekbones and the glint that pierces her eyes as I reflect on those un-tampered-with breasts. The girls from the recent models convention, parading themselves around the hotel like preening peacocks, don't even come close to the allure of this woman.

"There's always a few…" I say, sounding horribly smug. "DJ…?"

"No…nothing like that, let's keep it simple," she urges, as I note down the info.

"Marquee…no…band…no…" I mutter, ticking. "So are you still packed up in boxes - living with the bare essentials?"

"Yes…" she says, taking a sip of her coffee. "For some strange reason I've put everything in my bedroom and plan to branch out from there, so my bed is surrounded by mountains of boxes that I have to climb over every night just to get to sleep," she replies.

I would climb over the Himalayas just to get into the same bed as you, I think to myself. I would leap the giant hurdle of internet porn just to lie beside your nakedness! And I decide there and then that I want to dedicate myself to sexual intercourse for the rest of my life as it's the only thing I think and care about, my only road to true happiness. Fuck the planet; fuck the economy, the politics, the work, the dissemination of mindless information - let's all just fuck! With a slight personality makeover, a new set of clothes and renewed confidence, this is wholly feasible, given my youth and good looks.

The heel of Fiona's shoe disengages with the foot and hangs beneath the satin-stockinged arc of her in-step, the sight of which leaves me speechless as I observe discreetly from beneath the furrow of my brow making my attendance of P.E.S.T seem all the more pointless in the face of what is nothing short of blatant teasing. I stop writing and look up into those pitch black eyes and see a thousand starlit heavens, galaxies of infinite wonder awaiting exploration, a solar system of burgeoning life laid open for me to simply reach out and pluck its fruit if only I had the courage. She *is* driving me to madness.

I reel off the new arrangements, observing the slackness of her ankle which now rocks in unison to my words, causing the shoe that still hangs to slap gently against the heel of her sole.

"Fine," she says, adjusting her notes, uncrossing her legs, putting her feet out of view, giving me full access to the immaculate bone structure of her knees beneath the fabric of her hosiery that sparkles in the light. She sips her coffee and looks at me seductively from above the rim of her cup.

"Have you lost weight?" she asks, confidently.

"Me? I don't think so." I reply, uneasily.

"Maybe it's me…" she says.

Her quiet, continued analysis suggests she is unconvinced, but too polite to insist upon it.

"Do I look like I have?" I ask, secretly revelling in questions that have nothing to do with business and everything to do with the human condition.

"Does she fancy me?" I actually *hear* myself wondering.

"Well…yes," she says shyly.

She didn't hear.

"I'm unaware of it. I've been exercising regularly…maybe that's it?" I tell her, sensing 'a moment' between us.

Could the unthinkable be happening – is Fiona Dunne hitting on me? Has she been thinking about me since our last meeting? What *does* she do all alone at night in that Fulham flat of hers? Should I really be pursuing this line of questioning? Just as quickly, the cup is lowered and Fiona adopts a business-like attitude once more.

Circumspection dictates the remainder of the meeting, which is brief, as she has another appointment. The final details of the event will be posted forward with all costs pertaining to the changes with a deposit required three weeks prior to the event. I recite the rest of the details with servitude until she finally tells me she has to get going and calls the meeting to a close. As we gather up our things, I can't shake the feeling I've missed a trick; and the idea of asking her whether we should get together some time pesters me as I escort her back down to the main entrance where Caroline is trying to mollify an irate guest checking out.

"Well what do you expect? If you pay peanuts – all you get is monkeys!" he informs her as she nods helplessly.

Trying to stay out of ear-shot, I move Fiona to the door to say goodbye.

"Oh dear…" she mutters.

"It happens sometimes." I tell her.

Then, as I grasp the warm, moist flesh of Fiona's hand, a

deep human instinct takes hold of me, something borne out of the tender feeling of true love and affection, something beyond mere adoration that sweeps over me in folds, prompting me to lean in and attempt to kiss her on the lips. Surprised at my temerity, she subtly turns her head sideways using her hair as a barrier, preventing my lips from actually touching hers and leaving my nose buried in a freshly-washed mane of soft silver fibres. She's blushing again as I pull away, still clasping her hand.

"All the best," I say, releasing my grip, the sad realisation that her move was something akin to that of one trying to evade a leper's touch. "Any problems, give me a call," I tell her, as she smiles at me then departs through the revolting doors.

I'm rooted to the spot, unsure of where to look. Caroline is still with the guest, who seems to have calmed down sufficiently so as to allow her to explain the various reasons as to why he had cause for complaint. Wary of her having been privy to my inappropriate conduct with Fiona, I quickly leave her to it and head back upstairs, feeling leech-like and scabrous and utterly daunted at the prospect of spending the rest of the day in a stinking office.

Lisa informs me Klep is having his interview for the Sales job with Steph after I enquire about his whereabouts. The news dogs me for two reasons: one, its stomped its dirty boots over the effigy I had of Fiona and made it quite impossible for me to lose myself without distraction and two, it's stupidly reinforced the idea that Steph has forgotten about me and that Klep has bonded with her in a way that I'm unable to counterbalance due to my passivity towards the job and life in general.

After about an hour and a half he returns and quietly takes his seat, his face giving nothing away. He doesn't mention the interview and I and everyone else in the room, don't press for any answers. Further irritation follows: my computer is still unbelievably slow; my 'roids' have flared up again, leaving me squirming in the chair – not good news - as I need to be defect-free come Saturday's date with Danute, I can't shake the gorgeousness of Fiona from my mind and I can't do anything about it here at work, the temperature in the room feels like a hundred degrees, Klep won't stop commenting on his glands and how the fluctuation of inflammation is affected by his thought process, I can see the sweat patches staining the armpits of Suzie's shirt, made all the more alluring by her obliviousness to it. I am a rampant bull - I need to leave this room!

I pull myself away from the pit at lunchtime, foregoing the canteen and the smoking area and hide in the sanctity of my car which is unwise as the isolation and personal space makes me yearn for home even more. All my problems would be solved if I were back at home in front of the computer with Fiona. I pull out my phone and scan for porn, grabbing a sneaky peak at the new updates as my hand wanders down to my crotch. Not content to settle for seeing the images on a tiny screen, I put my phone away then lower the window and light up a cigarette instead.

After ten minutes, I get out of the car and head back to the office where I meet Danute who's going the same way. I feel awkward in her company, me being in her presence as having the effect of me cheating on somebody, namely Fiona. I observe her with greater scrutiny, looking for some awful biological or genetic deficiency, one greater than the touch of cellulite, the large nose, spots…one usually carefully guarded, yet exposed in shocking clarity on those rare occasions when the barriers are down, thus adversely affecting all future communications. And as we walk, I realise Danute and I will never be something long term, at least as far as I'm concerned. She will be an experiment, a means to finding out if two and two equal four - nothing more. My vanity won't allow anything less, reminding me of a comment made by Darren at P.E.S.T stating he could never be faithful to a bird unless he had her knocked up. I would have

Fiona Dunne knocked-up in a jiffy. Danute on the other hand will see things differently, that is obvious despite the rudimentary stage of our affair. She is honest, loyal, kind and above all, looking for a mate. What troubles me is that she thinks she's found one in me. I see it in her face; hear it in the sound of her voice, borne out of relief of what has probably been an arduous search. She's a step away from finding her man, but it isn't me.

I finally make enquiries about when and where we should meet tomorrow. Again I can sense the eagerness in her tone and an almost desperate need to confirm in her own mind that it's actually going to happen when what I really want is a display of *indifference* to the whole affair; to the decision of whether we end up having sex or not, which of course I want.

"There's a pub just around the corner called The Plough. I thought we could have a drink there first," I tell her.

"I'll be driving…" she says apologetically. "I suppose I could get a cab…"

"You can always stay at my place if it's a problem," I tell her openly whilst debating whether this is such a good idea, as I was hoping to get back to *her* place. "I'll call you tomorrow if you like – just to confirm," I say, *indifferently.*

"Okay…" she says.

As we reach the top of the stairs, Steph meets us on the landing coming down.

"Ah Alex…just the man," she interrupts.

Danute smiles and carries on up, leaving me alone with Steph.

"Interview Monday…two o'clock…" she says.

It takes me a moment to figure out what she's talking about or rather *who* she's talking about as she fixes me with her grey eyes.

"Monday…yes…no problem…" I say, realising she means me.

She's still talking but my mind is already racing. A good reaming from Steph on a Monday is just what the doctor ordered and will hopefully go some way in snapping me out of my stupor. I still can't tell how sore Klep's ass is but he seems to be suffering no physical defect judging by the way he's been sitting, which makes me think she went easy on him. My attitude towards the interview will determine how easily I can walk come Monday evening, meaning I have some work to do over the weekend in terms of preparation.

Steph's mouth continues to move and I watch distractedly… she crosses her legs and smiles wickedly,

"In which position do you intend to fuck me?" she asks.

"I beg your pardon!"

"I'll bet you've got a big penis – haven't you?" she says.

"What!"

"I'm forty-two going on nineteen you know…" she sighs.

"But…!"

"I'd rather be having sex twenty-four hours a day than doing the job I'm doing," she informs me.

"I…"

"Shall we conduct this interview in the toilet?" she asks.

"The…?"

"Are you a man or a mouse!" she teases.

"STOP…!"

Just as quickly, she's brushing past me, advancing down the stairs, treading tentatively in her heels.

12

"Excuse me, I'm just going to the toilet," I inform Danute as I rise from the table, leaving her to ponder over Martin's imminent arrival. As I relieve myself, concerns arise about the state of the flat and the condition I left it in before I came out. In spite of my attempts to make it half presentable in the event of Danute coming back, I'm certain I've forgotten to change the bed linen. I'm also certain of the fact that I haven't changed it for weeks. The hoovering is done, the kitchen washed up and the office cleaned and aired. I also cleaned up the pile of sick left by the cat that I found in the hallway this afternoon that he must have produced whilst I was showering. Having abstained from visiting the computer all day, I've also ensured I've left something in the tank for Danute tonight, should a situation arise. However, I'm convinced I've forgotten the crusty sheets.

As with all people outside of their work attire, Danute looks like a completely different person, as if this Danute is a friend of the Danute at work who's done me a favour of setting us up for the evening, one I recognise, with all the regular traits and idiosyncrasies, but with another element attached, revealed by the short skirt and extra bit of thigh on display and the bare flesh of the arms where she allows the hairs to unashamedly flourish and grow, not abundantly, but almost imperceptibly. Her face exudes the same radiance and a thirst though: the intense stare, those green pools nestled beneath thick eyebrows fixing onto my every move as I re-take my seat, revealing a sense of *history* to the person. The efficient, unwavering instrument at work has been left there until Monday morning where it will be plucked from the drawer and turned back on and re-set to fulfil the tasks it's required to do. Now Danute - the girl from Lithuania - sits beside me as real flesh and blood warming to the occasion.

"You know, you're right about the money," she says, continuing where we left off. "I could be earning more doing what I'm doing somewhere else."

"But you like the place?" I say.

"Yes, I do," she says. "The people are really nice and the area…"

She lets the words fall away, as if unsure about whether she's saying the right thing or if I'm really interested. When she sees I'm listening, she goes on.

"To be honest, I wasn't sure how long I was going to stay in England - a year, maybe two at the most…"

"And now…?"

"I don't know…it depends…" she says, expectantly.

I nod soberly.

"I've only been at Thorn Park for seven months…so we'll see," she says, taking a sip of her drink. "*You* must enjoy it – you've been there a while."

"It has its ups and downs – when it's down, it's usually concerning a guy named Marcus." I tell her.

"Oh he's funny."

"Funny! No he's not funny."

"He asked me once if I was albino," she laughs.

"He said that? That insulting - anyone can see you're not." I say, a little too defensively.

"He was only joking. He sometimes calls me Snow White. He says he wants me to introduce him to a girl from Lithuania. He really is funny."

"I'm sure your opinion would change if you worked in the same office as him."

"I think he has a good attitude to life! We need people that are a little different and make us laugh – especially in our office," she says.

"Yes…I can't imagine your boss inspiring mirth. Still, I suppose it's in the nature of your work." I tell her.

"What do you mean?"

"Well I mean, you look at numbers all day – it must get boring." I say, causing slight offence.

"It's not boring…" she muses.

"Well I suppose not – that's *why* you're an accountant."

"I'm not an accountant – I deal with the Sales Ledger."

"That's just a job description - you work the books - its accountancy."

"Ok, it's a step towards being an accountant – a qualified accountant."

"Which is where you want to be…?"

"Eventually – yes." she nods.

I sip my drink.

"I know…let's not talk about work," I urge. "We spend the better part of our lives doing it - why talk about it when we're not doing it?"

"A sense of perspective perhaps…?" she smiles.

Silence ensues as I ruminate over the width of her smile and the shape and colour of her teeth wondering what we *should* talk about without sounding patently obvious.

"Don't let the bastards grind you down!" I hear behind me before Martin's hand slaps my shoulder.

"Danute – fancy seeing you here," he says, grinning lasciviously, as he and Tasha move around in front of us.

"Hi Alex," Tasha says, before rubbing Danute's arm affectionately.

Feeling a little cheated, as I was happy working on Danute

in my own quiet way, I raise my glass in welcome.

"This trip has just cost us ninety quid. That or three points," Martin says, as Tasha dismisses the comment.

"Rubbish."

"It flashed. She's just been nabbed speeding." He tells us.

Tasha rolls her eyes.

"No I wasn't!"

"You were doing thirty-six." Martin persists.

"He just talks rubbish." Tasha tells Danute.

"You drove…?" I ask obviously.

"She's not drinking tonight, as she had a skin-full last night," Martin tells us. "All the more for us, eh…? Beer… beer…? He says, counting himself and me in, before lifting his eyebrows to Danute.

"Gin and tonic," she says.

"Gin and tonic…I like that." he says, before dismissing Tasha's choice as redundant.

I'm wary of being in the company of Martin on a Saturday night while escorting a date, as the last thing I want to do is get completely blotto and render myself a vegetable in the face of Danute's amorous advances. To say I'm sure of getting a look at that bush tonight goes without saying, on the proviso that I don't act like a complete arsehole, which means capping the amount I drink. That can be tricky with Martin.

"Alex, don't get wasted tonight…" Tasha pleads quietly as Martin walks to the Bar. "You're a bit more sensible than he is, so keep him under control. He's already had a few and he's got the bit between his teeth…"

"I wasn't planning on getting *too* drunk and spoil my dinner," I tell her, as Danute eyes me carefully.

"He's drinking too much," Tasha confides seriously. "It's that fucking job. He works all hours and then drinks when he comes home, to relax. I hardly ever see him and when I do, he's drunk half the time." she says, watching Martin converse with the barman. "I mean, I like to have a drink if I'm out with some friends and sometimes I get shit-faced, but I don't do it out of habit like he does."

"It's a stressful job," I tell her.

"Yeah, but that's not an excuse to just selfishly indulge and forget about everything else – like his wife! Life is stressful for all of us, but that doesn't mean we have to drink and smoke every night."

"Well how bad is it?" I ask.

"I don't know…" she says, evasively. It would just be nice to have a *conversation* once in a while, without resorting to anger and name-calling."

"Yes…" Danute says thoughtfully.

"Sorry, I'm being a real party pooper," Tasha says, making light of her grievances. "Ssshhh…don't say anything, he's coming back," she whispers, as Martin returns.

"We were just talking about the impotent effect too much drink has on man," she tells him, half in jest.

"Sounds like a solid step in decreasing the world population," he replies. "Too many people on this planet as it is…"

I observe Danute from the corner of my eye as she continues to ruminate over Tasha's problems, despite her seemingly full attention given to Martin as he speaks. Indeed, for the next hour, Martin holds forth, as the voice of reason, of angst, of condescension and hypocrisy, of outright foolishness, anger and even the voice of enlightenment, as we listen and interject randomly with opinions of our own that really do very little but serve to humour ourselves. It's Danute, with all her aplomb and deftness of touch that keeps Martin from stepping *too* close to the fire as I delight in the control with which she conducts herself. Sex with her is intense; like her stare - deep and unbarred - a search for the purest love and eternity in every sound and movement; it is slow and sensual and with trust established, experimental. Her eyes have bewitched Martin, I can tell; and with the beer beginning to take effect, I partake with a growing sense of greedy attachment towards her. After another round of drinks we head for the restaurant, which is a quick jaunt in the car, care of Tasha. Danute decides to leave her car in town where she will pick it up later, or not, as the case may be. I assure her it's safe where it is and that if it makes her feel better, she can always park it in my road where I know there is ample space.

As the Head Waiter shows us to our seat, Martin makes a point of wanting to see the chef. He disappears behind the scenes while we make ourselves comfortable. Bang on eight-o-clock and the place is already busy providing a warm and informal ambience. I make a note of the Waitresses as they pass our table.

"This looks nice," Danute says, observing her surroundings.

"Martin and I have eaten here before – when the old chef was here – and it was good then. Martin says the new chef is *really* good," Tasha assures us.

"Any recommendations…?" I ask.

"I had the monkfish last time and it was *superb*," Tasha says.

"I'm so hungry…" Danute drools.

Martin returns in good spirits.

"Good – he's nice and busy!" He declares, before taking a seat. "He says to have the duck liver to start and the lamb for mains."

The waitress arrives and hands us our menus before telling us about the 'Chef's Special' - Suckling Pig Pie. I open up the wine menu first and begin looking down.

"You were working here last time we came," Martin tells the young and extremely pretty Waitress with blonde hair.

"I've been here about six months," she says.

"Have you tried the Suckling Pig Pie?" he asks.

"No…"

"Don't they let you sample the menu?"

"Well…"

"You see this is what I'm talking about…" he says, addressing the table. "How can someone recommend something passionately if they don't know what it tastes like? Sorry, what's your name?" he asks the Waitress.

"Claire," she says, looking utterly sorry *before* we've even ordered anything.

"Claire…I'm not having a go at you – it's not your fault – but you should tell them they need to let the staff sample the entire menu, so they know what they're talking about, okay?"

"Okay…" she repeats, as Tasha glares at Martin. "Can I take a drinks order? Can I get you any water?"

"Still water please…at room temperature," Tasha says.

"Have you tried the lamb?" Martin persists.

"She just said she hasn't tried it," Tasha says, getting a smile out of Claire.

"No – she just said she hadn't tried the pig pie."

"I have had the lamb and it's really good," Claire adds.

"Claire, ignore him," Tasha says.

"I'll have a pint of your finest ale," Martin says. "I'll leave it to your discretion."

"I was thinking of getting some wine," I butt in. "The list is good."

"Well we can get some wine as well," Martin says.

Claire looks at me hopefully, but I remain undecided.

"What do you want to drink?" I ask Danute.

"I'll have a bit of wine," she says. "But I'm happy with water."

"Red or white…?" I ask.

"Water has no colour," Martin says before turning back to Claire. "Have you tried the water?" he asks.

Tasha intervenes.

"Stop being stupid…"

"I don't mind," Danute says, uncomfortably.

"I'll have a think and order when you come back," I tell Claire.

"Sure…enjoy your evening," she says, before leaving the table.

Martin's pressure seems out of place for the occasion serving only to make everyone else feel uncomfortable, making me wonder just how much he's had to drink. He looks troubled, on edge, as if still reeling from a pre-departure altercation with Tasha that has yet to be resolved. I look across at the table beside us and the young couple, both tinkering on their mobile phones, oblivious to the presence of each other and everyone else around them.

"Behave yourself will you!" Tasha tells Martin. "Everyone is looking. Why do you have to be so embarrassing?"

"Oh don't start. I'm simply making a point."

"Well make your point and be quiet."

Martin winks at me as we open up our menus and read in silence. I'm still undecided about which wine to choose as I don't know what I'm eating yet, but I'm leaning towards the Pinot Noir.

"Well I'm going to have the Suckling Pig Pie and the Cock crab to start," Martin says, closing his menu.

"Yes I'm going to have the crab as well," Danute adds. "And the Sea bass…"

"I'm going to have the monkfish, because I had it last time and I know it's good," Tasha says.

I decide to start with the crab and go with the lamb for mains as this will pair well with the wine.

"So come Danute…what's a classic Slovakian dish?" Martin enquires, out of the blue.

"Lithuanian…" I correct him.

"My apologies…Lithuanian," he says.

"Well, we eat a lot of potato…" Danute laughs. "We have something called Kukuliai, which is like a potato…how do you say…"

"Dumpling…? Martin says. "I know it…like Gnocchi."

"We also eat a lot of pork. That's really the most common meat. But there's beef and lamb as well. One of my favourites is Zrazai – beef rolls that you fill with vegetables, mushrooms or potato – they're so nice," she says.

"What about 'hot borscht'?" Martin asks.

"Oh yes!" I eat a lot of that…and 'cold borscht!'"

"That's made with beetroot isn't it? That's why it's a bright pink colour," Martin says.

"Yes…we eat it in the summer with some potato or egg. We eat many soups."

Claire returns with the water and Martin's beer and after priming her notepad takes our order, including the 2014 bottle of burgundy.

"You not having a beer?" Martin asks me, as Claire is about to leave.

"No…I said I was going to drink wine." I tell him.

"Lightweight…" he mumbles to Claire as she smiles politely and leaves.

"I miss the food of my country…" Danute goes on.

"Well you're going to have some good English cooking tonight," Martin says.

"You're lucky having a cook for a husband," Danute tells Tasha.

"He does his bit - when he's not working. I like to cook too. We take turns." Tasha says.

"Yes I like to cook…" Danute says.

"That's good, because old Alex here needs all the protein he can get. A frozen pizza from the local Supermarket is a treat in his household," Martin mocks.

"Don't be nasty, Martin," Tasha says.

"You don't cook?" Danute asks, incredulously.

"Not really…" I tell her.

"Never has the time. I'll tell you what he's got time for though…" Martin quips.

Danute ignores the jibe and affectionately rubs my arm.

"Which part of Lithuania are you from?" Tasha asks.

"Kaunas – about sixty miles from Vilnius the capital…" Danute replies, as Claire returns with the wine. "It's Lithuania's second capital city…"

Claire shows me the label and I nod approvingly as we all watch her bring the corkscrew up to the top of the bottle. She looks scared stiff as she locates the centre of the cork and begins to turn. Halfway down, she stops, realising she's off-centre, unscrews it and begins again as we continue to watch. She smiles a terrible nervous smile and I suddenly feel very sorry for her as she realises we are all going to watch with a perverse pleasure as she struggles to open the bottle. Bringing the lever down, she lodges it onto the rim of the bottle top and using the leverage, pushes down on the other end of the handle, but it's not budging. Thinking for a second, she decides to pull up. This of course is what she should have done in the first place, but it's locked in solid. Then the lever loses its grip and slides down the glass neck and *still* we all watch in silence. Turning a bright scarlet, she repeats the process, dithering between trying to pull then push the cork out, with the same result. There is a general feeling of acceptance that waiters and waitresses know how to do their job and that opening a bottle of wine should present no problems for them; it is this knowledge that usually prevents us from telling them, when at tableside, how to open a bottle of burgundy. However, there comes a point when it is obvious that a waitress or waiter is having a nightmare and one has to step in with some advice.

"Hold the neck of the bottle firmly and pull up gently," I tell her, trying to ease her suffering.

"Sorry," she whispers, taking heed of my advice, doubtless cursing why I couldn't have ordered one with a screw-top.

She apologises again when she realises she has to place the base of the bottle on the table.

"Go on give it a good tug," Martin chimes in, as slowly the cork begins to slide out.

There's a collective cheer as Claire finally opens the bottle with a pop before offering me the wine to taste. I nod approvingly, before Danute accepts a glass. She then takes our order and with relief, finally gets to leave our table, although not before Martin orders another beer.

"She's a sweetheart," Tasha says, watching her go.

"Next time, don't be so inconsiderate…ordering wine and giving the poor thing a headache," Martin says. "It's like some of the damn girls at work – can't open a bottle of wine for shit – just haven't got the nous, or the elbow power."

"At least she didn't break the cork. How do you like it?" I ask Danute.

"Very nice – I prefer red wine to white. I've only really started drinking more of it since I've been in England as we don't really drink wine in Lithuania. There really aren't many places that produce wine…" she laughs.

Martin raises his glass.

"Good fucking health!" he says, and we all follow suit

For the next hour and a half, our table is a picture of civility as four friends talk over an evening of fine dining. Indeed, the food exceeds our expectations as we agree unanimously that our choice of venue was spot on and that all compliments must go to the chef, a fact that Martin re-iterates with both an air of admiration and mild envy.

I smile and watch affectionately as Danute eats her food and laugh, as Martin mocks and ridicules with the various anecdotes that spill out of him involving us all, turning the air blue and brushing aside all airs and graces. All is going swimmingly well, with more ale, on Martin's part, working as a liked and trusted partner providing us with the caricatures that serve to add to the occasion – until we reach dessert. Whereas Danute and Tasha have remained obstinately dry throughout the meal and I, despite more wine, have managed to pace myself, Martin finally succumbs to the effect of the dreaded sauce and begins to turn noticeably ugly with a slew of references to the personal habits of Tasha that are completely out of place.

We finish desserts and Martin pulls Claire over, handing her his mobile phone insisting she take a photo of the group. We squeeze together on one side of the table and look up. Claire gives some artistic directions. Fake smiles all round. Snap. She takes another one for posterity. Claire hands back the phone and we clamour round to gawp at the device. We *all* look ugly. Before Claire can escape, everyone is handing in their mobile phones and we repeat the process another three times. She finally gets to leave with our dessert dishes, giving us all an excuse to sit in silence as we check our phones, tinkering away at nothing in particular, each one of us heads bowed, lost in our own little worlds, fearful we might have missed some vital piece of information. The silence becomes awkward and I'm thankful when Martin finally breaks it with a spate of jokes retrieved from his phone's memory banks.

Conversation ensues with Martin and Tasha going at it in heated discussion. Before long, it seems a full blown war has erupted at the table, spewing over a molten mass of vitriol with both Danute and I acting as peacemakers for the warring factions, resulting in the Head Waiter coming over and asking us to keep it down. This is then followed by Martin asking Claire for more drinks as she passes by, much to the chagrin of Tasha, who tells him in no uncertain terms that if he has another, she will leave.

"Fucking embarrassment..." she hisses.

"Coming from you, I consider that a compliment," Martin replies.

"Just shut up!"

Tasha and Martin continue to hang out their dirty laundry in public until their argument degenerates into nothing more than a monosyllabic rally, finally bringing the temperature down to something like normal, which I use as a cue for requesting the bill. Danute sits, reading between the lines, looking very concerned about the welfare of Martin and given the chance would probably work as a good intermediary between the two, but on this occasion remains stoically quiet. All I want to do is leave as I'm more concerned about how Danute is feeling and what effect the whole event will have on her decision of what to do with the remainder of the evening. Claire finally brings us the bill and after much deliberating on how much we should all pay and the different means of payment and an apology from Martin, we finally leave a tip and say our goodbyes.

The air remains icy between Tasha and Martin as we walk back to the car with a feeling that only the tip of the domestic iceberg has been touched and that its true size will reveal itself when they get home.

"Where do you want dropping off?" Tasha asks Danute as we drive back towards town.

"I thought we were going to the pub for a nightcap?" Martin says in all seriousness.

"No, no, drop me off near the car-park?" Danute replies, triggering alarm bells inside me.

"Alex, you'll have a drink…?" Martin asks.

"I think I've had enough, mate," I tell him.

"Of course he's had enough," Tasha tells him. "He knows when he's had enough – unlike you."

Martin blinks and gazes out of the window. His subservience makes me feel a little sorry for him as I know he's in for a roasting when gets home and all he really wanted to do was make a night of it. I also feel bad about not standing up for him a little more as a mate, but I have my own agenda to contend with.

Tasha pulls into the small car-park and beside Danute's car, leaving the engine running as we say our goodbyes, then exit. As Tasha pulls away, we speculate over the conversation she's having with Martin and how far into the night it's likely to continue. I look to Danute for some indication as to what her next move will be. The fact that she's waiting and not making a bee-line for the driver's seat suggests she's open to further discussion. I check my watch: 10.50pm.

"Poor Martin…" she says, looking up at me.

"Hmmm…"

After an awkward silence I finally ask, "Do you want to come back for a coffee or a drink?"

"Sure, a coffee would be good," she says, fixing me with her eyes. "I'll take the car – if it's okay to park?"

"No problem. Okay to drive?"

"Of course," she says, adopting the same sense of wonder that she had when the evening began.

13

There are a host of worries in my head that cause me to hesitate momentarily before turning the key in the door: has the cat shit or puked all over the carpet and will Danute step in it; have I left any visible signs in any of the rooms pertaining to pornographic use, does the flat smell, do I have any food and more importantly, coffee; have I cleaned the sink, have I changed the damn, crusty sheets?

Inside, I turn on the light and quickly scan the hallway floor for animal deposits. Danute seemingly does the same as if she were somehow *expecting* to find something untoward, a faint look of disappointment on her face. I usher her into the front room, a room that suddenly seems very unfamiliar to me and very small, where she stands beside the sofa until she's offered a seat. Her thighs are almost bursting out of her short, tight skirt, face whiter than white as her eyes peruse over the room, ingesting the details, picturing my relationship with each item as a means of acquaintance, before looking at me, just to confirm her conclusions are correct.

"So…coffee…?" I ask, moving straight for the kitchen.

"Yes please. Let me come with you," she says, lifting herself off the sofa.

"I can manage – you sit down," I insist, wanting to use the moment to check on the sheets.

"I want to see your kitchen," she persists.

The kitchen is by far the worst room in the flat, with its peeling work surfaces, shabby cupboards and general all-round, unfashionable décor. Danute however seems happy enough watching me prepare the coffee, taking it all in.

"Ooo…where's your cat?" she says, looking down at the bowl of barely touched food.

"Good question," I say, wondering where exactly he is and what he's doing.

"How old is he?"

"Thirteen…no fourteen…thirteen…thereabouts…"

"He's probably hiding under the bed," she says. That's where they usually go when strangers come?"

The chances are he *is* under the bed, only I daren't go in the bedroom to look for him for fear of Danute following me in.

"You know, the more I think about it, the more I feel sorry for Martin," she says, changing the subject.

"Don't feel sorry for Martin," I tell her. "He probably deserves everything he gets from Tasha - having said that, she's no shrinking violet."

"That's what I mean; he was just having a good time," she says.

"You have a generous personality. First Marcus and now Martin," I tell her.

"I just think people can sometimes all seem the same. I like it when people act on impulse - I don't mean in a bad or violent way or drunk – just different," she says. "Like you…I think you're a bit of a 'Steady Eddy'…you keep a lot of things to yourself and you're happy to run along."

I quietly take umbrage at her comments insomuch as she's implying that perhaps I'm boring and that a glimpse of that bush is out of bounds to people like me - reserved only for the brave of heart.

"Steady Eddy…where did you hear that?" I ask - a term I know Klep uses.

"Your friend, Marcus… He said there are too many of them in the world and in his office!" she replies, laughing.

I ignore the fact she's talking about Klep, concerned only with the fact that she's laughing, releasing more endorphins, easing herself into a state of comfort. She talks some more about Tasha and Martin and drinking, but I'm only half listening, concerned more about the pushing of time and a means of reaching my destination concerning the property between her legs. I warm up two cups and watch as she examines the immediate area around her, touching things and turning various objects over in a bored and restless way as if waiting for me to hold her, shove my tongue deep into her mouth. I press the coffee and invite her back into the living room, before pouring and offering her some sugar.

"No thanks," she says, taking the cup. "Do you mind if I take my shoes off?"

"Not at all…make your-self comfortable. I'll put some music on."

Danute pulls the shoes from her feet before bringing them up onto the sofa and tucking them comfortably under her rump, a sight that gets me moving over to the stereo to play some music and put things in motion. I stick on an old selection of acid jazz, inoffensive and generic enough with just enough credibility so as not to overpower the moment. Again my thoughts turn to the sheets.

"I'll be back in a moment," I tell her, excusing myself.

"Are you looking for the cat?" she asks, behind me.

"I'll see…" I call back, as I disappear into the bedroom.

Under the harsh light, in one swift movement, I pull back the duvet to reveal not one, but a series of dried yellowish stains covering the sheet beneath. In haste, I yank it from the mattress, fold it into a ball and bury it at the back of the wardrobe, deciding on how I'm going to pull a fresh one from the cupboard in the hallway without arousing suspicion or looking horribly presumptuous. I look under the bed to find the cat staring back at me in ridicule…defying me.

"Did you find him?" Danute calls from the living room.

"Forget the fucking cat – there's only one pussy I'm interested in tonight…" I whisper to myself, creeping into the hallway to procure a fresh sheet.

With great stealth, I'm back in the bedroom and aligning all four corners against the mattress before tucking them in and straightening out the duvet. Finally I bend down, look smugly at the cat, make a quick appraisal of the room then turn out the light.

"He's not coming out – he's under the bed being shy," I say, stepping back into the living room. "You can have a look at him if you like."

Danute is only too eager to take me up on my idea and is quickly up off the couch waiting to be escorted into the bedroom. Feeling giddy, I lead her through, her forgoing the usual scrutiny of her surroundings and going straight for the cat, squatting down, craning her head to catch a glimpse of the beast, trying to entice him out of his languor with a few clicks of her fingers. Her raised bottom looks big and inviting in the half-light and I secretly urge the cat to remain where his is so as not to disturb my view. Eventually she gives up and rises from the floor, commenting on how sweet he is as we head back to the living room. Despite the music playing, the mood seems a little too sober and sombre and I ask Danute if she fancies a beer as I'm having one.

"The coffee doesn't taste quite right. I don't know if it's the wine or what. How does yours taste?" I ask her.

"Fine," she says, taking a sip.

Pulling a beer from the fridge, pictures fill my head of every pussy I've ever saved in the 'Hairy' section of my favourite's folder as I try to ascertain which one Danute's most resembles; it certainly falls under 'mega bush', which puts her in the top flight, superseding everything I've seen before it – even Zilla. It's something so unprecedented I have trouble believing it's actually sitting in my living room waiting for me to join it and that all I have to do is tickle it and cajole it from its resting place before diving in. I swig on the beer which is cold and satisfying, contemplating the notion that it might all fall through as Danute seems perfectly sober and quite capable of driving home.

"How long have you lived here?" she asks as I pull up the wing-back, facing her.

"About two-and-a-half years…"

"And before that…?"

"I was living in a flat…near Reading," I tell her, omitting the fact I was co-habiting with Sarah at the time.

"This coffee is really good," she emphasises, lifting the cup to her lips.

"It's a blend of Arabica and Robusta; I have it specially prepared for me by the local deli in town. Coffee is the one thing I take seriously – I don't just drink anything," I tell her.

"The *only* thing you take seriously?" she says flirtatiously.

"I need something strong to get me up in the morning," I tell her, sounding cheesy.

She laughs anyway.

"I've seen you in the morning and I agree," she says. "I think you need something stronger than coffee. I mean, do you leave the flat five minutes after you've just woken up?"

"About ten…" I joke, releasing more endorphins. "Morning is not the best time of the day for me. Reaction time is slow, I look terrible, I feel terrible and there's nothing to look forward to but work. What's your worst part of the day?"

"The evening…I think," she says after some thought. "It's okay if you're with somebody, but alone, I find it quite depressing."

"So find somebody."

"It's difficult…"

The beer suddenly makes me hungry for a cigarette.

"Yeah, I can see that…" I say, rising from the sofa.

"What does *that* mean?"

"Oh no, I didn't mean it like *that*…I meant just the people you work with," I assure her. "Do you mind if I smoke?"

"Of course not," she says, as I open the patio door.

Danute joins me outside and observes the long-abandoned, ill-defined plants in their shabby pots under the dim patio light, then nods her head approvingly - out of courtesy, not admiration - before looking up at the night sky.

"You need to keep me company more." she teases "Otherwise how is a girl to make new friends with the people she works with?"

"For that, I apologise."

"It's only taken you seven months. Talk about slow. Are you slow with everything?"

I suck strongly on the cigarette, drawing more of the nicotine into my bloodstream, becoming giddy with her mocking. She stares at me, gently rocking her hips, expecting me to make a move, expecting me to grope her madly under the moonlight, except there isn't a moon.

"You enjoy things more if you do things slowly, don't you know that?" I tell her, knowing damn well that slow is for schmo and that going at it hammer and tongs is the only way I know and that I'm just talking bullshit because I won't make a move!

She continues to rock her hips with that wicked little smile, leaving me panicky and lost for words and for some reason I think about the friendly Romanian girl at work and how sorry I feel for her, having to cart that great trolley of towels and sheets and whatnot all day long and how it must play havoc with her fragile back and rather her than me. After this I quickly complete a self-analytical checklist concerning my wellbeing and if I'm fit and up for the task of Danute seeing me naked: the rash has cleared up around the underside of my balls, the ants have vacated my rectum, the backache has subsided, although not completely, and I'm washed and trimmed… checked and ready to go. All of this takes place within seconds as I notice how quickly my heart is pumping and wonder if Danute can hear it in the still of the night. I take one last drag on my cigarette then throw it to the floor.

"Are you sure you don't want a drink?" I ask, my voice wavering.

"No thanks…" she says as she reaches out and gently rubs the top of my arm.

I move in towards her shadowy face then place my lips against hers. Instantly my cock swells and feels huge in the confines of my pants and the silence of the dark, as she embraces me and hungrily sticks her thick, wet tongue in my mouth. Pressing her lower abdomen against me, she grinds as the taste of nicotine, beer and coffee fill my senses. Indeed, her hunger is too great and I have to disengage and peck her on the lips in an attempt to gain some kind of perspective, the first of which is getting her back inside where we can get comfortable.

We move towards the sofa where she begins again with the same gusto. Her heat penetrates my body and I grab a faint whiff of her odour, the same sweaty odour I detected when she handed me the papers that afternoon in the office, strong and singular. Awkwardly, we manoeuvre ourselves downwards, still engaged, tongues lashing furiously like two hissing serpents. Things are moving too quickly, the booze is kicking in, the rush of the cigarette and the thumping of my heart all make me feel light-headed. I want to savour this moment, I want it unravelled slowly; I want my Christmas present revealed to me with tiny rips of wrapping paper, not a single stroke of impetuous glee. Her buttocks hit the cushions and she flops backwards into a lazy repose whilst I remain on the floor, kneeling between her parted legs. She looks up at me, submissively, like a loose rag-doll awaiting my next move, at the mercy of my every whim. As

I wheeze and catch my breath, I decide I have to stop smoking. God forbid I should ever have to run for a bus! The intensity of the moment moves down a gear. I need more food, more sustenance! I look into Danute's eyes for permission - which is given - then run my hands along the sides of her pelvis and up along her ribcage until I reach the underside of her breasts. She emits a sigh. We disengage and she tugs at my top, before pulling it off completely then runs her hands across the smooth skin of my chest before quickly removing her own top revealing the bra beneath which she unfastens in one deft movement.

At this point a sense of unreality kicks in; her breasts, which are soft and formless, flop down like two lumps of white dough that fascinate me as I stare into their bright pink areolas, two tiny black hairs piercing the skin of both. The walls of the room close in, creating a strange claustrophobia that leaves me short on breath with the acid jazz that was so fitting earlier, now sounding like the cheesy soundtrack to some porn flick that is relentless on the ears and needs turning down, which I don't want to do for fear of breaking the momentum. I can *sense* the cat's presence in the room somewhere, tucked away in some vantage point, having come out from his hiding to watch the headlining act, "You don't want to miss this…" he says, scornfully to himself, taking his seat. I try to locate his whereabouts with a look here and look there, a glimpse of a swishing tail or relucent eye, but see nothing. It gets worse as I have no sense of who I am, kneading the two fleshy white handfuls before me and what it is I'm trying to achieve. In a panic, I dive down and begin to suck greedily like a baby on one teat then the other, to the sound of Danute's soft moaning, confirming to me that both she and what I'm doing *is* real and working some kind of magic. Her hand reaches down, groping for a feel of my cock - something for her to think about - as I move up and kiss the nape of her neck.

"Aahhh…" she sighs, rubbing her face against the side of my head.

I head back down, pecking at her like a pigeon, nibbling and licking the flesh, my heart thumping as I move towards the prize: the jewel in the crown, the gem to end all gemstones and any memory of gemstone before it. Kissing around her navel I slowly begin removing her skirt by pulling down as she unfastens the zipper, feeling it slide past her hips, exposing her panties that are visible through the tanned tights she's wearing. It's actually going to happen… I think to myself, as I rear up for a better view - a view that will highlight the enormity of what I'm seeing and provide enough material to keep me wanking for the next thousand years. My fingers curl around the inside of her tights and my heart skips a beat: it's a mossy cave, lost on the outskirts of the world, moist and pungent; a forgotten garden, overgrown and wondrous; a haystack a mile high, a steaming shag-pile, a woolly mammoth, a huge, untamed thatch, a pelt of finest mink; it's a grass-covered knoll with sheep grazing on it - it's the biggest pussy the world has ever known! I pull down - the last barrier between me and the Promised Land.

What confronts me next is nothing short of shocking. To my horror, instead of a huge mound of hair, as so surely predicted, as speculated over for aeons - she is as bald as a coot! Not a single filament, tuft, whisker is visible to the eye. In fact, to make things worse it looks as though she's patted and pampered and powdered it, giving it an unbelievably smooth finish with a soft baby-like scent. It's so perfectly smooth, it's as though the area has never even seen a hair; been devoid of hair for all existence. A thin, single line, parting the bulbous flesh, starting from the pubic bone and disappearing down towards her buttocks is all that constitutes a pussy. It can't even be called a pussy! It's not a pussy – it's the freshly picked crevice of a young peach.

The world literally stops turning; the gravitational force that keeps me grounded bolts and I swoon in a confused mass of silent hysteria. Surely there must be some mistake! Surely they've given me the wrong product. The assistant must have misunderstood me! Can I not simply go back and exchange it for the right one? Did I keep my receipt? WHERE'S THE FUCKING HAIR!

With lightning speed, I try and comprehend how someone so brazenly hairy on nearly every aspect of her anatomy can be so devoid of it on the place where it matters most. She has obviously cut away, trimmed, and soothed herself in an attempt to keep up with the vagaries of modern-day life as she sees them, but in doing so, fails to see the wonder of the entire picture. I want to scream. The rules don't apply to everyone!

Danute senses my hesitation and clamps her thighs shut, not forcefully, but carefully. Whether my shock is revealed through my expression, I don't know, but her own expression turns to one of concern, as if to say, "what have you seen…is everything alright…what's wrong with my vagina?" This in turn leaves me totally incapable of communication. I kneel before her like a dumb slap, mute, staring down as if I've never seen between a woman's legs before, my silence garnering more concern as she instinctively pulls up and adopts a more defensive profile while I try and summon up the power of speech and a suitable excuse for my reticence and strange behaviour. I blindly run my hands over her breasts, attempting to re-kindle the passion as everything that was once positive turns to negative. Her body begins to relax once more. But as I lean down to kiss the soft, white flesh, I can't shake the image of Klep drinking his foul brown liquid every morning. Now Martin's aggressive nature flares up, berating me for being a lame pussy and for lying to him about the way I use my free time, before the men at P.E.S.T turn into caricatures of themselves. I look up into Danute's face and those eyes that have the power to turn a man to stone and feel my body shudder and decide I have to get out of this room.

"Shall we move to the bedroom?" I say, in a completely foreign voice.

For a second, she looks perplexed, unsure why. She finally cups my hand after awkwardly half-dressing before following me into the bedroom where far from working as an aphrodisiac, serves only to invalidate the whole dynamic of the moment. The room feels stiff and frosty, even with the soft glow of the table lamp, requiring a complete re-start to attain the same kind of heat generated in the room preceding it. She flops onto the bed. I move back down, hoping my first encounter between her legs had been a mistake - a gross lie - nothing more than a hallucination and that this time the buried treasure will reveal itself to me in its true form. Wide-eyed and *actually* believing I'm about to expose the elusive bush, I pull past her thighs and with it, dashing all hope of a reprieve with the same revelation as before. Danute is too engrossed with her own efforts in trying to extract the dying cock from my pants for her to see the calamitous effect this has on me. Again, I inspect the area, as if trying to seek out a possible hiding place from which her hair does grow – a Shangri-La, detectible only after an indefatigable search. I look hard into the abyss and pull up My Favourites folder in the hope of finding a remedy to this unexpected mess. Running down the list of all the suitable candidates with which to apply their wares to the actual flesh in front of me, I pick and choose before reaching back down.

"Aahhh…" she sighs, as I shake my pants from my legs.

Still gripping my cock, she rears up and forcibly pushes me back until I'm lying face up, before moving above me and gently kissing her way down to my crotch. I stare up despondently, numb to the occasion. My body feels stiff and unresponsive with my position evoking images of a wax mannequin staring coldly up from blank eyes, whilst the giver of life attempts to resuscitate with her hot breath. I glance down and allow my imagination to go to work on the raised backside that remains obscured by the silvery-grey crown of Danute's head then fall back and close my eyes as she places my cock in her mouth. Her tongue works over the end of it with the same ferocious zeal and it feels as if a hot, wet worm is frantically running amok, either searching for a way in or off the edifice! The effect serves only to irritate and I struggle desperately to meet my humble seven inches as the worm releases more of its slime. Instead, I imagine my cock as a twelve inch monster, thick with blood, bone hard and livid with the staying power of a ten-thousand-metre runner, her mouth barely able to take its girth. I envisage the impressive erections I see every day, ploughing their way through an endless supply of women without fear or impotence. Why didn't I buy any Viagra? All of this is having the opposite of the desired effect as my anxiety rises and the more zealous Danute becomes, the more I clam up. I picture Sarah and all the great sex we used to have and how gaining an erection was never a problem then. The ends of my fingers and toes feel freezing. It's not working – it's never going to work! I place an imaginary guest at the side of the bed - one of Danute's lesbian friends - that has somehow happened in on us, holding her mobile phone and filming us while she rubs between her legs waiting for permission to join in, which Danute forbids as a mark of torment. This seems to work a little before she too becomes inanimate, resembling nothing more than a ridiculous blow-up-doll. I can hear my mum calling me to call her and remember the time I walked in on her just as she was about to step into the bath. Dear God. Somewhere underneath us the cat is listening, he followed us in – I know it. Danute's technique is all wrong! I was wrong about the fullness of her mouth. Delivering good blowjobs are obviously not a Lithuanian girl's forte! A new position is required; I have to see something new and *real*, something tangible.

After what seems like ages and to the relief of us both, I rear up slightly, indicating that a new course of action *must* be adopted. Danute politely abates, sighs, then looks up at me and asks, "What's the matter?" And as I stare into those eyes, the horror with which I acknowledge those three little words confirm to me that all hope has departed as far as this evening is concerned and perhaps, forever.

14

So I'm sitting at the computer with a raging hard-on trying to fight off the last vestiges of my disaster with Danute whilst watching a Tranny with a huge cock perform self-fellatio on itself. My watch says 9:25 am on a Sunday morning that sees me alone fifty-five minutes after her departure. I was feigning sleep when I felt the weight of her body leave the bed. Then without a word, she dressed herself, placed a hand on my shoulder and gave me some feeble excuse about her sister as the reason for having to leave early. A moment of bated breath and I heard the door go. It wasn't exactly a slam, more a bang of discontent.

I smoke, watching the Tranny gobble itself while I stroke my erection wondering what it takes to be able to contort the body to such an extent so as to be able to suck yourself off. I mimic the action on screen trying to lower my mouth down as far as it will go, feeling the strain in my spine as if it's about to snap at any moment and stop, deciding it's something I have to work on and is surely only a matter of practice before its perfected which gets me thinking about Gary at P.E.S.T and the motives behind his taking up yoga. Danute will probably be at home by now, in bed maybe, working frantically towards her own orgasm in some kind of mutual, distant, masturbatory standoff and cursing herself for asking those three diabolical words!

The Tranny finally comes in its mouth, prompting me to hit

'pause' at the moment of ejaculation, allowing me to saviour and let my imagination run away with itself while I stroke, yet still the unshakable question of 'what's the matter' torments me to distraction. By all accounts Danute was more than entitled to ask. I didn't perform – couldn't perform! The prospect of that being portentous of things to come terrifies me as I click from one film to the next, trying to validate, with feeble excuses, the reason as to why it happened. It was her lack of consideration by shaving away the very fibres to her soul that caused the problems in the first place! The whole date was based on the pretext that there was a bush of enormous proportions waiting for me at the end of the night, with the 'hair' being the key asset that made everything else tolerable. None of this however makes me feel any better about not being able to get it up for a good fuck. Nor does it make me feel any better about viewing Danute with such a lack of respect.

My anxiety rises. I stub out the butt of my cigarette and light up another, frantically searching for a film to take my mind off the dreaded facts of last night's encounter and keep my waning boner solid. Without the boner, I'm as good as dead! Ironically, I steer clear of the 'hairy' categories - a subconscious attempt at repudiating the disappointment of last night perhaps?

Behind the drawn blind, the sun is over-shadowed by cloud bringing a darkened presence to the room, enhancing the screen's resolution and accentuating the features of the performers. The rain comes down in sheets as more cringe-worthy details of last night reveal themselves to me in shocking clarity like little stabs in the belly, superseding the images I'm watching on screen.

"Nothing…" was all I could muster when she asked me those three little words. She continued to suck until I had to finally push her away, intimating that I wanted to fuck instead. When I did finally mount her with something akin to a 'semi', she told me to wait, before sliding out from underneath me to quickly produce a rubber from her bag which she had brought in with her when we first adjourned to the bedroom - something I thought strange at the time. I had taken it for granted that Danute and I would consent to unprotected sex, with the thought of using a condom never having crossed my mind. Of course she was well within her right to insist and, although sensible, this has always worked as a killjoy for me. So when she forced me to kneel in front of her to apply the contraceptive, I did so grudgingly. This feeling was compounded, despite her best efforts to make the whole procedure seem sexy, by my inability to get hard again. Tugging at me with her left hand and holding the rubber with her right, like a fly-swatter, she continued until I had gained sufficient size, then tried to slip the thing on again, only for it to crease and slip off something resembling a miniature, wheezing bagpipe. Of course the more she tried, the more she failed and the more my anxiety rose until my head was so dense with the cloud of confusion, all other attempts had to be aborted, much to the relief of us both. To her credit she was generous about it.

"It's okay…" she said. "Let's lie down for a bit. Have a cigarette if you want."

"Sure…" I replied.

I suddenly feel compelled to call Danute up, ask her if she wants to come back over as things will be very different this morning. I soon realise this is just incredulity at missing out on a 'real fuck', knowing full-well I have no intention of fulfilling this task, with a day on the computer sadly looking like my only option, where I don't have to move and where I can imagine Danute as I *wanted* her to be.

Like I said, she was generous in her suffering and we both tried to make light of the situation, without saying it, instead pointing out various idiosyncratic features on each-other's anatomy as I smoked: a birth-mark, a protruding rib, the lines inscribed into the palms of our hands, cleverly working our way around the erogenous zones. Her hand eventually wandered down below the duvet and onto my thickening cock which she took as her cue to slide the sheath back on, before quickly straddling me, looking down into my face with those intense green eyes that seemed almost demonic - a look I couldn't reciprocate. Her vagina felt enormous; prompting me to remember an old school friend that used to tell me about a girl he fancied but reckoned it 'wouldn't even touch the sides' if ever he got the chance. It was this thought and her urgency that caused my cock to whither and slip from her with a 'slop'. Frantically, she tried to stuff it back in. But it wasn't just that: it was the inhuman way my addiction to porn had chosen to deny me and that everything leading up to the moment had been an extension of my warped expectation that finally forced her to give up with an exhaustive sigh. I finally suggested we 'do it up the arse'.

"What…?" she said with surprise before instinctively sitting on her rump.

"Why don't we try it up…the bottom?" I answered, thinking perhaps it was my terminology that had scared her.

"Why?"

"I just think you'll enjoy it," I replied, suddenly feeling very turned on.

After looking around the room - for the exit perhaps - she finally answered, "I don't do that."

"I thought all girls enjoyed it," I replied, sounding like I was an authority on the subject.

"No!" she answered, defensively.

As we sat facing each other, I thought about all the girls I'd seen in the movies and how they had positively begged for anal sex and how some actually *preferred* it to frontal sex, so decided to pursue it with this line of reasoning.

"It's okay if you've never done it before," I told her. "I think if you try it, you'll really enjoy it."

"Maybe I won't…maybe I don't want to try it."

"How do you know if you've never tried it…?"

"I prefer it the other way – the normal way…w*hen* I do it…" she emphasised, alluding to the fact that I couldn't even get it up for that. "Maybe you've had too much to drink?"

"No…I haven't."

"Then what is it?" she asked, irritatingly.

"Nothing…"

"I can see that," she replied. "Maybe we should just sleep – it's late."

We crawled under the covers and held each other, the feeling of her hot, naked flesh against mine prompting me to try again, only for it to end with the same worrying result, after which we both drifted into sleep. This was only after some hellish introspective questioning on my part whilst lying in the dark, refusing to believe it was that anomaly highlighted at P.E.S.T of Danute simply not standing a chance in the face of the competition she was up against in the form of the computer. The 'real thing' was far better, surely…?

I release the grip on my cock and stare forlornly at the blind in front of me, growing more depressed. It is hard to determine how this will affect my relationship with Danute as we will never look at each-other in the same way again. To say she will remain discreet about the whole ordeal is certain as she's not the type to spread gossip, but forgiveness is harder to come by. Again I look towards the phone. I am desperate to talk to her, to share some breakfast with her, to look at her face again and above all, to fuck her. The smell of her still lingers and I re-engage with my cock once more.

An hour passes then another and another until fifteen minutes from midday, I bring the session to a brief close, to eat. Drinking more coffee and eating a sandwich, I pace the living room floor with a feeling of having returned to the scene of the crime, re-living last night's details with a step by step reconstruction of what was and what *should* have been. Remembering the cat as being instrumental in my feeling of anxiety, I search the room as I've not seen him all morning. I can't be bothered to look any further than my immediate surroundings and finish eating before venturing out to find him still curled up under the bed.

The session resumes with renewed energy and focus; open to personal forgiveness, jocular even. It's all a lie. The sun is out, reflecting off the rain water left earlier and creating a huge wall of brilliant white behind the drawn blind, making viewing of the screen difficult, but I'm rooted in the succession of films that follow one after the other as the debacle that was Danute passes into fantasy once more.

The room becomes an orgy of figures, bodies entwined, reaching out and groaning with pleasure, emitting the deafening cry of sex in every language from all four corners of the earth. At one point I have to stop as I'm hit with a mental picture of myself looking at myself wanking; an image seen from an elevated position somewhere in the room behind me that seems so absurd I have to take to the bathroom and splash cold water on my face. This is a brief digression however, and I am soon captivated once more by the filth spewing out of the computer. The fly in the room is a constant reminder of time and mortality and although I have succeeded in persevering with my task and done my best to ignore it, its presence is beginning to work on me. After five hours, my body is aching, causing a continual cycle of movement to find new and more comfortable positions in a chair that seems made of granite.

The session goes on. At ten past five in the afternoon, eight hours since its inception, I am irascible and nursing a headache, no longer turned on by what I'm seeing, yet compelled to continue, out of a sense of duty, compelled to finish, as evidence at least, of all my toil. '*Panties and Girdles*' is plucked from My Favourites folder - a fine collection of women - kitted out in specialised underwear that have perfected the 'art of undressing' and who recognise the concept of 'less is more' by revealing themselves with painstaking precision and pace. It works. I'm back. I pull up a film, simply entitled: '*Filthy Bitch!!!*' Exactly as the title suggests, this webcam girl has finished me off on many occasions and upon opening the film, I spring into new life. The girl's look is scornful, full of mischief, spiteful even. Her uncensored tongue knows exactly what I want to hear. I 'play' and 'pause', deciding whether to 'blow or go', repeated over and over until I'm close. My eyes interlock with hers as the whole of her life story unfolds before me. Then, past the dazzling blue of her eyes, she unexpectedly becomes very real. No more than nineteen or twenty, the daughter of a mother and father, somebody's sister perhaps, she cavorts around in what looks like her bedroom or some other makeshift crib, used soley for the purpose of licentious activity. Her brazenness astounds me. Do her parents know what she gets up to in her spare time? 'Ching''ching'…I can hear the money drop to the dulcet tones of 'thank-you', urging the hordes of thousands or millions out there to part with more if they want to see the hardcore version! Is she recognised outside of 'work'? Is she recognised when taking a simple trip to the Supermarket? Does she feel the weight of stranger's eyes baring down on her when rifling through the fruit and veg, turning over the cheese, scouring the sweets, all swearing to themselves that 'she's the one…it's definitely her'? Does the cashier short change her out of distraction? Does the trip turn into a sycophantic melee, bods clamouring for her attention with sweaty zeal? 'Ching…ching'…another penny in the slot thank-you-very-much…now I'll show you my arse!

The garish back-drop in her room averts my eyes and I'm back to the rubber-limbed whore working her magic over my dome. I'm close…I'm very close. The muscle proudly fills my hand and the eyes glaze over. A tingling sensation tickles the end of my knob – strange yet not unpleasant. As the feeling persists, I'm forced to look down. There, perched on the end of my penis is the fly. My mouth goes slack, body frozen in awe at the unexpected and alien image, one never seen over the course of my lifetime and probably never will be again. The picture of black against the shiny, pinkish purple of the head seems so ludicrous I can only stare in wonder, as if seeing some great work of art for the first time. Staggeringly my cock remains rigid as it sits there, rubbing its front legs together, performing its ablutions. In the background I can hear the 'ching…ching' and the hissing of the girl's tongue sparing no blushes. Then, snapping to the reality of what I'm seeing, a myriad of thoughts run through my mind: hygiene, the laying of eggs, fishing maggots and Instagram. Through bodily vibrations, the fly senses this, causing it to brace, and for one horrifying moment it looks like it's about to crawl down my Jap's eye – that's when I swipe! In a heartbeat, messages of searing pain coming from my penis are sent FedEx to my brain causing me to rise up in agony as the fly buzzes past my face. Instinctively I look down, my only concern being whether the fly has scuppered my chances of 'finishing off' on account of it being too painful. In a fit of rage, I pull up the blind, one quick wrench at the drawstrings, exposing the world beyond, the fly buzzing madly within the window frame as I claw at it, before it soars, coming to rest on the ceiling. I'm spitting and frothing at the mouth as I jump at it, causing it to take flight once more, to which I grab the nearest book at hand from the shelf - Kafka's 'Metamorphosis' - and hurl it at the pest, which does nothing but split the book as it hits the far wall, sending a flurry of papers to the floor.

"Fuck it!" I shout, genuinely annoyed at the destruction of a personal favourite.

The fly comes straight for me in brazen defiance and I brace myself for the attack, standing solid, waiting to see which direction it takes. He's coming straight for my face and when in reach, I lash out, clawing and slashing at the air until I can almost feel tears welling up in my eyes. Then it's back in the window, bouncing off the glass as if doing me a favour of trying to knock itself out. I quickly unlatch the window and try and direct the beast out, despite my anger telling me, nothing but death will do. Then, just when I think I have it cornered, it suddenly drops, a complete vertical drop with phenomenal speed, as if somebody had plucked its wings and applied weights to its body. It hits the sill, before buzzing past me again and to the back of the room, where it disappears.

An eerie silence pervades.

Breathless, I circle the room once, until I'm back in front of the computer, baring my nakedness to the outside world. As I look across to the rear of the houses beyond, a granny stares back at me from her kitchen window, indifferent to the spectacle she's obviously just witnessed. Then, just as a fat, balding man of about sixty, presumably her husband, walks into the room behind her, I quickly pull the blind down. I resume, unabated and the room morphs into a little night cave with the sky black outside and the desk lamp on and the clock reading 10:22pm and out of surrender, I finally orgasm, bringing the curtain down on the entire weekend.

Too spent to even think, I hobble into bed and pull the duvet over my head just as I hear something in the room move beneath me, a sound which carries over to the door, coming from what I can only assume is the cat, who is about to embark on his own nocturnal habits.

…I'm running across an expanse of land with towering steel on all sides of me and I can sense my pursuer, even though I can't really see him, is close. I can *feel* my fear; there is fear all around. My running is laboured, despite my action being fast, like I'm trawling through quick-sand, requiring great effort to actually get anywhere, but I'm getting nowhere nearer. I can feel my pursuer right behind me, his sole intention to do me harm. Now I'm in a room, queuing with others like me, amidst a scene of

ASH BRUNNER

chaos, all being herded towards a conveyer belt where we're segregated into groups before being despatched in various directions. Fear and pain fill the room, a hopeless sorrow emanating out from deep within the hearts of the people. I know where I am, yet recognise nothing. I look down and see I'm wearing an old pair of corduroy trousers favoured by my mother who used to make me wear them on special occasions when I was ten years old, set with matching red jumper, which all fit, despite me being of the age I am now, and I am a child again, even though I'm not. The great presence bears its huge, oppressive hand over us all, watching us, controlling, censoring all thought and yet I stand out as a figure of rebellion.

I'm bundled towards the conveyor belt, where my cat, clutched close to my chest, is suddenly wrenched from me and put into a cage and transported away. I watch as he turns on the spot, confused, looking helplessly for me as I scream for reunion until the basket disappears altogether. I'm pushed towards a queue of people, numbering hundreds, who are crying at the loss of their own loved ones and I realise there is no hope and that the whole world has become a brutal and savage place unfit for human love and kindness, a fact I want to tell my opposite number who looks at me and smiles a toothless grin, before affirming he understands me with a nod of the head, and I'm tossing and turning and when I wake up…

…Steph is sitting in front of me with a perplexed look on her face as if she hasn't understood a fucking word I've said for the past hour and a half as I digest the catalogue of questions she's just asked me: What image do you have of our hotel and this industry? What kind of goals motivate you the best? Tell me about a sales experience that demonstrates your work ethic. What is your sales process, given a genuine lead? Why the Hotel Industry? What was your greatest professional achievement? Tell me about it in detail. What personal qualities will you bring to the table and how will you incorporate them into your work? What drives you? What role do you think Social Media plays in the selling process? Are you a team player? Give me an example of your interaction skills. Tell me something about yourself – what do you do outside of working hours? (This was the hardest to answer). Why should I take *you* on, Alex? All of this on the back of trying to shake the nightmare I had last night and its portentous meaning that won't go away and that I have yet to understand.

Steph tilts her head thoughtfully, empathetically, before asking, "Alex one last question – how do you keep a smile on your face during a hard day?"

Currently facing this exact dilemma, coupled with the sleep-inducing temperature within the room, I realise my answer will be nothing if not economical. I decide this is not the time or place to go into one about my 'top five' or how coming up with ways of seeing Klep suffer is enough to put a smile on anyone's face.

"By being thankful I'm alive…" I reply, leaving a long, ponderous silence.

Steph's perplexed look finally softens, either from the fact that she's understood something I've said or in the relief that the interview has finally reached its conclusion, I can't tell which. In contrast, I am about ready to keel over. She closes her folder and smiles, giving nothing away.

"Let's leave it at that. Thank you Alex…" she says, extending a perfunctory hand which feels cold and tiny and strangely crinkly, prompting me to reconsider her age.

"Thank you," I reply, with relief.

"There's one more person I have to see this week, before I make a decision…" she tells me as we amble back towards the main corridor, my legs feeling very wobbly and my head in a confused state.

"Of course…" I say.

"Everything alright with Alpha6?" she enquires. "Anything

you need to know…any questions you want to ask? Getting along with Marcus alright?"

"Yes…no problems…"

As we reach the lifts, she bids me a cursory farewell after which I head straight to the toilet at the far end of the second floor corridor as I know it will be free of people. Concluding that this has to be one of the worst days of my life, I splash cold water across my face and steady myself against the sink. Was the interview really as appalling as my gut-feeling is telling me? Am I simply being hard on myself? Interviews always seem worse than they are upon reflection, right? I swear I saw Steph's red panties when she crossed her legs at that one point! My temples throb as I look up at my reflection thinking perhaps it really wasn't so bad after all.

I dry my face then slip into the toilet cubicle, lock the door, pull out my cock and begin to stroke. Steph's red panties – which I swear I saw – Suzie, the girl from Leisure, the tight-arsed Spanish girl, Caroline, even Danute all work at soothing my apprehension in spite of my unfamiliar and dangerous surroundings, eyes narrowing, mind drifting, shoulders relaxed – a good swelling. I look down into the cistern, conscious that perhaps a dirty little camera is looking up at me, having been placed in the bowl with a view to capturing the toilet habits of the unsuspecting and used for later viewing under the heading: 'Hidden WC'. Perhaps tonight, when I return home and log on I will unwittingly become the voyeur of *my own* nefarious activity. What a turn on that would be! I can feel an orgasm building. Then the sound of a thud, a door swinging open, a cough echoing out, sounding huge in the confines of the toilet, jolting me upright, forces my cock back into my pants. I listen to the sound of a forceful stream of piss hitting the urinal, the final zipping up, the obligatory look in the mirror, which seems like ages, making me wonder if it's Klep; no washing of hands, a bee-line for the exit then silence once more. I zip up and follow the same pattern as my unseen predecessor – but wash my hands – then head back up to the office.

Uncharacteristically, Klep shows me the same respect with regards to my interview, as I did him and makes no enquiries. However, his beady eyes work me over and follow me back to my desk, looking for a sign; the bleeding of any cuts, anything to give him the feeling of having the upper hand. He quietly mutters something to himself then picks up the phone. I decide to forget about the interview, let things take their course and stop worrying about things that haven't happened yet. What worries me more is my condition regarding my porn use and the fact that, despite my willingness to attend P.E.S.T, it's getting worse. Even now as I stare at a nondescript event template, all I can think about is getting home and in front of the computer – this, after an entire Sunday of exhaustive foreplay, *after* being unable to fuck the girl lying in my bed the previous night!

Down the corridor in the photocopying room, I hear voices muttering outside then the retreating footsteps of someone heading back to the offices. I pull the last sheet of paper from the machine and step out to find Danute loitering around the pigeon holes looking for post. I force a smile but her blank expression is a sour reminder of the horrors of Saturday night and brings me out in a cold sweat.

"Hi…" I say.

"Hello…" she replies with just a hint of malice.

Actually I'm shocked at just how cold and expressionless her face is.

"Listen Danute, I'm sorry about Saturday…" I begin, speaking in an undertone, aware of my surroundings. "I hope you weren't upset about anything. I know things didn't go very well…"

"I had a great time," she says briskly.

"Well I'm glad about that…"

"Don't worry…I won't tell anyone about your problem…" she says.

She's half-smiling but I can't tell whether she's joking or not as it's an expression I've never seen before.

"Sorry…I must have drunk too much. It does usually work – I swear."

She looks baffled.

"I meant your snoring. I didn't get much sleep. At one point I tried putting the pillow in your mouth," she says.

"Really…? I say, surprised and relieved. "I know, I know. I didn't realise it was such a problem."

I can tell Danute is thinking about the other issue but she won't say anything, she's too well-mannered. I feel terrible for her.

"Here it is…" she says to herself, pulling a small brown parcel from one of the cubby holes.

"Listen, we can do something again if you like…" I tell her, taking a step closer.

The cold expression is back and when she looks up at me I'm fearful of her answer.

"We'll see…" she says dismissively. "I have to go…"

"Sure."

She turns and heads back towards the Accounts office just as Caroline steps out of the stairwell on her way to the HR department looking as upset as ever, but I say 'hi' anyway.

My gut feeling is, there won't be a next time. She knows her radar malfunctioned on this occasion and honed in on a dud. We'll say 'hi' once in a while, maybe even flirt a little and keep the office machinery functioning at an efficient rate, but that's about all. What more could I expect? As I step back into the office feeling even sadder, Klep is at the head of the room beside his flip-pad wagging his finger at me and shouting: "Good Technique…!"

At home, I spend the evening with my book, still reeling from Danute's brief palming off and Steph's bullish questioning, As I am about to turn in for bed, a text message comes through on my phone from Martin, apologising for his behaviour on Saturday and stating that next time we should go out without the meddlesome girls if we want to avoid any hassle. On a whim, I decide to answer back with what is essentially a cry for help, albeit disguised in the cold and faceless format of text messaging:

> ME: I'm curious – do u wank off?
> If so how often?
> Please don't get wrong idea -
> just a question!

After a few minutes, comes the reply.

> MARTIN: Of course I wank off – I'm a
> bloke. Why, u want 2 watch?

Typically answered, I push for more than just his caustic wit.

> ME: No! I think I have problem.
> I wank too much. Getting out
> of hand!!!

I hesitate before sending this as there is no ambiguity to the declaration leaving me fearful of the answer. I send. After a few moments, he answers.

> MARTIN: WTF!!
> Contradiction in terms there!
> R U serious? As your doctor I
> advise u 2 have a wank and go
> 2 bed – you'll feel better in the
> morning.

I have to smile, stupid to think I would wean out something more sober from the man who confessed that as a kid he used to walk around with his finger stuck up his bum and then offer it to the adults in the room to sniff. Still, his response works as a pick-me-up and perhaps he's right – I will feel better in the morning.

15

With exactly the same people sitting in exactly the same places, I feel decidedly more at home as I listen with interest whilst Darren refers to what he describes as his E/D problem. The fallout from Danute has had a greater effect on me than I first thought, lamely coming up with every conceivable excuse to try and hide the real reason for my impotence, which I still can't fathom, hence my being here. I'm tempted to ask Darren what exactly he means by 'E/D' but afraid of looking stupid in front of the group, so wait for him to elaborate as my eyes wander to the words, 'Problems in Bed' scrawled across the flip-pad. Of course, as Jim rightly pointed out, 'there are no stupid questions in a group like this'.

"Sometimes I can fuck for hours – literally – without coming," Darren tells us. "Sometimes I can't even come. I've had a bird where we had to stop because she was knackered out! So was I come to think of it. It was that or the complete opposite, where I couldn't get it up at all because I couldn't get turned on!"

The group nod in unison before Jim takes over.

"Darren has just hit the nail on the head as to the reason why men give up porn," he emphasises. "When we can no longer get it up in the sack, it scares the shit out of us. The idea of not being able to make love to a real woman anymore will usually galvanise men into doing whatever it takes to quit porn – on the understanding that that is the root cause of their problem."

Jim turns to me as if addressing me alone and goes on.

"We become used to masturbating in a certain way, we know what we like, we know how to achieve a certain sensation that often won't be replicated when dealing with a real partner, resulting in the inability to gain an erection, yet when we view porn, we have no trouble at all."

He pauses.

"Alex, you look like you want to say something. Is there something you want to share with us? You've been allowed to reside in the shadows for long enough – it's time to step up and speak," he says.

Gary turns his oily face to me and smiles encouragingly.

"Well I've recently just had my own problems with what you call erectile dysfunction – this past weekend in fact. I just…couldn't get it up," I tell the group.

"Why?" Jim asks.

"I don't know…she just didn't turn me on."

"But you ended up in bed with her - so *something* about her attracted you."

"Well I realise now I wasn't attracted to *her* – the whole person I mean – I was attracted to…" I stutter, motioning to my crotch area.

"You were only attracted to the idea of having sex with her?" Jim asks.

"More than that… I thought she was hairy…"

"What made you think she was hairy if you'd never seen her naked before?"

"She just had the look about her. Also, I could see it on her arms…legs…"

"You like hairy women?"

"Well not everywhere – but down there…" I tell him.

"I've had that before…" Rob chimes in. "I like hairy

women…bushy eyebrows, hairy arms, bit of a 'tache, yet down below – not a speck. What the fuck's the point of that? That really dropped the bomb when I found out, I can tell you."

"Well, hold on Rob, Alex is speaking," Jim says. "Was it just the fact that she wasn't hairy that turned you off – or was it something else?"

"Well that was definitely part of the problem and the fact that she wanted to use a condom, which I don't like… and that I just wanted sex with her." I say.

"That's okay – we all want sex…" Rob mutters to no-one in particular.

"But you were still unable to, despite her not being hairy. How do you think your use of porn affected you in this?" Jim asks.

"She wasn't as much of a turn-on…." I reply.

"In other words – you had a pre-conceived idea of the things she was going to partake in *before* you went to bed with her?" Jim asks.

"Yes."

"Wasn't just being in bed with a woman a turn on for you?"

"It was initially…but as we progressed it became less and less. It all went wrong after the hairy thing. All of a sudden she wasn't the person I thought she was." I reply.

"But you said you were only interested in sex; surely it wouldn't matter if you had stuck a paper bag over her head – so long as you had the body? If sex was all you were interested in – why couldn't you get it up for her?" Jim persists.

"I told you – she wasn't hairy…"

"Does this preference apply to all women?"

"No. Not necessarily."

"She just ticked a certain box…" Rob butts in. "Or not, as the case may be. That's what you were in the mood for that night – only this time you couldn't just 'click' onto something else when you got bored of it."

"She must have been upset?" Jim states.

"Obviously…"

"How did that make you feel?"

I pause before answering, resolved to answering truthfully.

"Ashamed. Inadequate…like there was something wrong with me, which only made me feel worse and less responsive," I tell him.

"Is this the first time this has happened to you?"

I think back to Valeria, the Waitress I had managed to talk into the sack and what a dire affair that had turned out to be leaving her with the impression of me as a total pervert.

"No…"

"Again, you just wanted the body without the baggage, yes?"

"I suppose so."

"Who doesn't when you're young?" Darren chimes in. "We're all experimenting…we're all fishing about, finding out about ourselves…we don't want some deep, meaningful relationship with babies and the whole works. We just want to have some fun with our tools while we can."

"And there's nothing wrong with that, providing it's consensual and that both parties are on the understanding that that's all you want." Jim replies. "Most relationships and lasting marriages all begin with the mutual feeling of sexual attraction. We've already established how important and powerful those feelings are to human beings, but in order for that to happen - a man must first gain an erection. What porn is doing is making our brains become accustomed to a certain type of stimulation that's fucking up our sex lives."

"But let's be honest – we all like to spice up our sex lives. I mean vanilla or raspberry ripple?" Rob says. "My wife - or rather my ex-wife - developed a penchant for anal sex when she was pregnant, which carried over even after the birth of our daughter and then suddenly stopped, at her insistence, for no apparent reason one day out of the blue. I was mortified. It had been a welcome change in what was a pedestrian sex life."

"There's nothing wrong with spicing up your sex life, even looking at porn to do so – some couples do. But the strength of any relationship will be centred on a deep-rooted love and respect for one another. If that is absent, there are very few marriages that will survive on sex alone." Jim says.

"Yes well I know that and I'm in awe of monogamous people - I don't know how they do it." Rob goes on. "A man is going to have a fling one way or the other isn't he? Whenever I felt the urge, I'd go off with some porn just to get it out of my system, as opposed to having it with another woman, which seemed like cheating, out of love and respect for my wife, only for me to end up getting fucking hooked on it and leading to the break-up of my marriage. So how do you win?"

"But is watching porn instead of having it with another woman a mark of respect?" Matt quietly asks. "You're simply engaging in a virtual relationship as opposed to a real one ..."

"Too much stimulation will always affect a relationship, usually in a negative way - that goes for anything." Jim goes on. "This is especially true when it comes to porn, for obvious reasons. Artificial stimulation segregates, it weakens our need for bonding, causes promiscuity and the devaluation of the people closest to us, which affects every aspect of how we perceive them: how attractive do they seem to us, how intelligent are they, how great is their love and how good are they in bed - until we finally reach a point where we're no longer turned on by real people, but by fake ones. Look around you. Everywhere you go, people are no longer engaging with each other, they're engaged with their mobile phones or other devices. We'd prefer to spend our time interacting with a virtual world rather than a real one. What does that say about us? Where are we all heading?"

"Yes...a world of emotional detachment." Gary nods affirmatively.

"What is sex like without emotional involvement?" Jim asks.

"Shit!" Rob quickly answers.

"With all good sex, trust must first be established. For that to happen, a certain degree of bonding has to take place between the couple. Alex denied himself that bonding and simply sought an 'unrealistic whore' – albeit it a hairy one - with which to obtain satisfaction," Jim says, turning back to me. "When you realised she didn't match up and you were lacking emotional content, you suddenly found yourself struggling to become aroused."

I nod in agreement.

"With trust and respect we attain the things we desire, in terms of sexual preference within the bedroom. Most of the time…" he goes on. "Despite what you've seen on your computer screen, no woman wants to be treated as just a 'hole' for your self-gratification. Pornography makes us believe this; it lies to us and paints an unrealistic picture of what sex is."

"That's all very well – but that still doesn't get away from the fact that what we see on screen *is* a turn-on." Darren says. "These are the things we *want* to happen in the bedroom. That's how we like it. Reality is boring, like Rob said. Internet porn has opened up a whole new world of possibilities…introduced us to a thousand new ways of having sex that are better than anything that's happening in the bedroom - unless you're lucky!"

"I agree." I blurt out. It's impossible to stop looking at this stuff, because it turns me on and it's what I'd like to be doing with a real woman." I add.

"But you don't know if a real woman would be willing to try these things - you've substituted finding a real woman with which to do it by looking at porn the whole time." Jim says.

"Maybe I prefer just looking at porn," I say in defeat. "You don't have the hassle of having to find out…of having to ask questions…of having to wait until she's ready, porn is right there for you, no questions asked."

"Then why are you here?" Jim asks. "Why not spend your life looking at it and be happy about it? Accept the fact that

that's all you want to do with your life and live with it."

"Because I'm *not* happy about it, in spite of what I tell myself…" I retort.

"Exactly…" Jim nods. "You're here because it's having a negative effect on your life – remember?"

Sensing my irritation, Gary moves to place his hand on my knee in an act of affection and understanding, until he sees my disapproval and quickly retracts it before it touches me.

"You're a young man Alex…" Jim says. "Have you ever been in anything like a long-term relationship?"

"Yes…" I tell him, head filling up with thoughts of Sarah.

"Would you like to tell us about it?"

I shift uneasily, avoiding eye contact with the group and especially Gary as I try to find a suitable place to begin or whether to begin at all.

"We broke up over two-and-a-half years ago…" I start. "We started seeing each other during our second year at University, then lived together for about six months after we both graduated. That's about as long-term as it was."

"And were there problems in your sex life?" Jim asks.

"Not to begin with, no. The sex was great…we did most things…I was satisfied. At least I thought I was." I reply.

"What do you mean?"

"I mean, I realised I wasn't ready to settle down and get too serious…"

"Were you looking at porn during your relationship?" Rob asks.

"Yes…especially when we started living together." I tell him.

"Had you been viewing porn before you started the relationship?" Jim asks.

"Of course…. I've been looking at porn since I was about thirteen years old. Haven't we all?"

"Did you suffer any abuse as a child?"

"Not at all… good parents, good friends…I was popular… no problems."

"What about attitudes towards sex?"

"Completely healthy, normal…" I tell him pondering over this thought, before continuing.

"The ironic thing is, I only really started looking at porn a lot after I became sexually active…as a person I mean."

"At what age…?"

"Eighteen…nineteen…"

"Well that figures." Rob interjects, before singing the words, "Just a little taste…now I want more…"

"It was like a magnet, drawing me in, until it felt like that was all I was thinking about. Then when we started living together, it became a daily thing, until it got to the point where it became the most important thing, until I got to the point where I couldn't wait to wake up and turn on the computer."

"Was your girlfriend aware of this?"

"No, I managed to hide it quite well."

"But surely she must have seen a change in your behaviour?" Rob goes on. "One minute you're there – the next you're constantly on the computer."

"I told her I was working. Most people's lives are spent on the computer nowadays."

"And she believed you?"

"I became a good liar…"

"What about your sex-life… she must have noticed the change?"

"She became the initiator and it became less and less. I was more interested in watching porn."

"How did that make you feel?"

"Well I didn't feel good about deceiving her. She didn't deserve that. In retrospect I realise I was becoming more irritable towards things and her silence just made things worse between us; arguments would escalate from the smallest of things: the T.V channel, the washing up, not doing the hoovering…even the fucking Christmas tree lights and how to arrange them on the tree…" I confide.

"We've all been there mate." Rob says.

"…Culminating in a huge argument one night when she thought I was seeing someone else."

"Which of course you were," Rob states. "Numerous in fact: Tracey, Laura, Chantelle, Rachel, Christine, Love-potion-number-fuckin-one…shall I go on?"

"Was this developing obsession with porn the reason your relationship broke up?" Jim asks.

"I don't know. It was certainly a factor. Like I said…I didn't think I was ready to get serious and I used that as an excuse. I didn't care as much. It certainly went to pot after she caught me looking at it one night."

Jim senses my reluctance to talk, but nods at me to go on.

"We had a second room…like a small, second bedroom in the flat that we used as office space, with a desk and stuff. We each had our own laptop, so we would use it whenever one of us needed it. I was in there on my computer looking at porn. Sarah was in the living room watching T.V, or so I thought, and either I must have been so engrossed with what I was watching and didn't hear her or she deliberately crept up on me - it's amazing how ultra-receptive your ears become when you're constantly at risk of being busted. Anyway, I didn't realise she was standing right behind me in the room watching me. Turns out she had simply come to offer me some biscuits she was eating."

"You had your dick out?" Darren asks.

"Yes…" I reply. "It wasn't so much that, I don't think. It was what I was looking at."

"Which was what…?" Rob asks.

"Cocks…" I reply.

"Please…no more chickens…" Matt whispers.

"No, no – cocks." I repeat. "I was looking at images of cocks."

"You mean penises?"

"Yes…oversized, big dicks. It was a website featuring

amateur guys with big dicks," I confess.

The group ponder over this for a moment before I answer the question I can feel they're all dying to ask.

"No I'm not gay...or a closet...nor was I ever fearful of becoming gay," I inform them.

"But she thought you were?" Rob asks.

"I think she put two and two together and came up with three. I think my lack of enthusiasm towards her in the bedroom coupled with the images I was viewing, made her wonder."

"Why were you looking at male genitalia?" Jim asks.

"Because I was in awe more than anything," I say, looking up and receiving a gentle nod of the head from Matt. "How many of you here haven't looked at a well-endowed man out of awe and appreciation and marvelled at the size of it and been turned on - not by the thought of the man, but by the thought of that cock and the effect it has on a woman? That's all I was thinking about...imagining it in action. Forget the guy...it was just the dick. Penis envy, if you like."

"Because you're led to believe that's what all women love and crave...right?" Rob says. "It leaves you feeling just a little short-changed, doesn't it?"

"Do you have an issue with the size of your manhood?" Jim asks.

"Not at all," I stress. "I do alright - I'm about average. I've never had any complaints."

"But like Rob says...pornography can give us the feeling of not matching up. Every day we see these huge pumping rods of iron that never seem to whither, resulting in anxiety which affects the way we perform in the bedroom," Jim tells us. "Did you explain this to your girlfriend?"

"I tried to...but I didn't articulate it very well and Sarah sometimes struggled with a sense of humour." I frown. "I think her angry reaction was more to do with the feelings she'd been supressing and her suspicions about me viewing porn all the time, confirmed. After that, the whole dynamic of the relationship changed and I don't think she ever really looked at me in the same way again."

"Did it not curb your porn use – the thought of it jeopardising your relationship? Did she not try and help?" Jim asks.

"No, on the contrary…I just kept looking at it…I couldn't stop. And I think Sarah was going through her own doubts about everything to do with the relationship. Then one day, by accident I found a picture on her phone of her holding another guy. She eventually told me she had started seeing someone else."

"And how did that make you feel?"

"I just put it down to the fact that we weren't meant to be and that we were young and not ready for any of it…"

"At no point did you stop and think that you had lost somebody very close to you because you were more interested in looking at porn?" Jim goes on.

"I did…but I was powerless to prevent myself from doing anything about it; by now, the need for porn outweighed the need for her, symbolised by my solitude after we separated and moved out – a situation that pleased me to an extent - because I was free to watch porn whenever I felt like it, without the burden of someone watching over me and instilling within me a sense of what I was doing, as 'wrong'.

"This of course being the great lie that *any* addiction feeds us…" Rob butts in.

"I started seeing less of the people we both knew, I moved away from the area, found a new job and did very little else but retreat into my own world. At one point, I did try to patch things up…but it was over." I say.

"It's the isolation that fucks you up." Darren states. "I got to a point where I was having fucking panic attacks when I was in the pub or outside with a lot of people. I felt like everyone knew

I was a wanker and hated me for it until it got to the point where I just didn't go out anymore. I kept forgetting things: pin numbers, telephone numbers, things I had to do…"

"Long periods of isolation imbue a sense of detachment within us bringing about many of the symptoms you've all described." Jim tells us. "This applies to *whatever* you're looking at on the computer. We live in an 'age of distraction' where the capacity for concentration is becoming more and more difficult and where 'real' interaction with others is becoming less important with regard to how we operate in our everyday social and working lives. How do we get around this? Modern technology isn't going anywhere. In fact, it's only going to become a bigger part of our lives. How do we tear our eyes away from the damn computer, i-Pad, or smart-phone? What's round the corner? How do we stop the younger generation - who know no different - from befalling the same fate as us? Paradoxically, more people, especially the young, are doing more things with their time – both intellectually and physically than the older generations did. What does that tell us?"

"There's another side to the coin." Darren answers.

Jim turns to a new sheet of paper then writes 'A WORLD TO EXPLORE', before re-taking his seat.

"At the risk of stating the obvious - there's more to life than masturbation!" He declares. "Our attention spans are being dragged away from the glorious world we inhabit. Let's look at this. It *is* a glorious world, isn't it? Ask yourself the question: Am I satisfied? Is my world a satisfying place? Does it interest me…challenge me…give me a sense of purpose? Is my viewing of porn simply a manifestation of my dissatisfaction at the world…MY WORLD?"

Again, he turns his attention to me.

"Alex, what do you do for a living?" he asks.

"I work in the Conference and Events department of a large hotel," I tell him, tiredly.

"At least you work…" Rob mutters.

"I imagine you meet a lot of different people every day," Jim goes on.

"Yes."

"Do you love your job? Does it satisfy you?"

"Yes…" I say.

The lack of conviction with which I answer resonates throughout the room and through me, prompting me to question the motives for every action I've ever taken over the course of my entire life.

"Really…?" Jim asks sceptically.

For a moment I can't speak with the smell of the chair permeating up and the classroom lights and the predatory eyes of the group fixed on me due to Jim's persistent use of me as his whipping boy.

"I'm after a job in the Sales department. It's a step up," I finally tell him.

"So you're unsatisfied with your current position?" he says. "Is Sales what you've always wanted to do? Is it what you studied for?"

Again, lack of conviction prevents me from answering. Jim goes on.

"My point is Alex: does it provide sufficient stimulus so as to keep your mind occupied and focused, with a sense of purpose in those moments when you're alone with nothing but time on your hands or is it simply a means of paying the rent?"

Jim's face softens slightly. He goes on.

"A man must have some purpose to his life. It is this that we must try and get back – or find. What are you all waiting for? It goes with the old saying: 'time waits for no man'. We have a finite amount of time with which to achieve this. All of us here have watched the hands of the clock tick by as we sit at the computer holding our dicks, telling ourselves: 'it's okay – there's always tomorrow'. There is no tomorrow… only the here and now. "I'm not trying to single you out Alex – I simply want to know what makes you tick."

"I don't know…" I tell him, confused.

"It's amazing, the things you'll find of interest that you thought you never would," Gary butts in. "Everybody has to start somewhere and it's important that we don't let our pre-conceptions – which are usually wrong – dictate the way we live our lives. Everything is connected. You'll find, once you start the process of 'giving' yourself to something – something wholesome, I mean – you begin a chain of events that lead you to 'giving' yourself to other things until you reach a point where 'the self' is no longer important."

He pauses to reflect on this for a moment.

"I also believe in the old saying: 'what you give is what you get'. I believe, if you're in a constant state of negative thought then bad things happen to you; your outer being reflects your inner and vice versa, even if you can't see it. I'm not free yet…" he says, moving forward as if he's about to touch my knee again. "The cleansing process takes time; coming to these meetings are a constant reminder to me of where I was and how desperate I was and where I want to be. It's not just about me though, Alex; it's about helping others who are going through the same thing."

Gary shares a look with the big man then wipes the palms of his hands along the length of his thighs. He goes on.

"Rob has been to my house a few times now to play on the Scalextric. I know that must seem like a really stupid and childish thing to do but it's getting him out and taking him away from the computer, getting him to interact with real people again."

Rob emulates Gary by wiping the huge palms of his hands along the length of his thighs, whilst nodding his head. Jim points to the flip-pad and comments.

"There's a world out there to explore. It's all about gaining a sense of accomplishment and thereby boosting self-esteem –

something you'll agree, we have all lost. Remember, change requires a conscious effort."

The preachiness of the whole affair is beginning to grate on me as my ego fights against the prospect of what lies ahead, but therein also finding a soul: a nucleus of warmth that spreads through my body, struggling to re-shape the thought-process, but strangely up for the fight.

What I need is freedom: a break from the established order I'm currently in. Like the hero of my book…a free spirit…a stranger in a strange land… I need a journey of my own.

I observe each man in the room. I *am* one of these men, I tell myself. I am human spirit in the midst of discovery.

"Time is moving on." Jim says, looking up at the clock. "How did we all get on with our weekly trackers and daily counters? How did we manage those cravings?" he says, turning to Matt.

"Not so good…" he begins. "I left last week's meeting, thinking I was in good shape. The next day went well, very little in the way of distraction, met up with a work colleague for a drink in the evening, discussed some work-related issues and the merits of some films we'd seen recently, came back home, without any urge to turn on the computer and went to bed. The next day, the girl from dispatches came up to see me just before I was due to finish work with some business about one of our overseas customers. Well, she had on the tightest skirt…"

Matt's face scrunches up into one of pain until it looks like the skin of a prune as he re-lives the cataclysmic moment in his mind.

"After that I couldn't shake the image and fought for the best part of two hours when I returned home until I finally gave in…" he says. "The rest of the week turned out to be just as much of a struggle. In fact it's fair to say it was a disaster from beginning to end. My willpower is shot to pieces. It's a hopeless situation."

"It's alright Matt…" Darren chimes in. "I had something similar happen to me. I got home and tossed off, but I didn't use the computer – I just used my imagination. Mate, it was one of the best feelings I've ever had. Trust me, you should have just held that thought, gone to the toilet and got it all out."

"Bravo!" Gary applauds. "Well done Darren. Quite right – you're thinking about a real person, who's had a real effect on you."

"We're meeting up this Saturday night." Darren beams.

"Double bravo!" Gary shouts.

Darren's story of success is infectious, but my eyes remain on Matt who seems to have been forgotten in the celebrations and I'm quick to follow on from his lament, unconvinced that he won't just keep falling prey to the same images he's bound to see every day.

"So that's the answer to Matt's problem is it?" I ask the room "Go home and *think* about it as opposed to turning on the computer? Matt, you say you've relapsed, due to seeing the woman from dispatches in a tight skirt. Every bod I see at work is wearing a tight skirt as far as I'm concerned! How do I get around that? What's to say I'm not going to be relapsing for the next fifty years? I can't ask all of them out?"

The room is silent once more.

"How do we get around our perpetual state of horniness?" I ask.

"In some ways you don't - you're a young, hot-blooded male. However, it can be controlled, by doing something else…by conditioning your mind; just as your mind has been conditioned to the allure of porn every day, so it can be undone." Jim says. "Remember Alex, your brain is currently wired for all the porn you can get, a festival of novelty. Your dopamine levels are constantly screaming at you for more. Your 'sexualising' of everyone you see out in the street or at work is your brain telling you it would rather be in front of the computer, jacking off."

"Fine – better that than getting done for sexual harassment." Rob butts in.

"We have the power of self-control Rob – it's what makes a decent society," Jim says. "Matt's problem was triggered by a woman he saw wearing a tight skirt. This could be one in a thousand images we all see every day. How do we get around this problem? We don't. God forbid there should ever come a day when we don't feel attracted to the opposite sex, or the same sex, and where we no longer think about what they look like naked. The problem is, Matt then went home and immersed himself in a virtual world that had nothing to do with the woman he saw at work, whereas Darren kept the thought of the girl alive and real, thus intensifying his feelings for her, without the use of any artificial stimulants. Sure, his dopamine levels were jacked up, sure he whipped it out… but he kept it real."

Matt remains engrossed in the structure of his knees while Jim keeps a sharp fix on me, before turning to the group.

"To all of you – there is something very powerful about being away from technology and being in a natural environment; outside in the world, in the air, in nature, dealing with real people and the real challenges they present to us. It makes us feel like we're part of something important. The man-made, artificial world of technology doesn't compare to the vast sky or the setting sun; it is the most powerful force there is. It makes you feel glad to be alive, to be a part of the human race with all the beauty and troubles that come with it. Do something less boring instead." he stresses, eyes gravitating back towards me. "Alex, did you clear your hard drive?"

"No…" I reply bluntly.

I can hear the quiet disapproval coming from Gary's corner and see the exaggerated shake of the head from the corner of my eye.

"Why not…?" Jim asks.

"I couldn't cut myself off completely. It was too much of a

move." I tell him. "I deleted some things. I'm sorry."

"Don't be sorry – don't spend your life being sorry," Jim says. "Is that how you want to live your life…by saying sorry to everyone…sorry to yourself?

"Divorce that fucking bitch, man," Rob tells me squarely. "She'll ruin your fucking life."

"Rob is right," Jim nods. "By not doing it, you're telling yourself that everything is okay. You need to get a divorce. Inaction is inexcusable and only causes suffering. Alex. I'm sure you've entertained some very dark thoughts at various points simply because you did nothing to ease the problem. Inaction is inexcusable… otherwise don't waste our time and your time by being here. There is no pill to make you feel better – not for this. The only thing that's required is action: a concerted effort on your part to put changes in place. You've already taken the first step… it's time to take another."

He addresses the flip-pad again and writes: 'THE BATTLE – NOT THE WAR'.

"How do we make those changes happen? How do we push ourselves to *not* do something when we're all alone without the aid of others, like the people in this room for instance? Where do we find the self-motivation for change?" he asks. "Gary?"

"I use reminders," he begins. "I have a knife that I keep at the side of the bed encased in a laminated box with the lid open - it's merely a symbol – but it serves as a reminder of the time when I was at my lowest and thought about taking my own life. It fills me with shame every time I look at it."

"Rob?"

"For me, it's the sense of loss…" he says. "…my wife… my kid…my job…they've all suffered and I've paid the ultimate price in losing them. Having said that, I've managed to turn my life around and be there for my child. That's my motivation right there."

"Darren?"

"For me it's a challenge every day mate. I'm twenty-two years old and I'm fucked if I'm going to sit in my room jacking off until I'm fifty and missing out on the best things in life. That's my inspiration. Get it while you're young mate… do me a favour…" he says.

"Matt?" Jim finally asks.

"Like Darren – like you all – I find it a challenge in withholding my urge to sit in front of the computer," he begins. "Boredom is my greatest problem…and the fear of boredom. I've heard you all discuss the ways in which you alleviate the tedium of everyday life with your games and yoga and reading and what-not. My problem is I have yet to find something to surpass the excitement I feel when that first window pops up. Of course, this is all rooted in a far deeper problem: the transitory nature of our existence forever lurks in the back of my mind, rendering all other ambition as utterly pointless. Are not the endeavours you all undertake just as futile as sitting in front of the computer fapping all day long? All are meaningless in the face of death. Life is simply 'time to be filled' until we die, therefore making it pointless."

There is a collective sigh from the group, as if they've all been witness to this before and all tried exhaustively to coax Matt out of his nihilism, yet still he persists in digging up same corpse, prompting one to think that perhaps he's at the wrong meeting. Jim reassures him.

"On the face of it Matt, we are simply custodians of this rock for the next generation to inhabit; it's our obligation to look after this world and to make sure it's a safe and peaceful place for the years to come, just as the generations before us did. We have no power over the facts of life, but we have the power to make life beautiful…"

"I know…I know…" Matt whines.

"Let this be your battle – at least you are fighting," Jim says.

"Come on Matt – don't be so fucking defeatist," Rob adds.

"Easy now…" Jim croons, re-taking his seat, addressing me once more. "Alex, ask yourself – where do you find the self-motivation for change? What makes you tick? Is it simply a case of us all having to lose to know how to win?"

16

The string of red tail-lights glide seamlessly through the dusk, hypnotising and inducing within me a cool, mellow feeling as I follow its course home. I light up a cigarette, roll down the window and take in the night air which is warm and mysterious. My calm is such that I begin to lose distance on the fireflies until they finally vanish altogether over a black horizon, reducing me to nothing more than a lone, ghost rider. Jim is still talking to me, despite the miles between us, about how important it is to have a visual reminder of one's progress. 'Make your trackers beautiful…make them stand out' the voice echoes. 'Remember, you *want* to keep looking at them'. I can't help but smile as I envisage the various shapes and forms of what constitutes as beautiful. Am I seriously going to make some half-arsed chart, hang it on my wall and tick the boxes of each day as I go? A big gold star for not being a naughty boy! Am I big enough to set aside my ego and feel a sense of pride at such an accomplishment? Am I ready to see a chart filled with gold stars or black or red, each colour denoting a different outcome?

I blow smoke out of the window, noticing how dark the sky is already and it's only late August. Of course there will have to be prizes…and booby prizes; simple incentives to keep pushing the boat onward, little treats, one of which might be a whole day of wanking with all the trimmings, guilt free. Friends will come in and ask: 'Oh what's that?' And I'll reply, 'that's my daily wanking tracker – to monitor my progress – every day of abstinence is a step closer to God'. Remember it must be proudly displayed – if hidden away it will only be neglected and forgotten. 'Make your trackers beautiful…'

My determination to follow through on all that was highlighted at P.E.S.T remains unabated even at home, a feeling that has me chuckling to myself as I turn on the television. Laughter expresses itself in the smallest of things and I realise I haven't engaged in this simple pleasure for ages. Working through the process of elimination, I weed out the good and the bad as alternatives to spending time with the computer, falling on nothing very substantial, realising it will require more thought. It doesn't matter: I'm laughing, simply at the expense of laughing All porn shall be deleted and done away with, there will be no need for it any longer; time on the computer will also be reduced to a couple of hours a day! My failing eyesight will return, my posture will right itself once more and hard-ons will be hard again. I'm laughing! I shall continue my work unhindered, put all my energy into becoming the best seller in the department. I'm laughing at the brilliance of P.E.S.T and what a coup it was stumbling across a place where others like me are struggling with their own obsessions and who divulge their secrets with courage and candour. I'm laughing at the slick image of Gary's face and the languorous air of Matt and how I ever came to be in the same room as these people. I pull a beer from the fridge and laugh some more at nothing in particular, helped along by more alcohol. I'm still laughing as the clock hits midnight, that nucleus of warmth that I experienced earlier in the evening, still prevalent, still thinking about the future. Before I turn in, I groggily approach the cat in the hallway and whisper in his sleepy ear: "Goodnight my friend. Sleep tight."

Morning brings the vocalising of a cat in great distress; a painful monologue in cat-speak that is telling me something terrible. Am I dreaming? I've heard this sound before - it's definitely the cat. The clock reads 7:04am. It hasn't gone off yet. The sound is a wail, a dreadful moaning punctuating the silence, turning the air painfully blue.

In the hallway the cat is crouched low with his face close to the floor, addressing the floor it seems, howling down into the cracks of the wooden boards at some invisible tormentor. I bend down and hold him, lifting him from below his forelegs to examine his face just to confirm it's coming from *his* mouth. His eyes are scared. He *is* in pain. I stroke him reassuringly, waiting for his purr to kick in, but it doesn't come. His eyes are pre-occupied with the hellion inside his little body, something I have no knowledge of, but clearly something serious.

"Shit…" I mutter at the inconvenience already unfolding at such an early hour.

I'm the first one in the Veterinary Clinic and the young Receptionist, who is blonde and desperately pretty, is still taking off her coat as I approach the desk, observing the name Hayley pinned to her uniform.

"My, my, aren't we noisy this morning," she says, as she comes to the window looking down at the basket I'm carrying.

"He seems to be in some pain. I'm not sure what it is. He needs to see the vet this morning." I tell her.

She punches my details into the computer then tells me to wait until the vet is ready, just as a man with a muzzled German Shepherd walks in behind me. After about ten minutes, the vet finally appears in the form of a handsome, greying man of about forty, named Wycombe who calls me through with an assertive voice.

On the examining table, he feels along the underside of the cat's body, squeezing firmly, working across the internal structure he has pictured in his mind, searching for any abnormalities, ignoring the growls of objection then working his way back, his fingers digging deep into the fur until I can almost feel him rooting around inside *my own* body. The sensation makes me weak and a sudden pain above my left kidney forces me to lean back against the wall.

"Has he been eating alright?"

"On and off… Sometimes he doesn't seem very interested."

"Any blood when he goes to toilet? Does he seem lethargic?"

"I haven't noticed any blood, but he does vomit occasionally," I reply.

As the vet continues his examination, I notice how much weight the cat has lost and how scrawny he looks leaving me shocked at how this has gone unnoticed by me at home. Filled with sudden guilt that comes with neglect, I sense the vet now regarding me with suspicion and doubt.

"Does he go out often?" he asks, lifting the cat's face and looking into his eyes.

"Not really. I have a small garden that he sometimes uses," I tell him.

"Have you noticed him to be in any discomfort? Does he seem to sit awkwardly? Does he cry a lot?"

"He's cried before, yes. He also seems disorientated and forgetful. I was wondering if he was showing signs of dementia." I say.

The vet seems unmoved by my unqualified diagnosis as he asks me to hold the cat while he checks his information on the computer.

"Excessive vocalisations can be the first signs of dementia; and I don't just mean a simple meow. It will sound unfamiliar and strange. Of course this could also be due to pain. He's what…twelve, thirteen years old?" The vet asks reflectively as he checks his data.

"We were unsure," I tell him. "We took him in as a stray."

I can see the vet is unconcerned with speculative dementia,

but concerned about something. In keeping with the poker-faced silence that doctors seem to be so adept at when their suspicions are aroused, he leaves the computer and asks me to hold the cat while he takes his temperature. One up the bum and the cat lets out a disgruntled growl before it's over. The vet checks the reading then stoically returns to the keyboard and types in his conclusions thus far, which seem to be a lot.

"Right…" he finally informs me. "I can feel something around his lower abdomen and the stomach…which concerns me. It could be nothing more than constipation, an abscess…I don't know. What I want to do is run some tests and perhaps take an X-ray. That way we'll know for sure."

"Well what do you think it could be?" I ask.

"I don't know…the tests will tell us all we need to know. He has a temperature and he's visibly underweight."

"Will I be able to pick him up tonight?" I ask.

"Drop by tonight and we'll be able to tell you more from the tests," he says. "Has he eaten this morning?"

"No."

I take one last look at the cat who is gingerly seeking a way off the table, but fearful of the height. The vet prevents him from moving any further and reassures me once more before I leave him to it, stopping by Reception to tell Hayley I will be calling in later this evening and to leave her my mobile number, should there be any problems.

The optimistic mood I had intended to carry over from yesterday into today has been blighted by the cat's complications, leaving me on a downer and convincing me that higher forces are conspiring against me. And walking past the smoking area, the idea of creating a tracker to monitor my progress seems like another futile venture as I feel the old shadows beginning to crawl over me once more.

Suzie immediately enquires about the cat's welfare as I enter the office, sharing with me her own experience of having to deal with illness and how expensive vet bills can be. I thank her for her concern, whilst I concern myself with the tight skirt she's wearing, one I've never seen before, which reveals the true magnificence of her buxom figure. I simply can't be dealing with it today, I tell myself. The focus for today is to keep all sordid thoughts at bay!

"We need to get our heads together over Alpha6… when?" Klep asks me matter-of-factly as I sit down.

"What about Friday…?" I say.

"Fine…bring whatever you've got on them and we'll crack on," he says, turning away very seriously.

Mid-morning Danute walks into the room and straight into Prasad's office. Her presence throws me completely as I wait for her to emerge, causing a stream of errors as I type. When she does finally appear, I try and catch her attention by looking up, but she blanks me completely, instead making a bee-line straight for Klep whom she shares an affectionate smile with before she leaves the room.

I'm still thinking about the exchange on the way to the communications meeting with the Heads of Departments having decided not to elect Klep to cover for me, coming close to questioning him on what that smile with Danute was all about - the whole thing exacerbating my apathy towards work and hatred of the man, leaving me two throws from calling it all a day. In the meeting, I watch Martin - who delegates for the kitchen - play on his phone without listening to a word that's being said. Then just as the tedium is about to overwhelm me, the Operations Manager finally calls it time. I leave with Martin and we walk together as he enquires about my text message.

"What?"

"You brazenly said you thought you had a problem with too much dinner service…" he informs me. "I was going to bring it up in the meeting, but thought I'd save you the blushes."

"You didn't take me seriously…?"

"Actually I did. I just wanted to confirm my suspicions about you," he says.

"It was something I was reading…about a bloke who confessed to having a problem with masturbation. I wanted to see what your reaction would be if I told you. It was a wind-up." I tell him.

Martin smiles, remains unconvinced.

"It's okay… I wouldn't frown upon it. Everybody needs a fucking vice. Lord knows I've got mine; we're bigger than that aren't we? I tell you what, if I could sit at home tugging it all day, I would," he says.

"How are things with you and Tasha?" I ask, changing the subject.

"Oh she's fine," he says dismissively. "She can get a bit sensitive sometimes and a bit upset when I drink too much. She's only looking out for me. How'd it go with Danute?"

"She came back for coffee…we had a chat…and that was about it. Then she went." I lie.

"Really?" he frowns. "I thought she'd be all over you. You just can't tell, can you?"

"Next time, maybe… perhaps next time…" I tell him.

"Listen, did I tell you I was leaving?"

"No, you didn't…" I say, surprised at the news.

"Yeah…job at the Four Seasons. It's a lot more money than this place… and a bit more prestigious."

"Congratulations… sad to see you go."

"Yeah…we got to keep moving haven't we? Stay in one place too long and things get boring. You only live once and all that. Don't worry, we'll still see each-other."

"Sure…"

Martin's news only saddens me even more. As I pull out of the stairwell, and onto the upstairs corridor, I'm astonished to see the route blocked by Danute and Klep engaged in conversation. I pause, confused, observing them from a distance, before walking down, their voices becoming noticeably quieter. As I pass, Klep acknowledges me with a smug nod of the head, whereas Danute remains bowed, pretending to be looking at the papers she's holding. My legs feel as if they're about to give way as I enter the office trying to interpret what I've just seen, passing it off as nothing more than conviviality between two workers. When Klep eventually walks back in looking pleased with himself however, I'm convinced it's something more, with my first thought being whether Danute has divulged any information about our Saturday night together and whether she really is a witch and one-hitter with a bitchy streak that stops at nothing in exposing the foibles of men.

At four-thirty, after having been reduced to nothing more than a silent witness for the entire day, I walk into Prasad's office to tell him I'm about to depart, leaving him looking at his watch in confusion until I have to remind him about the vet before he grudgingly lets me go.

Suzie sends me more well-wishes and tells me not to worry – everything will be alright.

The drive to the vet however is gloomy, as anything that's connected with illness usually is, much like the guilt that surfaces when confronted with the possibility of losing something.

Still wary of the dream I had a few nights ago that took place in some dystopian hell that I only vaguely recollect the details of now, one of which being how my cat was taken from me, I meditate as I drive in the hope of transferring some positive energy instead, all tied in with a sudden resolve to become a better father to him. Still, no matter how great the well-wishing, I can't shake the ominous feeling that the vet will be the harbinger of bad news.

Hayley has been replaced by an older, but none-the-less attractive nurse with raven hair, by the name of Val. I give her my details and watch her, trying to interpret mood and expression, but she seems just as adept at keeping things close to her ample chest. She finally tells me to take a seat and wait for the vet. After ten minutes, the vet walks in and calls my name, his handsome face, serious and absorbed.

I'm lead past the consultation rooms and into the bowels of the building, down a corridor and into a section lined with cages, housing around six felines, all connected up to various drips, catheters, some bandaged and stitched. A young nurse is checking on each cage and tending to the animals and when she sees me she smiles. The vet leads me down to the very last cage where my cat is curled up at the rear, staring out vacantly. He has a tube strapped to his front leg that leads to a small bag of clear fluid, held fast with tape that every so often he laps at, as if trying to smooth down the foreign object that's become a part of his body. The sight of him alarms me as he remains docile to my presence coupled with the vet's expression that seems grave and I'm loathed to hear what he has to say.

"What's wrong with him?" I finally ask.

"He's not a well boy, I'm afraid. Let's go in the other room." the vet says, leading the way.

The vet props himself up against the table and folds his arms then gets straight to the point.

"Your cat has a tumour. It's basically a tumour in his stomach roughly the size of my hand," he says, lifting his hand and clenching his fist to illustrate.

He takes a large envelope from his desk and pulls out the results of an X-ray, exposing the huge area taken up with the growth which looks to be about a third of the cat's body and I'm shocked at how something so big went undetected by me for so long *and* how something can still function with such an anomaly inside of them. He explains to me the type of tumour we're looking at and how easy it was to detect just by physical examination. He then explains what effect this is having on the cat's body, involving the upper and lower gastric regions, stomach, digestive system and abdomen area. All of which he tells me would have accounted for the lethargy, loss of appetite, weight loss and the 'howling'. The vet lowers the X-ray and looks hard into my face before he goes on.

"The tumour is at a very advanced stage and to be honest, I'm surprised he's made it this far," he tells me, pausing briefly.

"So...where do we go from here?" I stutter.

"Well the prognosis isn't good – there isn't a lot we can do," he says. "Taking into account the cat's age and the late stage that the tumour is at, I think any method of treatment wouldn't do a lot of good and certainly wouldn't prolong the cat's life by any considerable means. This would include surgery...removal of the tumour...which wouldn't work, as it's just too big. There is radiation and chemotherapy, but the issue is that it tends to be ineffective against large tumours, not to mention the traumatic effect all this would have on the animal."

I nod solemnly as he goes on.

"Then, of course there is the cost to consider. Now some might argue that cost isn't an issue when it comes to saving lives, but, taking into account the small amount of time we're talking about - three to six months max, if successful – it might cause you to reconsider." he says. "The fact is, with early detection, we might have been able to do something about it. Unfortunately, at this late stage, I don't think it would be fair on the cat."

"So what are you saying?" I ask.

"That it's time to start saying your goodbyes..." he replies softly. "It's for the best."

"Would it be worth getting a second opinion?" I ask.

The vet is professional enough not to be offended by this and magnanimously nods his head.

"Of course, that's your choice. However, I'm satisfied that the physical examination we've done and the radiography has told us all we need to know about the cat's condition," he says.

I take the X-ray from the vet and have another look at the dark shadow filling the tiny frame where once there was transparency and light. The last thing I want to do is prolong the pain.

"Is there nothing we can do?" I ask desperately.

"There *is* nothing we can do except surgery, with no guarantee that the cat will make it through. At the end of the day, it's not the length of life that is of prime concern, but the quality of that life," he says. "I'm sorry."

After the vet talks me through the process of putting the cat to sleep via anaesthetic injection, I finally give him my consent. I'm surprised at how easy I find it to make the decision. The process requires me to fill in a form certifying that I have agreed to allow the vet to carry out the procedure. After this he punches more information into the computer then asks me if I wish to be present when he administers the fatal dose.

"Is that normal?" I ask.

"All depends on the individual. Some like to be there in the final moment – others don't," he tells me.

"No I don't want to be there. But I'd like a few moments with him now, please." I tell him.

"Of course," he replies. "I'll leave you alone until you're ready."

We make our way back to the rear of the building and the nurse walks past us and smiles again, only this time I detect a hint of sadness to it. I'm told to take all the time I need as the cage is unlocked before the vet too disappears. The cat is still seated at the back of the cage, hooked up and motionless, looking out as I peer in and seeing him again, brings about a feeling that I'm about to cry.

"I'm sorry…" I whisper, as I reach in and gently touch his body.

I leave my hand resting on his side and feel the warmth permeate up through my palm as I feel his purr begin to kick in, growing louder. He looks at me expectantly, as if I'm about to provide him with his dinner, or ask him a question or produce something for him to play with, only now he remains solidly fixed in his position, debating as to whether those things actually happen in the strange environment he currently sits in. Reading his thoughts, I shake my head sadly, still struggling to accept his fate and in two minds as to whether to tell the vet to call it all off. As if reading my thoughts, the cat attempts to sit up, gingerly forcing the body to cooperate, to do what it used to do so easily with grace and agility, only now for it to slump back down in resignation and rearrange itself into a comfortable state.

"Please… no…" I whisper.

Reaching in, I unfasten the collar around his neck and pull it away, keeping it locked tight in my right hand, savouring its warm velvety texture. We spend the next few moments looking at one-another, me gently stroking him and recalling the past and the time spent together and I'm saddened at how very few moments I can recall, moments of real significance, recalling the words of Jim in my mind and the importance of grabbing time while we can and not waiting for tomorrow. And now here we are, in the moment, after which there will be no more tomorrows. I stroke his little body and he continues to purr. Would he have fared better had he gone with Sarah when we split, I wonder? Would this day still be a future event, months, even years from now had he gone with his mother instead?

"I'm sorry…" I whisper. "…please forgive me."

The urge to cry is strong and I'm still unconvinced about the decision I've made, even though it will come to pass. I can hear movement nearby, just outside the door. I can't stay here forever pondering over the whys and wherefores; the vet has other patients to see. I clench my teeth and suppress the pain and our eyes meet for the last time.

"Time to say goodbye, my friend…"

The flat is dead still when I re-enter. I place the empty basket down in the hall and move stiffly and silently forward. Every room is suddenly silent; too quiet without the quiet presence of *you*. I paid Val as quickly and as coldly as I could and I got out of there and didn't look back. I balked at the price of death then forgot about the place. Now, as I sit in respectful silence, anaesthetised, watching the second hand crawl across the clock face, I am aware from somewhere in the back of my mind that things need to be done, promises have to be fulfilled; I remember some vague idea about having to go shopping. It will all come back to me. Silence first - the simple joy of silence!

My grief lasts for precisely two hours and thirty-eight minutes before the image of Suzie wearing her tight, new dress, usurps the image of *you*, spreading and multiplying within me like a virus, immune to the sensitive antibody of *your* passing and has me in front of the computer whacking off to a new set of updates with a bloody-minded ferocity and determination that is both exhilarating and frightening. Somewhere in the back of my mind things need to be done, promises to be kept. The trick is to stay busy, keep the mind and body occupied and not allow the injustices of the world to stay embedded too deeply for too long - nothing will come of grieving any longer. I will consult the computer – this is what I'm good at, this is where I excel, this is what I know.

I have four windows on the go and my boner looks like a red, pulsating gear stick attached to a high-powered machine. The computer screen is iridescent and bursting with life and I'm moving up the gears as the sound of the fan works tirelessly at cooling the guts, working to counter-balance the demands of its venomous user. The sound becomes deafening as I push further, perversely attempting to see how much pain it can withstand before it too dies on me. Every bit, byte, megabyte is stretched to breaking point and still my gear-stick of an erection juts out, twitching and throbbing and snapping at the heels of the machine like a tormentor of evil. Flies whizz past my face and putrefy the air around me and I inhale greedily as my body attaches itself to the leather chair like sucker pads, tearing the flesh with every movement; and the sound of the fan becomes even louder and I'm lost in the melee with my sweaty skin and thumping heart. The heart of the machine heats the tinder dry desk beneath it, sending out signals that it's about to catch, that it's about to go up and rise into a giant conflagration and burn us all to a crisp; and still I push on and up the gears, choosing films at random, using the element of surprise and spontaneity to keep my boner engorged with blood and my hunger sated. I give off a booming laugh and thrust my pelvis back and forth and the sprawl becomes frenzied. There is no pain here; all pain is forbidden! I will toss away all pain! All pain will be tossed into the central processing unit to be deciphered, logged then spewed out as a cure in the form of 'Wanton Mary' and co. This thought triggers an alarm in the back of my mind that screams, 'lie'. I begin bellowing at the screen to drown out the sound of the voices coming from inside my head, telling them not to interfere - especially when there's been a death in the family. No pain - remember! My mobile phone suddenly lights up and begins ringing and I pull it from the desk beside the computer to observe the number and see its Martin trying to get hold of me. I place it back down, cursing at the distraction. Then, just as I'm about to get back into my stride, it goes off again. I look and see its Martin once more and realise that for him to call twice, he must be desperate for a beer. The voices in my head are telling me to pick up, to get out; to share my grief with another. I'm twitching and debating, cock still filling my hand. This sways it for me - Martin should have called earlier. I shall do the right thing and apologise to him tomorrow, telling him I was in no fit state to socialise on account of a sudden bereavement. Half an hour passes before the phone rings again. This time it's my mother. What on earth could she want at this time of night - are they all calling to offer me their condolences? Do they all have some intuitive voice telling them of my troubles? The call is ignored and I shift back up the gears bringing myself closer. Piss away the pain, my friend. Let it all out and start afresh tomorrow. The world will be very different tomorrow. The computer dishes out more dirt: garbage in – garbage out – and like a gutless wimp I eat hungrily, stiffening to the point of no return just as I begin to pray. Then, as I ask for forgiveness, I come.

I step outside of the room and listen in the darkness, venturing forward and down the hall in the black, then into the lounge, stepping over to the bay window to look out. The full moon is up and suspended above the rooftops in brilliant yellow; a perfect sphere, large and luminous casting an eerie light over everything before me. In the silence, I walk through and into the kitchen where the moon's brilliance sheds just enough light for me to see *your* food bowl in the corner on the floor. Everything will stay where it is, including the uneaten supply of food still in the cupboards. I walk back into the hallway passing the litter tray and realise it needs changing. Everything will stay as it is for now. These small insignificant objects are not *you*, but they belong to you. I shall keep them with me tonight. Finally, in bed, in the quiet and the dark and very much alone, I capitulate, turn my face into the pillow and cry.

17

Suzie is the first to console me by wrapping her arms around me as I walk in, a move that makes me want to cry again; this time in the warmth of her bosom. Her body fills my grasp and I can smell the sweet, fresh morning scent of her hair as we squeeze together and all at once my sorrow is replaced with the desire to look into her face and kiss her madly.

"Oooo Alex… I'm soooo sorry…" she coo's, overemphasising as usual.

"I know…I know…" I lament.

"Sorry Alex…" I hear Lisa call out.

Suzie keeps her arms locked around me and looks up into my face, intensely searching for any last remnants of pain to soothe over in a way that only a woman knows how.

Klep is watching us from his chair and even he seems grieved by the news.

"That is soooo horrible," she says before finally disengaging.

The weight of her departure leaves me feeling naked to the bone and I quickly take to my seat so as to evade prying eyes. As I take off my jacket, Prasad pokes his head out and offers me more condolences.

"Sorry mate," Klep says, turning in his chair. "You could always get another one."

"It's not the same Marcus…" Lisa tells him shortly.

I'm still feeling the vibrations of Suzie's touch as I open up my e-mails and realise it won't be long before normality is resumed and that the wheel of life just keeps on turning, pushing forward, ever forward and that we must move with it.

"No, I know it's not the same…obviously. I'm just saying - everything is dispensable."

"Marcus, that's a horrible thing to say!" Suzie retorts. You make it sound like a razor or a cloth or something you just toss away after it's been used. You obviously know nothing about losing something close to you - something that's alive!"

"Not true – I lost a dog when I was sixteen years old."

"Then you should know what it feels like."

"I'm just saying – there comes a point when you accept what's happened and replace it, or not, as the case might be." he says. "That was my point."

"We know that – but you don't say that when someone is still getting over their loss." Suzie goes on.

The persistent talk about the cat is the last thing I want to hear and all I want to do is keep thinking about the figure beneath the clothes of Suzie in a quiet and stress-free place.

"Please guys don't argue over me. It's okay." I interrupt.

The phone rings, forcing me to pick up and thus taking me out of the equation, even though I can still hear Suzie laying in to Klep as I listen to a client trying to book an event for Christmas.

The rest of the day is spent in a kind of private limbo as I'm given a wide berth from the rest of the office out of what I can only assume is a mark of respect. This only makes me more reflective as the day wears on and as I head down for my late afternoon appointment I bump into Danute on the stairs who adds her own penny's worth of condolence.

"Ooo…Alex…I'm so sorry to hear about your cat," she says.

"I know…" I say surprised at the fact that the news has already filtered down to her, making me think that perhaps the entire hotel knows about it.

"I didn't realise he was unwell."

"Neither did I…" I tell her.

"What was it?"

"Tumour…inoperable…"

She shakes her head sadly.

"These things happen, I guess." I tell her.

We hit an impasse, both struggling for more words until I finally tell her I have to go. As I hit the stairs going down, I glance up at her ample behind gliding upward, until it vanishes somewhere on the second floor landing.

On the way home, the car judders, lets out a loud grating sound, as if its tubes are filled with phlegm then heaves and coughs its guts out, trying to release the bile before it wheezes and slows. There is enough momentum in its legs to see me pull over into the lay-by before the whole sorry thing comes to a halt as the five-thirty, homebound commuters carry on by, observing from their windows, the poor misfortunate stuck in the middle of nowhere with nothing but an RAC job to look forward to, all thanks to my neglect. I start her up and give it some revs only to hear the same calamitous sound; a sound that suggests it would be impossible to get her back home to the garage without more trouble. I reach for my phone and call the roadside service.

After just over fifty minutes, an RAC man turns up and after much questioning and testing tells me it's something to do with the transmission *and* the radiator and that I won't be able to drive her back as there's nothing he can do and will have to wait for a pick-up which could be a wait of anything up to three hours. I want to tell him my cat's just died and that I'm in no fit state for any more bad news, but instead pull a cigarette from my pocket and light up as he slithers back into his car and pulls away, leaving me loitering roadside as if waiting to partake in some 'dogging session'. I light another cigarette.

After just over an hour the pick-up truck arrives and hauls me back into town where I decide to unload the car unobtrusively in the forecourt of my local garage where I can call in first thing tomorrow morning and ask them to have look at it. Again, it means calling in late for work. Exhausted and run-down and dreading the solitude of my flat, I decide to stop off in the pub for a drink in the hope of erasing the last twenty four-hours from my mind. After three drinks I can feel the veil of depression beginning to descend and decide to go home. The gloom stretches out into every crevice, every tree branch, every distorted street lamp and the myriad of sounds that fill the evening air and it's with relief that I close the front door behind me.

Inside, I remove the cat litter tray from the hallway, empty and clean out the contents then store it away in the cupboard. In the kitchen, I wash out the cat bowl and store it away in the same place. The cat food is pulled from the cupboard and thrown away as are the various playthings and other cat items that I've accumulated over time, but were rarely ever used. The only thing that remains is the collar and an old picture I have of him meowing into the camera lens, frame full of teeth making him look as ferocious as the larger species of his kind but is really only a trick of perspective. This needs a frame that I will buy at the weekend when I shop for the bits I need for my tracker. Cold acceptance of the fact that he is gone has now replaced sorrow; and although his life has been reduced to nothing but a memory, I am grateful for at least that.

The computer holds no sway over me – that feeling of being in limbo having carried over from work leaving me maudlin and quietly unresponsive. There is only bed, where as I begin to warm up, the scent of Suzie's flame-red hair fills my senses. And as I begin to drift off, the sensation dissipates, becoming nothing more than a thought… just a thought.

So on Friday morning, it's with quiet distrust that I look back at Klep, who looks across at me with his beady little eyes from the comfort of Prasad's chair – he having vacated for the rest of the day as time in lieu – as we run over the formalities concerning Alpha 6. The man in the garage was unapologetic when he opened his shutters this morning, informing me it was doubtful my car would be ready by the weekend. To top it all off, they were completely out of courtesy cars due to the sheer volume of work they had on, saying there might be something on Saturday, but no promises, leaving me calculating how I would get in to work for the big show-round first thing on Monday.

"We'll introduce ourselves at Reception then move on up to the Bar," Klep goes on, matter-of-factly. "I'll have chef prepare them a little welcome gift, some kind of decorative truffle assortment on a slate that will look really pleasing on the eye and go well with the coffee. John will come and introduce himself and give his usual introductory bullshit, telling them how great we are without trying to come across as an arrogant prick."

"Which will be difficult," I mutter.

"Doesn't matter, they haven't come to listen to John. We'll sit and nod our heads and laugh at his bad jokes until he disappears. You know the score…" he adds, observing me through the slits of his eyes.

"Agreed…" I tell him, before he reels off the rest of the news, mostly concerning the planned route, demonstrations and sales pitch. I nod as we both dismiss Steph's proposal of us working like a comedy duo as ludicrous and agree to stick to the facts with charm.

"Don't talk over each other," he urges. "Don't be too eager, don't be anxious, don't rush, but don't draw it out to the point of boredom. Look smart, act smart. Remember to tell them why they need us, thus incorporating a little bit of knowledge about their company from our end and describe past successes and why they're relevant."

The corners of his mouth curl into a grin as he reaches into his back pocket and pulls out his wallet. He opens it up, extracts a miniature playing card.

"This is for you," he says, handing me the King of Hearts. "I've got the diamond. We're a couple of kings – remember that."

He taps his wallet, signifying that he has his mojo tucked away inside and that if I'm smart, I'll do the same with mine. For a moment I actually soften to his snake-like charm and follow his lead by slipping the card into my wallet.

"Remember, we're the dream-team. Winners!" he concludes.

He offers me his clammy hand and I accept with a feeling of having just made some Faustian pact, reinforcing once more the colossal distrust I have of the man. Indeed, I'm reminded of his little meeting in the corridor with Danute and wary of what he knows about our date together. Klep, I think senses this and over the course of the day, plays on it, with masked references to impotency, sentences filled with double-entendres and surreptitious little glances over in my direction, all without actually implicating me, or himself, in any way. 'Did you hear the one about the bloke with brewers droop…?' he begins, innocently telling the room, all the while scrutinizing me with those beady little eyes.

I try to ignore what I can, but he's playing it well, working on me like a dirty, little pest, a filthy fly, buzzing around the room, building within me a wall of fire and hatred that is about ready to topple over by late afternoon. I manage to pull through; and by five-o-clock, people's thoughts turn to the weekend and the promise of what Saturday and Sunday will bring. I too am relieved at the prospect of two days off where I can re-group and get my head together and work at fulfilling those promises that haven't yet come to fruition.

I'm the last to leave with Suzie; and just as I'm about to say goodbye, John the Director walks into the room to make final enquires about our preparations for the show-round on

Monday. I offer him bullshit reassurances before he slopes off to the back of the room to talk with Suzie who is reluctantly forced to re-take her seat in what she presumes will be a dressing down of some sort. I hang around long enough to hear the beginnings of John's slimy diatribe which is nothing more than a sleazy come-on to one of his employees, pinning his hopes on a little something for the weekend I imagine, prattling on about some exhibition of supercars and what a worthy event it is.

Hemmed in and cornered like a frightened animal, Suzie looks gorgeous, with her flame-red hair and voluptuous body, her subservience as captivating to me as it is to John. She shoots me a glance, worried at the prospect of being left alone with the monster, before I head for the door, unsure of whether to hang around and wait perversely for the excuse she comes up with for her flight. The whole scene strikes me as farcical and I opt for a quick exit, leaving Suzie to work it out for herself, although not before blowing her a kiss goodbye.

And so that kiss goodbye and all its intentions remain with me as I suppress the state of arousal I find myself in at home, shunning the final destination that is the computer, *again.* My count has officially started; I'm on the wagon, despite the picture of Suzie that suggests otherwise. Those great pendulous breasts shall have no domain – not tonight. And that 'voice' with all its sway and persuasion keeps telling me: 'it's okay…you haven't created your tracker yet, therefore your abnegation of porn hasn't officially stared. You're allowed to stray just this once!'

I wash and eat with cold detachment, succeeding at keeping the voice at bay then for the remainder of the evening, read. Not five or six pages, but half a book, equating to eight or nine chapters, drawn out, drawn in, occupied. Again, a deep yearning for travel germinates within me, much like the hero of the book who seeks knowledge and self-enlightenment across the vast stretches of land and sea. I too have much to learn and much to see. And the more I immerse myself in the character, the less fantastical the notion seems. Then, before midnight, sedated, heart filled with longing, I turn out the light.

I'm up early in the stationers sifting through the card, paper and pens, revelling in my little secret of why I'm buying such items and what their intentions are as I visualise how the tracker will look, making each version even grander than the one preceding it, until I finally have something resembling the finished thing. It's an embarrassing task for sure and one most people would surely cross the street from if they knew what these innocuous little items were for. However, it's a small price to pay if it's a step closer to getting my life back.

Back at the flat, I lay out the materials on the living room floor and have another coffee with a cigarette while examining the stencil that will be used for the lettering. After a long, drawn out couple of hours, the tracker is complete and fixed to the wall in the spare room beside the desk. Tacked on, it is easily removable should anybody pay a fleeting visit with a gap just behind the bookshelf for safe storage. Then, as an act of defiance, I turn on the computer and settle down to check my e-mails, update my Facebook page, with a masked reference to the fact that I'm still alive, check the website of our clients for Monday's meeting and generally surf just to see if I'm capable of doing it without resorting to old habits. It's difficult - a world of filth awaits me just a click away. I turn to my tracker, scrutinize the gold and green livery, the bold lettering and the symmetry of the boxes and for some reason it reminds me of a Christmas decoration, pulled out, faded, dusted down and out of place in this unseasonal time of year. I'm fading.

Defiantly, I pull up My Favourites folder and begin randomly deleting. Still unable to delete the entire folder in one, fell swoop, I work on eliminating all but the very best, the ones that have transcended mere acts of porn and everyday human behaviour and reached enlightenment. Click, click, click, click, click, click, click; without remorse, each one confined to the 'recycle bin' then emptied altogether into the wasteland of cyberspace. Click, click, click, click, click, click…the list goes on. And after three hours, where once, my Saturday was reserved for the very best viewing experience, I am finally left with a reduced menu that is readable on one page.

I stick a gold star in yesterday's box and the day before that and confidently predict another one for today. With the same determination, I remain on the computer and scour the jobs market, curiously making notes, subconsciously looking at life beyond the Thorn Park Hotel, pushing forward…being pro-active. For the remainder of the day I walk around the flat for a bit, watch T.V, eat, and finally finish the last few chapters of my book. And I'm happy at how these little things leave me feeling contented, no pressure to commit myself to anything other than being…living in the moment.

And as Saturday bleeds into Sunday morning, the first thing I do is place a gold star in yesterday's box then admire the three gold stars juxtaposed together symbolising my good behaviour. The urge to turn on the computer is strong though which stems from a dream I was having, the details of which I can only vaguely recollect, but involved a past one-night stand who took to blowing me whilst talking to her friend on her mobile. The answer is to set about making breakfast. There will be no cigarettes this morning, only energy and vitality and a desire to do something physical – something actualized outside, not in front of the computer.

This eventually takes shape in the unprecedented step of going for a walk. Indeed, my remit is to take one step at a time, to place one foot before the other on another fine morning along a bridleway I have often seen but dared never to venture down. And as I walk, I'm struck by the tiny figure of a blonde female coming towards me with her dog. The dog reaches me before she does, lower half caked in mud, a big, excited fuss around my feet, yelping at the approaching owner, a form I now vaguely recognise from somewhere. She calls out the dog's name in a conciliatory tone, but the dog ignores her. After ruffling his furred head, I look up and recognise the girl as Hayley – the nurse from the vet. She is even more attractive than I remember her to be, a fact that soothes my annoyance at being accosted by a mutt on this perfectly fine morning

"Sam, get off! Come here!" she commands.

The dog turns its backside towards me and continues to thump my leg with its tail before it's pulled away by the collar and reprimanded with two sharp slaps on the rear, the strength of which surprise me coming from such a petite girl.

"I'm really sorry…he gets a bit excited," she says.

"It's okay…he's just enjoying himself."

"I know, but he needs to learn he can't do that," she insists. "I hope he didn't get you all dirty, he's been down in the woods."

"No, it's no problem," I tell her examining my trousers as the dog mooches towards me once more, this time more sedately.

"He's gorgeous…" I lie. "How old is he?"

"Two…he's at that age…"

"You work in the vet don't you? I was in the other day with my cat." I tell her.

She nods instantly, recognising my face.

"How is he…?"

"I had to have him put down."

"Oh, I'm so sorry."

"Yeah, it was for the best. He was very ill."

"It's always hard when it comes to saying goodbye. But it has to happen one day." she shrugs.

"You must see a lot of it…" I say, the dog looking up at me forlornly, as if affected by the news as well.

"I do…it's always sad. We become so attached to animals…"

The dog is mobile again, sniffing at the ground, restless.

"I'm sorry, I don't remember your name," she says shyly.

"Alex…"

"You're not dating Jenny are you?" she asks out of the blue.

"No…I'm not dating anyone." I tell her, having no idea who Jenny is.

"Sorry… you look like somebody else…"

"I hate it when that happens. You're standing there thinking, is he…isn't he? Should I say something? What about that story I heard about him…" I say.

She laughs at this and her face becomes even more attractive and I take the opportunity to look at her figure which is tight and well-proportioned.

"Do you always come this way?" I ask.

"Most mornings…round the block. I'll usually get up early before work."

This time *she* looks at *me* suggestively, more an assessment as we begin to relax. We engage in more small talk, she, a lot about animals and how much she loves being around them with her work and how much she loves horses and hopes to have one very soon; she's sweet and open and comfortable to be around and its obvious to see why she does what she does. Before I know it, she's inviting me to pay a visit to the surgery at some point to look at finding me another cat until the dog finally gets her moving again, leaving us heading in opposite ways. The meeting leaves me on high as I resume walking and I grab one last look at Hayley's rear which is just as tight and well-proportioned as her front.

The encounter with Hayley works as a major distraction back at the flat and I find myself hovering around the computer and the spare room, pretending to be busy with other things. And although the walk was a revelation, it's inadvertently placed me under pressure when I was doing so well. A 'quickie' in the bathroom just won't do, so I force myself to go out and get the Sunday papers, opting for a stop-off in the Italian café for a coffee before heading home and settling down on the sofa to read with my chaste violinist.

After more resistance, I set about completing tasks in preparation for tomorrow so as not to have to burden myself with it first thing in the morning: shirt, trousers and tie are all ironed and hung; files, notes, tablet are tucked away into my leather holdall; cash is on hand in my wallet; body is showered and scrubbed, hair washed, nails clipped, only a shave will be required after waking up. Bus timetables are checked quietly and methodically until all that's missing will be my presence at work.

I retrieve the small miniature playing card from my wallet, handed to me by Klep and turn it over in my hand, eager to throw it away, but slip it back inside, a part of me believing in Klep, believing he means to hold good on his word and that it is I who has been wrong all along. Beside the card is the picture of Sarah which I pull out and look at for the last time, before scrunching it into a ball within the palm of my hand and throwing it in the bin. And with the same quiet, steely resolve, I see out the remainder of the day with a few beers and a fertile imagination, culminating in one of the best night's sleep I can remember.

18

Something about 'Monday, Monday...' and not 'trusting that day' goes the song - an excerpt of 60's nostalgia that the newscaster tells us was an anthem of its day. I watch the feature with my breakfast, whilst trying to suppress the extreme feeling of danger I'm experiencing due to the potentially disruptive elements that could ruin *my* day: the show-round, no car and having to rely on public transport, the weather girl – who's wearing a very tight-fitting red dress - declaring that today and tomorrow are going to be scorchers due to a wave of hot air coming in from Africa, Klep and lastly, the high state of arousal I find myself in.

I'm already feeling the oppressive weight of the heatwave envelop me like a hot blanket on my naked skin. I finish my breakfast, shave, then head into the office, double checking the bus timetable, calculating how long the walk will take from the flat to the bus stop, then the journey itself and how much time this leaves me before the appointment, which works out at about ten minutes, which I realise is cutting it fine. Way ahead of schedule due to my pre-emptive moves yesterday, I place my watch on the desk beside my wallet and take a seat. Unsure of what my intentions are, I turn on the computer.

Whatever compels us to commit such acts of stupidity in the face of adversity is surely one of life's great enigmas. Is it the desire to push the boundaries of all recognised order just to see what will happen or the inherent self-destructive nature of man? An unjustified over-confidence perhaps with regard to the show-round, knowing in my heart of hearts I don't really give a damn, or is it the fact that one is so stupid, they have no idea of what it is that's good for them, despite being told the contrary? Whatever it is, I decide, after all my renewed efforts to regain a life, to open up my habitual porn website that begins all sessions with a view to satisfying nothing more than vague curiosity.

I observe in a composed, confident and detached way. And had the succession of new updates continued in the same unremarkable vein, I would have dismissed the whole thing as a minor lapse in concentration and turned off. Instead, I'm presented with a new batch of unseen films – totalling eight - featuring the internet goddess herself, 'Wanton Mary'. As I scan down the collection of thumbnails, unbelieving in what my eyes are seeing, time and the universe suddenly cease to exist. By default, I pull out my cock and check on the watch which reads: 7.45am. This gives me just over twenty-five minutes of viewing time before I have to leave, nowhere near long enough to see all the films in their entirety which means an abridged version of each – a taster - will have to suffice, which means a restless day of expectancy at work until I crawl back in through the front door tonight.

Clamouring for my cigarettes, I extract one with a shaking hand, light up and click on the first film. Immediately 'the voice' pipes up in the back of my mind and reminds me of the absurdity of what I'm doing, before it's dismissed as interference. As is to be expected from the greatest performer of our age, the films are of exceptional quality; so much so, I'll have trouble getting through one let alone eight. I draw on my cigarette, procuring more of its effect and move onto the next film. Ten minutes have elapsed already and I curse at the fact of me having to go into work as the second film is even better than the first. Lured in by Mary's' thunderous thighs and womanly loins, I become a dribbling puppy, panting and wining, my drool hanging off my loping tongue as I venture forth into her cavernous hole. I tear my eyes away for a split second to read, 8.02am on the watch before venturing deeper. All manner of nocturnal creatures fill the void, obscured, lost in the shadows, signalling to each other with their mating cries as I pull on my torch and shine my beam toward the far reaches of her vagina. Stalagmites and stalactites glisten in the dark and all at once I'm confused as to which ones are which, before remembering my teacher telling the class that 'tites always come down'. I venture deeper, the torch hot in my hand; head giddy as I run the tips of my fingers across her jagged, wet, limestone wall; her dank, womanly scent fills my nostrils and I can feel my balls beginning to tighten up. I check on the watch: 8:02am, then click on the next film.

The perspiration already feels like it's pouring out of my skin, the pulled blind doing nothing to alleviate the heat and resplendence of the rising sun. And as 'Mary' opens herself up to me once more, I am hit, like a bullet in the head, with the feeling that something terrible is wrong. I look back at the watch which reads: 8.02am. Initially, this seems perfectly fine, giving me another ten minutes or so, but it *feels* like I've been sitting here longer. I look around the room for a sign of something out of place as panic begins to set in, then back at Mary, where more creatures howl from the depths of her hole, then back at the watch, which *still* reads: 8.02am. Staring at the clock face, my heart stops as I discover the second hand has stopped also. I hone in on the digital clock in the corner of the computer screen which gives me a true reading of: 8:16 am. Despite the evidence, my confused brain still doesn't register – or doesn't want to - and I remain where I am watching Mary cavort butt-naked on the bed, before the penny finally drops.

At once, my mind is a blur, as a mass of information streams in from all channels and explodes into chaos, sending me frantically dancing around the room, unsure of what to do first. Realising I'm not wearing any clothes; I lunge into the bedroom, unwilling to accept the fact that I am going to miss my bus and dress hurriedly. The heat is stifling as I throw on my neatly pressed clothes that stick to my moist skin, mind already planning ahead on what to do next, calculating the speed with which I will have to run. My cock is still swollen and Mary is still cavorting on the bed with her thunderous thighs and enormous vagina as I rush back into the spare room and hit 'shut down'. Then, before the screen turns black I check on the time, grab my bag and rush for the door.

I feel sick and light-headed and the sudden exposure of being outside makes me deeply conscious of the way I look, undoing all the preparatory work I put in yesterday. I hit my stride, trying to look as unflustered as possible, cursing over and over, like a mantra…"I can make it…I can make it…I can make it…" then curse at the amount of people beginning to materialise on the streets, breaking my momentum. The air is thick, making breathing difficult, like the first time you step off a plane in a hot country, hit with that unfamiliar, foreign heat that finally tells you you're on holiday. The sweat is soaking my armpits and staining my shirt which will only hinder my movement during the show-round and I curse again at how my life has come to this whilst pondering over which side of the family my stupidity comes from? Running now, I'm a minute away as I check my watch which still fucking reads 8.02am! I'm running, wheezing, listening to the sound of my flat feet slapping the hot tarmac, chugging for breath, the sun as bright as burning magnesium. Then, turning the corner onto the main road, and feeling like I'm about to faint, I make one last concerted effort for the bus stop which is just around the corner. For some insane reason I'm feeling confident I'll make it, that it'll have been stuck in traffic or that I've got my timetable wrong or that something like this couldn't possibly happen to me. Then as I round the corner, I see a bus having just departed, crawling away in the distance – my bus.

I continue to run, thinking I might catch it at the next stop, until I finally give up the chase and come to rest at the side of the road, my chest heaving as I suck in air, one hand resting against the window of an antique shop to save myself from collapsing. An elderly lady passes looking alarmed, unsure of whether to stop and assist, until I wave her on, like I'm directing traffic. Having failed to adjust the time on my watch, I have no idea what the time is and finally catching my breath, manage to ask.

"Eight-thirty-five…" a stern-looking woman informs me, before I adjust my watch.

It's even later than I expected and I'm resigned to the fact that I'm not going to make it in on time as visions of the future flash before me: penury, bent pride, angina, hell and damnation! The first thing I do is pull out my mobile and call the office but staggeringly, no-one answers. Then I realise I don't even have Klep's number so I can't call him either. The next bus isn't for another hour which means my only other alternative is getting a cab – something I should have organised for myself in the first place. Unsure of where I'm going or where the taxi stand is, I take off down the main road thinking about asking somebody - anybody - for a lift to the Thorn Park Hotel. I move vaguely in the direction of where I remember the taxi stand to be, trying not to think about the consequences of failure whilst working out the approximate time of my arrival and what I intend to use as my excuse. I dodge a lorry's wing mirror that almost takes my face off as I step into the road, realising I forgot to put a gold star in yesterday's box. The day is growing hotter by the minute and the taxi rank seems a lot further than I remember it to be and I can feel my chest growing tight once more and my mouth dry as hell. When I do finally arrive at the lot allocated for the small fleet of cars that operate out of town, I'm alarmed at the sight of empty spaces and no cabs visible. I approach the small booth and a blonde lady who must be in her fifties, but seems much older, with a craggy face and smoking a cigarette, comes to the window already shaking her head.

"Hi. I need a cab to…"

"I've got a lot on, luv…" she interrupts, with a coarse voice, her smoky breath hitting me full on, making me ravenous for a cigarette as I look into her craggy face, recognising something that is entirely fuckable. "Won't have anything for about another twenty-five minutes," she tells me.

"Twenty-five minutes!"

"Got the festival up at Woodstock for the next three days – my guys are flat out," she says, checking her watch. "I should have a car back at about nine-fifteen."

The woman retreats back into the booth to answer the phone leaving me to ponder my next move. She finishes talking then returns to the window.

"You can try calling Courtesy Cabs – they might have something available," she says, handing me a card.

I have to laugh at the irony of this, in the fact that I *don't* have a courtesy car that's put me in this mess in the first place. Pulling out my mobile, I dial the number where I'm put straight on hold to the sound of classical music that sounds Russian in origin until a voice finally replaces it telling me nothing is available for another twenty minutes to which I decline. I turn back to the craggy-faced woman, who is bending over inside her booth looking for something and giving me an eyeful of her slim rump and tell her that I'll wait for the first cab to come in.

"It's up to you…" she tells me, after enquiring where I need to go.

I check my watch then pull out a cigarette and spark up before calling the office again. This time Gemma picks up.

"Gemma it's me, Alex…"

"Hi Alex," she replies nonchalantly.

"Gemma is Klep there… I mean…Marcus?"

"No he's with the show-round." she replies, her voice perking up. "I thought you were supposed to be there as well?"

"I was…I mean I am. I've missed the fucking bus. Is there any way you can get hold of him and tell him I'm going to be late?" I ask. "Better still, have you got his mobile number?"

"I haven't no. Wait a minute, let me ask Lisa – she's just walked in."

The line goes quiet for a moment but I can just make out Gemma's voice posing the question to Lisa plus a load of other talk that I can't quite make out but which I presume is a mockery of my plight. She finally returns.

"Alex, she hasn't got it either. He's with the clients at the moment. How are you going to get in?" she asks.

"I'm waiting for a taxi," I tell her, feeling a sudden urge to cry.

"John was in earlier asking after you and I don't think he was too happy," she adds.

"That's his fucking problem - the bus left way ahead of schedule and the taxis are all out!" I cry. "If you get hold of his number, give me a call please."

"Prasad will be in soon – he might have it," she tells me, as I cut the line.

The craggy-faced woman is back on the radio and I'm looking at her and feeling horny as hell and I toy with the idea of jacking it all in and heading back home where I can relax and devote the rest of the day to watching the new 'Wanton Mary' films after which I'll have plenty of time to decide what to do with my life. I stub out my cigarette then light another, which dries my mouth out completely leaving me desperate for fluids. Then, as I'm about to get some water from the newsagents, a taxi pulls in. I approach it immediatcly and the driver seems startled at my sudden presence and peeved at my eagerness and the last thing I need to hear is that he wants a cup of tea before departing on his next journey. He doesn't bother lowering his window but continues to fill in some form as the woman in the booth says something to me of which I have no idea what and when I look at her she seems totally pissed off with me as well. And just before I'm about to start shouting, the driver lowers his window and I tell him where I need to go before I finally get in.

The journey is taking twice as long as it should due to the volume of traffic, squeezing my insides into fits of rage as I try desperately to ignore the unremitting voice of the driver who talks about nothing else but the festival. Despite my monosyllabic answers, he keeps talking like some programmed machine on default, configured for the duration of the ride. The interior of the cab is baking despite his window being open and I move to the centre of my seat to avoid the sun's glare as it streams in from all directions. I can feel a headache coming on. I voice my disgust at the clogged up roads as veiled remarks for getting us to the hotel quicker via shortcuts, but he remains on auto, keeping up the trite banter which only irritates me more.

By the time we reach our destination, it's almost hitting ten-o-clock and my bowels are moving uncontrollably. The sun glints off the parked cars and dazzles my eyes as I step out of the cab and all I can hear is the constant drone of muttering from the driver even after I begin walking away. I pass two Housekeeping girls chuffing away in the smoking area who laugh at me as I hurry across the small parking lot and towards the staff entrance and I want to tell them to 'fuck off' but the movement of my bowels dictate otherwise. After relieving myself in the toilet, I work on tidying up, hurriedly dabbing at the sweat patches staining the armpits of my shirt with paper towel which already give off a heady smell, the action of which makes me sweat even more. I look into the mirror and see my face red and livid and splash it with cold water before meditating for a moment to clear my head and give off the impression of having a calm exterior.

"Alex you're late," Lisa states obviously, as I enter the office to drop off my bag.

"Where are they?" I ask, pulling out my folder and tablet.

"I don't know…" she says incredulously.

Both Suzie and Prasad are out of the office and Gemma looks at me like I've committed a murder or something as she watches my every move while Lisa simply looks sad.

"Right, I'll see you later," I tell them, heading for the door.

"What are you going to do?" Lisa asks.

I don't bother answering before I walk out.

Klep or the clients are no-where to be seen in the Bar as I approach the counter where the Spanish Waitress with the peach-of-an-arse is putting dirty coffee cups into the washing machine.

"Hello," she smiles or perhaps it's 'Hola', I can't tell, as I lean over.

"Morning…" I say. "Have you seen Marcus down here with some clients?"

"Yes…they leave already," she says.

"Do you know where they went?" I ask.

"I no no…I sorry…" she says, flirtatiously.

I pause briefly to look into her green eyes then head down to Reception where Caroline is talking with the assistant from HR in a low, hushed voice and looking visibly upset. I can see she's been crying; a fact that would usually trigger feelings of arousal in me, in so much as the open vulnerability requires an intimate response. However, seeing her face, moist and puffy, under the harsh lights of the ingress, I feel nothing but pity at how ugly she looks and decide not to bother them and head straight for the Conference Theatre. The first thing I seize upon entering is Klep, gesturing at the expanse of auditorium in some over-dramatised, operatic fashion as the two clients look on. I remain at the back of the theatre, unseen by all as he points to the lighting rigs up in the roof and across from the AV office and catch snippets of sentences as he pontificates over the importance of rhetoric in the modern era. He is bold and confident and my hatred for him is propelled to new heights. Firmly grasping my tablet and folder and clearing my head of all that has happened I descend the steps towards the stage and despite there being no-one else in the vastness, it's not until I'm two feet away and standing like a lemon waiting for the speech to end that Klep finally acknowledges me.

"Hello Alex…" he says, distractedly.

"Hello…I'm sorry I'm late, I…"

"Ah Rebecca…Max…this is Alex…he works in the Conference office with me," Klep interrupts. "Alex this is Rebecca and Max with Alpha6."

"Hello," I reply, offering my hand which is accepted indifferently.

They look shorter and less important than I imagined. Rebecca is a redhead – more ginger than auburn – with very pale skin and a tight body for a woman in her forties.

"Are you going to join us for a bit?" Klep says, with surprise.

"Of course…" I reply, just as taken aback.

Max and Rebecca turn their attention to Klep as another torrent is unleashed, gushing forth and flowing over the two clients like a dirty great river leaving me hanging around like some extra on a film set. Every so often Klep pauses for breath, giving me a window of opportunity to have my say only for him to jump straight back in like a hungry terrier and freeze me out, doing it so as not to seem like his intervention is obtrusive whilst keeping me at a distance. Self-abasement, anger, insecurity – the old ghosts - all leer over my shoulder as he hits his stride leaving me without a leg to stand on due to my poor punctuality.

"Shall we see the Grand Ballroom?" he asks.

I politely allow Max and Rebecca to pass first and Max looks on gratefully as if I were one of the Housekeeping girls about to clean up after him. I'm eager to ask Klep what he meant by 'for a bit' as I'm suddenly in the mood for confrontation, but he's still talking to the clients, despite trailing a few yards back. Then, as we exit the theatre he turns dramatically to me and using all the charm he can muster asks me if it would be possible for me to go up to the office and fetch a new brochure that has just been printed, highlighting the Grand Ballroom that should have been delivered from Reception.

"Sorry…?" I frown.

"Those new brochures – I asked Reception to bring one over when they arrived and it should be on my desk by now. Could you grab one for us Alex – it would be great to show Max and Rebecca. Thanks…" he repeats before ushering the clients away.

I can barely believe my ears as I duly comply with his request and head upstairs, unsure of what brochure he's talking about. In the office, I search his desk as the girls look on quietly. I finally ask them if they know anything about it, to which they both shake their heads. Lisa asks me if I made the show-round, which I make a point of ignoring before I depart and head over to the far Reception where I know all incoming post is held. Then, after what seems like a ten minute walk, I'm confronted by a girl I've never seen before and have no idea what her nationality is, but I think it's either Spanish or Italian. Whatever it is, her English is terrible and I try to read her name badge but can't make out the writing, but it looks like Madeira or Marissa or Medusa and the first thing that pops into my head before I ask her anything is whether she goes in for anal sex as she looks like the type. I tell her about the brochure and ask her whether she's delivered anything to the Conference office this morning to which she replies, 'no'. Then she hunts around for a while, back and front, becoming more flustered and talking to herself in either Spanish or Italian, as I glare at her silently over the counter until after much apologising, she finally hands me a brochure that looks something akin to the one Klep is talking about. I decide she's not very attractive and leave without thanking her then make my way back towards the Grand Ballroom. Then, across from main Reception I pass Danute who is doing her rounds of collecting last night's cash. I smile at her thinly and she gives me a look filled with pathos and regret, and I sense in that look her warming to me once more and wonder whether it wouldn't be so brash of me asking her to grow a bush after all, as I sense a second bite at the cherry.

Klep is nowhere to be seen in the syndicate rooms and along the corridors and through the windows I can see the sun is bright and clear and the sky is a giant blue ocean that goes on forever; and through the pane of glass I feel the sun's heat and all I want to do is stand and close my eyes and bathe in its warmth and dream about far-away places like the hero of my book, until a foreign voice belonging to a young boy wheeling a stack of chairs, interrupts my reverie. He nods at me respectfully before I leave and walk over to the Grand Ballroom. The Ballroom itself is already set in preparation for a function tonight and Klep is a figure of animation in the centre as he sets the scene for Max and Rebecca. I sense his displeasure at seeing me again as the torrent continues to flow, the dirty tidemark staining the walls climbing higher and higher. He pauses briefly as I approach and fakes a smile as I hold aloft the brochure to which he indicates to the table that Ernesto the C&B Manager already had one prepared for him.

"Thanks for your trouble Alex…" he says, before blanking me and proceeding with his selling strategy.

After another ten minutes of listening to his blandishments thrust upon the client, without having added anything myself, I'm relieved to see one of the lads from Leisure poke his head into the room and motion to Klep.

"Ahh…here he is…" Klep says, interrupting himself. "Our golf buggy awaits us… Max…Rebecca…"

This confuses me as my understanding was that the bedrooms were to be looked at next, not a trip to the Leisure

Club. Klep ushers the clients to the door and all I can do is follow like a puppy.

"Are you happy with everything so far?" he asks.

Rebecca seems unsure, but with Klep's persistence, finally nods her head. Outside, I can see the buggy parked up, waiting to ferry the clients up to the club. I can also clearly see the buggy only seats four – including the driver. My initial thought is that Klep wants me to *walk* up and join them, however he doesn't even offer me that privilege as he turns to me coldly and says: "Thanks Alex for dropping by. Perhaps you can join us later on in the Bar after we've finished…"

At this, Max and Rebecca both smile at me courteously before they're escorted to the buggy by Klep. A profusion of calculations fill my head spanning seconds: What does the future hold for me? What is my name? Did Klep really just do what he just did? Am I retarded? Can I ever show my face at work again? Do I really give a shit? I finally conclude that if I had a gun at this very moment, I would happily shoot Klep before turning it on myself.

I watch the buggy kick into life, tootle away and disappear leaving me stranded like a lost acid casualty. I'm desperate for a cigarette – anything to quell my flames of anger. Forcing my body to move, I detour through the dark, unseen corridors and canals of the hotel until I reach the smoking area that is bathed in bright sunlight. I quickly spark up then turn my face towards the sun amidst the stench of cigarette smoke and conclude that I can do one of two things: go home and finish watching the films of 'Wanton Mary' in complete quietude and vow to never set foot in the Thorn Park Hotel again or head back up to the office and continue as if everything is perfectly alright. I decide on the latter.

"What the fuck happened?" someone says behind me as I'm about to open the door to the office.

When I turn around, John the Director is glaring at me, his

skin red and irritated, eyes solid and glassy. "I've got Marcus down there doing a show-round with potentially, one of the biggest clients we've ever had and you're not with him," he spits. "Why the fuck is Marcus telling me this morning that he doesn't think you're up to the job?"

"Why did he say that? I stammer.

"You tell me. Why were you late this morning?" he barks.

I search for some feasible excuse, but can come up with nothing better than the truth.

"I missed the bus – or rather the timetable had changed and it was early. I had to get a cab in as I'm without transport at the moment."

"Why the fuck didn't you tell me – I would have given you a lift in myself," he spits.

"I'm sorry…the traffic was terrible and I couldn't get hold of Marcus…"

John nods cynically before leaning in closer.

"Okay, I'll tell you now – nobody is indispensible. Is that understood?" he says.

"I don't know why Marcus said that…" I begin, before I'm cut off.

"Right, forget about Marcus. Leave him with the clients – he's going to deal with them. You've got ten minutes to get down to Reception for a client enquiry about a possible future event. It's Kelly's meeting, but she's busy dealing with IPP. Everything is fucked up this morning – so you get on it!" he emphasises.

I'm confused for a moment until I realise he's just referred to Lisa as Kelly, but think it best not to correct him.

"Just do that for me, will you!" he orders, before storming off.

In the office, Lisa hands me the piece of paper outlining the details of the person I'm supposed to be having the meeting with, as referred to by John, which I take with me to read on the way down. I pass Prasad's office and he gives me a stern look whilst he's talking on the phone. Downstairs I muster a fake smile and approach a woman by the name of Janet Engstrom who's supposed to be meeting Lisa, but gets me instead. And as I approach her with my extended hand, she rises from her seat and I notice the wonderful shape of her breasts under her tight-fitting jumper…

After an hour and a half spent listening to Janet prattle on about the success of her small business over the past year and how she wants to repay her small workforce with a do at the hotel as a reward and with me answering her queries in the same robotic manner as the day before and the day before that and the one before that, whilst keeping one eye on her chest, I head for the toilet with a throbbing head that feels like it's about to explode.

The toilet is baking hot and I remove my jacket and wipe the damp sweat patches covering my armpits then bring my hand up to my nose to smell. One of the lights continuously flickers at the far end and hurts the eyes inducing the feeling of one about to have an epileptic seizure. I'll have to get onto Maintenance about changing the bulb. I run cold water over my hands then bathe my face, head hung impassively. The water drains away as does all feeling I have for the place I'm standing in, unsure of where my place is – I'm sure it doesn't belong *here*. I close my eyes and remember the sun and the distance it travels to warm my face and how that same distance gulfs me from the far shore of reconciliation with the world as drops of water intermingled with sweat run down and seep into the crevice of my mouth leaving a salty taste reminiscent of the same taste procured from the soft white flesh of Danute.

"*Idiotule…idiotule…idiotule…*" I mutter.

Somebody enters. The noise of the door opening startles me into pulling back sharply and straightening up. I don't turn to look at the intruder, instead watch from the corner of my eye as

258

the figure moves over to the urinals. Pulling paper towel from the dispenser I dab my face and hands and wait for the intruder to finish. When I do finally turn around, Klep is standing before me zipping himself up, smiling. And all at once my hatred of the little man washes over me in a giant wave of flame.

"What the fuck do you think you're doing?" I ask him, my voice sounding coarse.

"I could ask you the same thing," he replies smoothly.

"What does that mean?"

"It means exactly what it says – *what are you doing?*" he replies. "You were due in this morning at nine-o-clock and guess what - you weren't there."

"I was running late – I couldn't get hold of anybody…"

"Running late? Your transgression *could* have cost us the deal of the century," he butts in.

"Transgr…?" I begin to repeat, scowling.

"Transgression…!" he butts in. "Luckily, I was on hand to deal with it. Do you have any idea what you did to poor old John's arsehole this morning? You fucked him good and proper. Frankly, I don't know why you were on it in the first place."

"Is that why you told him I wasn't taking this thing seriously," I say, moving a fraction closer.

"Well it's the truth isn't it? If you had been serious about things, we wouldn't be having this conversation right now. You're lackadaisical, you're unfocused and your commitment to the client is always half-baked," he lisps. "You do *just enough* to get a result, to see you through, but that's as far it goes. It's 'just a job' right? Do you seriously think you're pulling the wool over Steph's eyes, or John's or mine for that matter…?"

"I couldn't care less about you…" I reply. "You're no more in it for the client than I am – you're in it for yourself…"

Klep makes a beeline for the mirror but has to get around me first.

"Do you mind…" he says, as I step aside and observe while he checks his appearance.

I can feel the sweat trickling down my back and every time I move, my shirt becomes stuck and unstuck. And despite no windows, I can see the sun, bright and glorious, a giant fireball in that vast, azure sky and the heat is stifling as I listen to the sound of running water as Klep opens the tap and washes his hands then dries them off with a paper towel before checking his appearance once more. He steps past me again and adopts the same position he had before his act of vanity. And as I watch him, I can hear the ringing in my ears growing louder.

"You're nothing but a show-boat," I tell him.

"That's part of the job..." he replies, opening his arms pompously. "Sales is about giving off the right impression and then convincing the client that that impression is right for them. That's why I'm joining the Sales team and you're not..." he informs me. "Did you seriously think you were in with a shout? How deluded can one man be? Steph laughed you off after the interview but gave you the time out of courtesy. She said you had that 'vacant look in your eyes' - the same one you walk in with everyday..."

The ringing becomes louder.

"You didn't even tag the card I gave you, did you?" he goes on. "The King of Diamonds - the suicide king, that's you alright. Take a friendly piece of advice and do something else. This isn't for you...somebody needs to tell you..."

Every muscle in my body becomes taut, like somebody has just injected me with artificial filler as I adjust my mind to the sheer effrontery of the wretch standing before me. I could withstand this news from anybody...anybody except Klep. Anybody but Klep! I shake my head. Everything pertaining to the disaster of my morning surges through me like a sudden, mad rush of adrenaline: 'Wanton Mary's huge cunt rises like a beast under a mad moon, viciously gnashing its hairy teeth at me while the taxi driver spells out the repetitious humdrum of his existence; the gargantuan effort of wheezing my way to the bus stop, only to miss the bus by seconds; the clear blue sky and African sun as predicted by the weather girl whose dress captures my imagination every morning as I innocently eat toast and sip coffee; and the sum total of my life, hung up on that wall in the form of a tracker minus one gold star…

"You're finished here old chap…you're a hapless fool. I guess I'll be the one to tell you." he concludes, brushing himself down.

The red mist descends; and like the feeling of a bow having been drawn back for countless years and then suddenly released - I lash out. My fist connects solidly with the side of Klep's face emitting an extraordinary metallic sound that ricochets off all four walls of the toilet; a sound that shocks me into thinking that perhaps he is a robot after all and that the flesh isn't covering bone, but a state-of-the-art cyborg system designed to infiltrate and destroy. The blow is unleashed with far greater force than expected and in the split second that I watch him go down, I am both shocked and impressed by my punching prowess. I follow him down. Then crouching over his body, his arms flailing, I punch again and then again, emitting the same metallic sound that rings out in the confines of the sweltering toilet…

19

Gary stares at me with watery eyes, his body absolutely still, save for the slight twitching of the hands resting on his thighs.

"I kind of just looked at him for a bit until I eventually went to tell somebody, making up some bullshit story about knocking him over by accident." I go on. "After that, I left the building, got the fuck out of there…"

"Shit…" Rob mutters.

"And then what happened?" Jim asks.

"Klep eventually came round and gave everybody the real version of events and the police arrived at my flat later that day and charged me with assault. I told the police the way I saw it, in so far as Marcus had insulted me and remonstrated that I had acted out of provocation. In court, I was charged with ABH and ordered to pay a four-hundred-pound fine…on account of good character without previous convictions." I explain.

"Mate, I know a bloke got three months for that…" Darren says, snapping his fingers.

"What else?" Jim asks.

"He was in hospital for a few days with concussion, or so I was told. I don't know… it all happened so quickly…"

"What about work?" Jim asks.

"I was suspended, pending an enquiry and then dismissed…"

The group stir, a low moan resonating around the room, like

the sound of a lost herd of cows wondering which field they should be in.

"Shit…" Rob mutters.

Gary's hand moves along the length of his thigh at a slow tempo and he has that look of affection that he dotes on me when he feels for one in need of consolation. Indeed, my own thoughts turn to Klep and my feeling of compunction coming on strong at having hurt him in the way I did out of nothing more than a hatred for myself - so much so, I consider getting up and leaving the room.

"How do you feel, knowing, that the chain of events that led to your dismissal – the ones that you've just described - were as a direct result of you turning on your computer that morning and tuning into porn?" Jim goes on.

"Honestly? Relieved…" I tell him.

Jim looks at me quizzically.

"Something had to happen…something had to give…" I tell them. I guess I just took it all out on Marcus…"

"Are you a violent man?" Jim asks.

"Not at all – it was completely out of character," I tell them. "I think it was a combination of a lot of things coming together at once: my cat dying, Danute, the boredom at work and my pre-occupation with porn at home. But I refused to change anything: I carried on doing the same shit, day in day out with vague promises about changing my life… Sarah used to say everything happened for a reason, well perhaps she's right, perhaps this needed to happen… I don't know…look at it how you fucking want. You ask me how I feel about it, I feel relieved. I'm relieved it's out of my system. I'm relieved I'm out of that job. I'm just sorry about what happened to Marcus."

Jim straightens up, looks over the room and begins to applaud. In seconds, the rest of the group have joined him; and this time when Gary leans over to pat me on the arm, I let him do so.

"You're wrong when you say you refused to change. You coming here was a huge act of recognition. It was fear that prevented you from committing yourself beforehand." Jim says, addressing the flip-pad before writing: 'Fear of the Unknown'.

"It is fear that prevents us from finding our true selves," he begins. "Fear of losing your job and not knowing how you're going to pay the rent…fear of not fitting in because you dress differently or say different things…fear of rejection that prevents you from asking that girl out…fear of not getting enough 'likes' on your Facebook page…and fear of quitting your porn use because, what on earth will you do with yourself then?"

Gary nods emphatically as Jim re-takes his seat.

"We've planted the seed inside our heads before it's even happened. We've cut ourselves off from our full potential before we've even taken the step or spoken the word. This is our greatest enemy," he says, tapping his finger against the side of his head. "Prolonged viewing of porn is simply used as a means to relieve the tedium in your life. It simply means: you have nothing better to do. People with a sense of purpose to their lives do not have this problem. Alex has described to us his sense of un-fulfilment, which began with a job he had little feeling for and a home-life devoid of company. Was it any wonder he was going to turn to something like porn to fill the void? Remember sex is a powerful and fundamental drive! The point is: Alex has taken another step to finding his purpose – without fear."

Jim pauses briefly before continuing.

"However, fear can also be a powerful ally – it pushes us to do things we might not normally do. I had a friend who was nineteen years old when her mother died from cancer. She had no father and very few relatives, but one older brother. She described to me the fear she felt after this happened. Aside from the terrible grief, she suddenly felt very alone in the world. She could very easily have given up or fallen prey to all sorts of things, like drugs or alcohol but she didn't; she was *forced* to take the initiative, to go out and work and earn money, to look after herself and to become responsible. She was forced to grow up very quickly."

The room nod in unison. Jim goes on.

"Like Alex said, sometimes bad things happen; but that can force us and push us to do great things – like quit porn. Now I'm not saying Alex has suddenly seen the light or that God has kissed his brow or that he's had some kind of epiphany – although I think he has. Violence is never the way and hardly an example of a positive change. Who knows, perhaps the guy deserved it… "

"It was pent-up aggression resulting from sexual frustration…" Rob chimes in.

"Right or wrong, it was going to manifest itself in some form sooner or later. How long are we going to carry on living lives of quiet desperation? How long are we going to keep ourselves locked away as we grow old and wait to die? Life is short fellas! Step out of yourselves and have the courage to be the person you want to be," Jim says before addressing me.

"It wasn't the work colleague that Alex hated so much, or the fact that he had to work for a living or even the computer; it was his repugnant self…"

He taps the flip-pad.

"Live your life without fear," he goes on. "Think clearly and question what you want from life and what you consider to be a good life; don't let internet porn become the substance of your fear…"

Opposite me I can see Matt looking tense and troubled as he stares at the ground in front of him. Jim notices also and picks up on it.

"Matt? Do you want to say something?

"I can't sleep." Matt states. "As soon as my head hits the pillow, my mind goes into overdrive…won't shut down…every image I've ever seen, buzzing around my head, like flies, stopping me from sleeping. I'm just tired that's all."

"Have you tried melatonin…diazepam…temazepam…? It works for me. Knocks me out like a light," Rob says.

"I don't put that shit in my body…" Matt replies evenly. "Give me something to stop me feeling horny all the time."

"Has anything happened in the last week for you to lapse like this?" Jim asks.

"Not at all – I just feel horny all the time." Matt replies, looking across at me and holding me with his gaze. "There's so much beauty inside of me, so much love that I want to share and it's this struggle, this suppression of everything beautiful, that leaves me constantly feeling miserable."

I want to tell Matt the flies aren't a figment of his imagination, they really do exist. I want to tell him he's going to need a good swatter beside the bed, poised for swift access – that or a good book, but preferably not one of his favourites. And I want to tell him, as a result of my studying, that flies are seasonal and that the summer months are always the worst.

"Keep fighting…share your beauty Matt. Remember it's about being the person we want to be." Jim says. "It's important that you realise, from the moment you wake up, you're going to be in for a fight; that is simply the way of the world. There will be days when you feel weaker than others; but the important thing is to keep trying and not give up and not to be so hard on yourself. Nobody said this would be easy…"

"Trust me Matt, there will come a day when it does get easier and you'll wonder what all the fuss was about," Gary adds. "Focus on the positives. Engage in a positive state of mind. The world can often seem like a negative place and the more we allow ourselves to become absorbed by it, the more depressed we become. It's like a ball rolling down a hill gathering speed, getting bigger - a huge speeding ball of ugliness.

"Absolutely…" Jim says. "Allow your body to shut down at night. Drink a cup of camomile tea to relax nerves and muscles. Set aside all thoughts – they'll still be there tomorrow. We have to be tough on ourselves…but not too tough."

"*I've* been clean all week, Matt." Gary goes on. "There was one day when I couldn't get an image out of my mind – an old favourite that I couldn't get enough of and I came close to telling myself that because I had been a good boy, it was okay to have a quick look. Well…even though it's been deleted, I know how to retrieve it. So I left the computer, sat down in the bedroom on the cushion that I have placed on the floor and meditated for half an hour – cleared my mind completely. Then, I went back to the computer and carried on with my work and freely thought about the picture again without the slightest urge to bring it up on screen. In fact, the idea seemed ridiculous to me. Works for me every time…and it will for you."

"Good for you," Rob says with a hint of bitterness. "Mine's been a painful week.

"Why?" Jim asks.

"About a year ago I slipped a disc in my back working on the house. It took a few months to heal, but every so often the pain returns. It only takes a wrong movement or lifting something heavy to aggravate it and last Thursday I woke up in pain. I don't know if I was sleeping funny or whether it was something to do with the fact that I had been on the computer that evening. I wish I could say that I'd been doing something worthwhile or constructive, but unfortunately I can't. I lapsed a little and had a bit of a session and to be honest I think I niggled it then. Since then, I've been walking around like an invalid," he tells the group.

"Punishment perhaps…?" Jim says.

"I guess you could look at it like that," Rob says. "Actually I'm beginning to see things like that. If ever I do lapse, I deprive myself of certain things – a drink, something to eat, whatever."

"That's a great way of losing weight," Darren chimes in.

"It's not meant as a way to lose weight," Rob says seriously.

"He was just joking Rob," Jim reassures him.

"I'm sorry…it's just…my whole life feels like it's been a joke and it's time I got serious about a few things."

"Its fine Rob…that's why you're here," Jim replies. "Was it just the one occasion?"

"Yes."

"Well that's better than the week before."

"It was made good by seeing my daughter at the weekend," Rob goes on. "We went to see the animals at the wildlife park and had lunch and she said I reminded her of the Panda bear we had seen earlier. Then I took her home and she kissed me goodbye and said she was going to tell mummy she'd had one of the best days of her life. And as I drove home, I just felt so ashamed, you know…"

Rob reflects on this for a moment.

"I tell you…if ever I come back here and say I've fallen back into old habits again, I give you all permission to kick the shit out of me."

"Don't worry Rob we're not going to do that. We're only interested in your attempts at becoming the man you want to be," Jim tells him. "How did your date go?"

"Not so good," he tells us. "We didn't really get along from the start – it's not that we didn't get along - we just intuitively knew we weren't right for each other. There was no chemistry between us – you could tell straight off, which is always better than going on blindly pretending. There was a time when I probably would have pursued it, just to try and get some sex out of it, but I didn't want that. I'm fine about it now."

Rob shrugs his big shoulders casually and stares at the space between his knees and as I watch him I'm struck at how accurate his daughter's observation was and how he does indeed look like a giant Panda bear and that all that's missing is a stick of bamboo for him to chew on. I suddenly feel sorry for him and for the rest of the group and despair at the thought of me still attending these meetings in, say, a year's time.

"Darren, how's your week been?" Jim asks.

"Clean all week mate…" Darren says, straightening himself up. "I didn't even fucking think about watching porn. I've been out nearly every night…I've been seeing more of Melanie…on Saturday night we spent the night together…and I'm in a good place."

"Well done Darren. Everything in working order I trust?"

"Spot on. She's a lovely girl…and I like her a lot."

"Good for you, Darren…" Gary says affectionately.

"Are you still working out?" Jim asks.

"Yep – two nights a week and I feel great." He nods. "Trick is to keep yourself occupied. Do things, mate. Even if I'm indoors for the evening with nothing to do, I still don't feel like sitting there jackin-off all night. It's like a bullet in the head and I think what the fuck was I doing with myself all that time?"

Darren goes on and I listen as I read 'Fear of the Unknown' over and over and wonder how much of it really applies to me. Sarah used to say, "If you don't try – you don't know". And as I recall the preceding years of childhood, adolescence and the formative years of adulthood, I wonder if that was my biggest bugbear; was it that that prevented me from being nothing more than the 'quiet man' – a king in my own world, too afraid to venture out into the real one? I look at Matt, who is staring across at me with his grey eyes and wonder how many more of him are waiting in the wings; how many more kings of their own world are staring out through the windows of their dark night of the soul?

"It's like I was at work the other day…" Darren goes on. "This one bloke, he shows me his phone and this load of porn that he'd been looking at and wanted to know what I thought, and I thought what a load of bollocks! And I'm thinking this bloke just seems a twat for showing me a load of porn and I used to do exactly the same thing. What did others think about me? It just seemed so depressing…"

"Absolutely…" Jim says, before turning back to me. "Alex, in light of recent events – where does this leave you? How have you been coping? It's been a month since we've last seen you – I thought we'd lost you."

Gary shifts in his seat beside me and a faint whiff of stale urine wafts over as Matt lowers his head once more.

"The truth is I feel better than I have done in ages," I tell him."You talk about the unknown, but that doesn't scare me, in fact, I welcome it. I feel excited about things again and I realise I haven't been excited about anything for ages. Porn doesn't even excite me. Well…not all the time… I have no job, no girlfriend, very few friends and I'm trying to stop myself from watching porn every day and I feel fucking great. I have no idea what's going to happen. I've hardly looked at any porn for nearly four weeks, at least not to the extent that I used to and when I do, I think nothing of it because I'm confident I'm not going to fall back into old habits. I've come to terms with *something*, but I don't what. If it was losing a job that I loathed – fine. If it was losing a girlfriend – fine. If it was finding out a little bit about myself – fine. All that matters is that I can see a future. *You* say I've had an epiphany – well maybe you're right. Gary was right when he said there will come a day when you'll wonder what the fuck you were doing with your life. I've measured out those spoonfuls of shit and asked myself what the fuck I was doing? And suddenly the whole thing was a joke. The laugh was on me…but it was nothing worth dying over."

Gary sighs - a long effeminate sigh – that sounds almost comic and pitched so high, I'm forced to look at him, just to confirm his gender.

"Everything's been deleted…" I tell him.

"Everything…?" he asks.

"*Everything…* I read again, I go for walks, I look at people; I'm thinking about perhaps carrying on with my studies. I'm thinking about what I eat… the wanking chair has gone; the entire spare room has been cleaned up, I've bought myself some new clothes. I shower more often and I actually speak to mum from time to time…" I say. "I'm living one day at a time - it's as easy as that."

"I'll take my hat off to that," Rob says, looking up. "I've been telling myself that for the past six months and I'm a fair bit older than you are. You're a young man – anything less than living, out of the pure joy of living, would be a crime," he tells me. "Keep thinking that way because things only get harder as you get older."

"It doesn't have to…" Jim says, still observing me.

"How can it not. *He* brought it up the other day," Rob says, referring to Matt. "Age takes over – it reminds us that the days are getting shorter, that your hair is never going to grow back, those six pints that were once easy to hold down have now been reduced to two because you just can't deal with the hangovers anymore. Every trip to the mirror reveals a little more decay and there's nothing we can do to stop it. All of this fucks with the head!" Rob says, tapping the space above his left temple sharply.

"Age has nothing to do with it Rob. We are all aware of the facts of life; any one of us can die at any time. It's our attitude to life that matters," Jim says.

"That doesn't stop it fucking with your head…" Rob persists.

"But Rob, you're contradicting everything you've just told us about your strength of will with regards to your daughter…" Gary butts in.

"Wait a minute…we're allowing the negative aspects to dictate the way we think. This is nothing short of media propaganda. We're allowing ourselves to be ruled by the new order…" Matt calls out.

"You're one to talk…" Rob replies.

"Don't think so much – just enjoy your fucking life! Darren interrupts, talking to no-one in particular.

"You wait till you're *my* fucking age – wanking's the only good thing left in the world," Rob insists.

"No! There's more to life than dollies and dildos! Our calling is sacrosanct…" Gary informs us.

"Let's not get morbid…" Matt tries to tell us.

"Who's being morbid…?"

"Hey…hey…everyone calm down…" Jim pleads. "Last week we were talking about ways in which we can put the computer to good use…"

I listen as the group descends into disorder and watch with detached impartiality before declaring myself done and taking myself out of the fold.

The green, neon clock on the dashboard reads past nine as the last vestiges of day slowly descend to make way for the burgeoning night-time sky. The roads are free of traffic. I'm relieved to have left that room and those lights and all those words scattered about the place and plastered to the walls that are there to fill our heads with new insights and keep us attuned to the true music that is there to lead us to our state of grace. I shall miss that smelly chair in some perverse way, just like I shall miss Gary, Rob, Darren and the quiet Matt. There will be others like me to fill the space; people who will wander in, sit down and try and fathom the reasons as to why they're there. I'm not saying I won't return – I might. The goal though is *not* to return. A separate tracker will be needed and a new purse of gold stars. To say, in the short space of time that I've been attending the meetings, that they haven't had an impact on me though would be false. For that I'm grateful. I'm certainly in no position to judge the members of the Old Pavilion and the rhetoric of Jim. All have had the courage to stand up and be counted; all have been kept awake at night by the same melodious tune, only to discover it was a song penned for the damned. No! I shall not return to the Old Pavilion out of spite. I'm glad to be out of there and that comfortable smelly old chair; it's very easy to become comfortable in a chair like that and accept the medicinal cups of tea as an essential part of your re-programming, until you're just as reliant on it as the thing that brought you there in the first place. No….the Old Pavilion is not for me, in spite of its good intentions. Out with old and in with the new, fortune favours the brave, a new broom sweeps clean, a rolling stone gathers no moss, a watched pot, never boils…I can think of a thousand clichés that best describe my motivation for change. It really was as easy as that! There comes a point in your life where you say, enough is enough – and actually mean it.

I didn't tell them about my travel plans and the journey I'm about to embark on across South-East Asia, starting in Bangkok then working my way down to Phnom then across to Phuket until finally ending up in Bali. I didn't want to jinx the trip by revealing things before they've happened - there's always been a small part of me that's superstitious. The visas are being processed and the flights and connections finalised. I shall be gone for the best part of two months and with a bit of luck won't be too affected by the monsoon season. It will be an adventure. I *need* adventure. Like the hero of my book - I need to get out. I intend to lose myself in a place that has no memory for me and to walk freely and without direction and sap the juice out of the world around me until I'm shit-faced. I will wear different clothes, smell different scents and walk among people of a different race *away* from the confines of the Thorn Park Hotel. I have the money; if there is one redeeming feature to spending every minute of your free time in front of the computer, it's that you don't squander your money on other frivolous activities. Yes…I want to see a bit of the world whilst I'm a young man. Cover all the continents perhaps – see if those innumerable women of diversity really do look as good in the flesh? Perhaps I'll work abroad. My eyes are open. The best way to unravel is travel…isn't that what they say? Perhaps I'll send the Old Pavilion a postcard. Yes…a postcard with a thank-you message, that's the least I can do.

Ahead of me, a Roe suddenly breaks free from the bushes and scrambles across the road. The oncoming car barely misses it and I catch a still of the driver's female companion, gasping, terrified, arms all akimbo. I slow down, as they usually come in twos and keep one eye on the side of the road. There really isn't a lot you can do when one does decide to bolt – it all comes down to luck, I suppose. I reach a junction and stop for the lights. Two girls, dressed up for the night, and teetering on stilts, cross the road and look into the car, as if recognising me from somewhere, their mouths forming words that I can't hear, only snippets of their laughter. Initially, I recognise one of them as Suzie, until I realise it isn't. I watch them stagger away as the lights turn green and press down on the accelerator that little bit harder thinking about the now defunct My Favourites folder and the buxom redhead that always reminded me of Suzie; then the others in the list, from top to bottom, arse to tit, cock to cunt, until I'm satisfied I've included everything that was once the elixir of life, but now nothing more than relics plucked from the annals of my own personal little history. To say these little sojourns aren't tinged with a hint of regret would be a lie; but then we are creatures of habit and letting go is always difficult. I shall definitely send the Old Pavilion a postcard! Perhaps I'll even send Klep one. He is after all a good salesman whereas I am not. I can live with that. In a way Klep got what he deserved, we both did. What he got was more than a whack in the face for arrogance; it was a detoxification, a toppling of the old walls to make way for a new order, the peeling away of one skin to reveal the shiny, newly formed of another, a final farewell to childhood perhaps, the transmutation of boy into man. We both learnt a lesson and for that I'm also grateful.

Sarah always said I had bad karma, that the fruits of my past actions would one day come back to haunt me, but that we all had the power to change it. Of course I laughed off her suggestions and she accused me of being a non-believer and a cynic which was why, she said, I was doomed to fail. She also said there were certain blockages in my mind, preventing me from reaching my full potential, the seeds of which were probably sown during adolescence. What these were, she didn't explain, made all the more baffling by my inability to come up with any explanation of my own, despite my spending the rest of the night in private, cognitive regression. This, she said, made me weak and susceptible to meddling outside influences that would always work on taking me from my true path, which accounted for what she called, my 'detachment' from the world, a restlessness, borne out of failure to recognise what I wanted from life, something she said I would one day find or forever be without, depending on my willingness to embrace my fellow man. She was wholly sincere when she told me these things.

To say my detachment remains would be fair though. Even at the age of thirteen and in the throes of losing my virginity to Vikki Gibbs two years after my friend Bobby Goodright had shown me that picture in that magazine, it was evident. To say I was losing my virginity is a slight exaggeration; it was more a fumbling for the light, casting out your line in the wrong part of the lake… singing amidst a hurricane. It had been hot that summer and Bobby and I and a few others, including Vikki and her friend, had spent a good part of it hanging out together, playing football in the park, swimming, and kicking up dust around the old broken-down and derelict Power Station, smashing new holes into old windows and tasting our first cigarettes together. My brother never joined us on these excursions, being three years older than me; he partook in more important things with his own set of pals. He had a computer then whereas I was still shy of getting my first one by two years. He never let me use it on my own and when he did let me have a browse, it was with him in the room and used for nothing more than school work and other curiosities like music and film, certainly not porn – that he kept to himself. So when Vikki made it clear to me one afternoon that she fancied me and was willing to show me just how much, it was to that dog-eared and stained girly magazine that I turned to for inspiration. Despite not being much of a looker, she still managed to impress upon me great excitement with her allusions to the things I would eventually see and do with her as we walked back from the park. We stopped occasionally to snog, our destination: the old Power Station. Bobby and our friend Dean were the only ones with us and were happy to tag along, quietly revelling in the prospect of quietly seeing your mate trying to make a go of it, despite the false tales of bravado that were told concerning such matters.

And so loitering with intent in that old decrepit place and sensing Vikki's impatience, I finally took her round behind the back wall that led into another worn-out room, festooned with junk. It was here I knew the magazine had been stashed, behind a plank of wood leaning against the wall and where access to it would be easy. We faced each other, her back against the wall, me looking into her tomboy face, trying to forget about the fact that I didn't fancy her in the least but was being pushed on by more powerful forces. Her big mouth clamped over mine and she sucked greedily, me sensing the forces driving *her* were even mightier. She was a good kisser – I'll give her that. She'd had practice, or so I'd heard. In fact, it was common knowledge Vikki had done the rounds with quite a few of the boys, making her something of a pro in the snogging department despite her tender age. It certainly had the desired effect bringing about a sensation in my pants I had never experienced before. I remember my hands reaching down and rubbing the coarse gusset of her jeans and her pulling back and grabbing my other hand and bringing it up to her breast for me to caress. And when she reached down to rub the straining bulge in my pants, I knew I was ready. It was then I decided to take the initiative by telling her to turn around and face the wall, which she complied with eagerly. Thinking about it, this was a bold move and somewhat advanced considering most first encounters are performed face to face where the eyes of trust can be seen and felt by both parties. My agenda fell short of this.

Vikki undid the button of her jeans and pulled them down past her buttocks and I remember the sight of her bare flesh seeming strangely familiar to me as I quickly did the same. It was then, with Vikki turned away from me, face pressed against the cold wall that I bent down and retrieved the magazine from its hideout. I flicked through its contents until I found the picture I wanted then placed it on the ground, face up for me to observe, whilst doing the deed. Vikki seemed utterly oblivious to the move – or perhaps didn't care – and remained where she was, poised for connection. Shifting up behind her, I braced myself then stuck my erection between her thighs and pushed. I wasn't sure what I was aiming for or if I had hit the target, all I knew was the feeling of it being warm and moist and of me feeling like a dog when I finally began to rock back and forth with quick, jerky movements. And there I was, head bent down looking between the legs of that blond girl in the magazine for all I was worth, jerking like a dog with the cool air hitting my buttocks, attempting to reach a destination I was unsure of. All of this was interrupted by the sudden sound of laughter as I looked up and saw Bobby and Dean peering round at us from behind the wall, forcing me to quickly pull away whilst Vikki remained, happy to be the mannequin she was and not in the least bit bothered by their presence. And so it was, as we drifted back home, the whole experience having left me a little confused, but proud as well that Bobby curiously enquired:

"Did you do her up the bum?"

"Dunno…don't think so…" I replied, unsure of where I put it. "Why?"

"You had her round the other way…" he said, the two of us strolling like a couple of gentlemen engaged in serious conversation.

"I just prefer it that way…" I remember saying, leaving us both to contemplate in silence.

I remember feeling terribly lonely after we'd said goodnight for the evening and I was making the final part of my journey home. I remember the feeling of regret at not having looked Vikki in the face during our engagement despite me not even fancying her and I remember that strange feeling of detachment as being something that perhaps I would never shake. Even now, the grass always seems greener on the other side…an illusion? We'll see. Who knows, perhaps one day I'll stumble upon a rock, take stock, plonk myself down and decide: this is where I want to be. Perhaps this whole porn thing really was just a phase I was going through. Something I needed to get out of my system, something where I could say, "My 'season in hell' has come and gone and I survived, lived to see the blooming of a new flower and made me a better man for it." Perhaps that's just pretentious bullshit?

The window shakes with the speed of the car and the wind whistles in my ear and I hit the automatic button to my side to lessen the influx of air as 'Wanton Mary' spreads her womanly thighs. I smile to myself and think about Hayley and her dog and the day I went in to see her, as promised, and how we got along famously and plan to see each other again and I think about the tracker on my wall and how it *really* looks like an old Christmas decoration now with its green and gold on account of me being a good boy. I'm four weeks out of the mire, not cured…but I *have* been a good boy.

Dark has suddenly descended, come out of nowhere like the fly that's slipped in and begun buzzing around the interior of the car, hither and thither off the windscreen, the roof, the door, past my face and around my ears making a nuisance of itself. And I smile, un-vexed because it's not the harbinger of doom, the modern technological version of Armageddon or the smutty appliance keeping me up at night. It's just a fly.

The road narrows to a single lane and I slow down, lower my window and watch as it disappears into the night just as I approach a sign indicating I have 'Right of Way'. Yes...I have definitely been a good boy.

I'm vacating the capsule.

I'm getting out.

I hope you enjoyed this book.

Leave A Review

Reviews of their work are the lifeblood of any independently published author. I know time is precious, but if at some point, you could head over to Amazon and leave your honest opinion about the book (long or short) it would be much appreciated. Peace and love.

Get Your Free Book

Visit Ash at www.ashbrunner.co.uk and SIGN-UP to the monthly newsletter for updates on promos and new releases and to get your FREE COPY of the novelette 'BUST' – a gritty tale of bent pride, fighting and loss in small-town England.

About the Author

Ash Brunner is a British writer of Contemporary Fiction. Ash grew up in Richmond, South-West London, where he studied Graphic Design before travelling and working numerous jobs, including: photographic lab-assistant to wine-seller and enthusiast. He also spent eight years singing with various bands on the London club scene. After studying Screenwriting at Goldsmith's College London, he began to write in earnest, producing numerous screenplays before writing his first novel PEST – a visceral, darkly comic and often repellent story of a young man's struggle with porn addiction. Ash lives with his wife in Oxfordshire, England where he is currently writing his next book.

Printed in Great
Britain
by Amazon

31377516R00170